The Way Things Fall

a novel

Liz Torlée

blue denim press

The Way Things Fall

Published by Blue Denim Press Inc.
First Edition
ISBN 978-1-927882-55-9

This is a work of fiction. Resemblances to persons living or dead, or to organizations, are unintended and purely co-incidental.

Photo by iStockphoto / Credit: den-belitsky
Cover Design by Shane Joseph.

Library and Archives Canada Cataloguing in Publication

Title: The Way Things Fall: a novel / Liz Torlée.
Names: Torlée, Liz, 1950- author.
Description: First Edition.
Identifiers: Canadiana (print) 20200275356 | Canadiana (ebook) 20200275380 | ISBN 9781927882559 (softcover) | ISBN 9781927882566 (Kindle) | ISBN 9781927882573 (EPUB)
Classification: LCC PS8639.O78 W39 2020 | DDC C813/.6—dc23

DEDICATION

To Pauline, the very first believer

Judith

Thank you! Really hope you enjoy it.

Liz

Ah, Love! could thou and I with Fate conspire
To grasp this sorry Scheme of Things entire
Would not we shatter it to bits —and then
Re-mould it nearer to the Heart's Desire!

Omar Khayyam, The Rubaiyat
Translated by Edward FitzGerald

PROLOGUE —OCTOBER 2011

Rachel was late for the opening of the art exhibition. She couldn't find parking and, in desperation, left her car on a side street a few blocks away. It was October. The air was crisp and cold, and a playful wind spun the fallen leaves around her feet as she hurried to the gallery. Clutching her open coat to her chest, she glanced in the windows of the red-brick Victorian houses, most of them converted to studios, art and sculpture galleries, and felt bad about her cursory interest in her need to rush by.

She had almost forgotten this art show. She was supposed to write a five-hundred-word critique for an art magazine she contributed to but she hadn't received the prospectus and felt totally unprepared. Her friends, Nigel and Philippe, had been enthusiastic about this painter's work so she tried to psych herself up for the cocktail party ordeal and all the "meet and greet" that she was not very good at.

The door to the gallery was partly open and she could hear the buzz and chatter of multiple conversations, one or two voices spiraling above the others, one or two bursts of deep laughter. She checked her coat and accepted a glass of champagne from a server as she entered. It was warm inside and oppressive. She tried to avoid eye contact with anyone and went to the far wall to study what were mostly landscapes and strikingly personal country scenes.

One painting she approached drew her in immediately: *The News,* read the caption at the side. Two cedar chairs on a lawn; two glasses of white wine on a table, one of them knocked over, the clear liquid darkening the wood. A book was lying on the grass as though it had fallen, its spine bent backwards. The colours were strong, exaggerated, fauvist in their intensity but the style suggested a profound sadness. The painting kept pulling her closer. She felt she could smell the spilled wine.

Next to this, *Stranded:* a man, alone at the side of a road, his back to the viewer. Ahead of him, the road curved sharply upwards to the left. The man was in motion, leaning forward. His hair was blown back. Behind the trees that bordered the road, the sun was settling into the horizon. Rachel studied the colours. The leaves of the trees, the blue denim of the man's jeans, even the lowering sun, all had a faint greyish tinge, as though the colours of the day were bleeding away. There was a clandestine, mystical aura to the painting, as though something was about to go wrong. *Stranded.* Perhaps it was only the title that kindled the strange sense of anxiety she was feeling. She turned away then sharply back to look at it again, a technique she often used to recapture her dominant first impression. She felt a tiny squeeze in the pit of her stomach. *Have I seen this before? Surely not.* This was a first serious exhibition, and the painter was only just becoming known. But something was tugging at her memory.

Behind her, a brief commotion over a spilled cocktail brought her back into the moment. She realized she hadn't eaten anything substantial since breakfast and abandoned the half-empty glass of champagne on a nearby tray.

It was the next painting that took the breath right out of her: a stag, full grown, leaping out from a stand of trees. It was captured in full flight, its front hooves curled up tight against its huge body, its back legs stretched out behind, its heavy, antlered head turning to stare at her. The animal was painted with photographic intensity, demanding all the attention, while the surrounding scene was rendered extraneous. Erratic brush strokes suggested dense woods, a splash of dark grey was perhaps a stretch of road. Rachel felt her whole body go rigid. How slowly that giant head turned, how angry and terrified those luminous eyes as they locked onto hers. She tried to step away but was frozen in time like the magnificent stag, a captive in the painter's field of vision. She was out there on that lonely country road, feeling the same chill of the evening air, not here, in this gallery on this October evening.

She pivoted slowly, fearing her knees would buckle. The room shifted back into focus, the voices rose to her ears, and she saw the painter. He was walking across the room but turned as she was turning and looked directly at her. Their eyes connected for the briefest moment in inexplicable recognition.

Someone kissed her on both cheeks. "Rachel, I began to despair." It was Nigel, in full sail. "Philippe said you'd be late. Called you a philistine. Come, come, you must meet—" But she was looking past him at the painter who was coming towards her now. He was dressed like any other artist at a downtown show: black jeans, black sweater, a grey scarf hanging around his neck. His hair was untidy and fell over his eyes. She reached to take his outstretched hand.

"The man himself!" said Nigel. "All alone for a change. Steven, let me introduce you to my good friend and possibly our most exasperating freelance writer, critic, raconteur, Rach—"

"Rachel Covelli." The painter was still holding her hand, his head tilted slightly to the side. "I don't think we've met before. Or have we?"

Nigel rolled his eyes. "Of course not, Steven. You've hardly met anyone. Socially, you're a serious challenge."

"Thanks, Nigel. Great intro."

"Don't worry. Rachel ignores everything I say. Isn't that so?" Nigel turned to her. "Are you all right, my dear? You look a bit peaky."

The painter had released her hand and she felt suddenly cold. She was relieved to see the familiar purple streak of Philippe's hair as he jostled through the crowd towards them.

"*Enfin,*" he said, stopping in fake surprise, his hands at his heart. "*So*, what do you think? Amazing, *non*?"

"I haven't seen it all yet," said Rachel. "I was just working my way round."

"Then come with me, *Cherie*." He grabbed her hand. "We'll go upstairs. And you are hogging poor Steven. Look at all these people desperate to meet him."

She was whisked away, half wanting to linger and half so anxious to get some space and clear her head.

Philippe left her on the floor above. She seized a couple of canapés from a passing waiter, hoping a little food would make her feel better. The paintings on this level were a dramatic departure from the other work. Large, symbolic, confrontational, they reached deep inside, tearing out raw hunks of emotion and skewering them to the canvas. Visitors stood well back, not just to absorb their impact but as though they were afraid to move closer.

She stopped in front of one painting in monochromatic greys: a naked man, falling, swinging towards her, his legs trailing awkwardly, his hands clutching at the emptiness. He was looking straight at her, a defiant, accusing stare.

Next to this, *The Abyss,* large expressionistic: a steep slope, suggesting an immense drop, a bottomless pit. Strange shapes were scattered around the vortex as though someone had flung them there: trees, bushes perhaps, but blurred and crashing into each other, growing less and less distinctive as the eye followed them down. High above, a pale moon hung lifeless in a darkening sky. A small blue smudge was hidden in the centre at the bottom. What had made him put that there, she wondered. It didn't belong. She stepped back. It looked like a suggestion of water, a lake perhaps, or maybe just whimsy. The blue wasn't right. It didn't fit. As she stared, she had the sensation of falling, as though she had leaned too far over to figure out what that blue was. She put her hand to the wall to steady herself. The loud, angry sound of a fire engine filled her head. It was coming close. She looked around the room but no one was paying attention to it. Two cellists played unconcerned and unnoticed over in a corner. Had it stopped, she wondered. She glanced over to the street window. There were no lights flashing.

She was sitting on a low bench in the middle of the room. An elderly man had his arm around her shoulder. "Half way down before I caught her," the man said, addressing a few curious onlookers and rather enjoying his role as modest hero.

"I have to call 911," Rachel heard herself saying.

"What's that, honey?" A woman, the man's wife perhaps, leaned towards her. "No, no, you just had a dizzy turn. I'll get you some water. You sit here a minute."

PART 1: A FATAL DECISION

Chapter 1

Eleven years earlier, in June, 2000, Rachel was working in Egypt. She was anxious to track down a contact she'd been given, someone whose experience might be helpful to her project, but all she had was a scrap of paper with the man's name and address written in Arabic. No one had been able to help with a telephone number. The front desk at her hotel gave her a map with directions and, as it didn't seem far, she decided to walk.

The day was hot and bright and she kept in the shade of the squat, dusty palm trees that lined the banks of the Nile. Following the map, she turned away from the tired elegance of the embassy district and moved deeper into the noisy market areas. The narrow streets teemed with the clamour and colour of copper and brass workers, carpet weavers, gold and silversmiths and stores selling leather, jade, ivory, perfume and jumbles of decorative arts. She picked her way through the cheerful chaos to the ceaseless honking of horns, jumping from the path of the reckless cyclists who swerved over the cobbles and around the old cars, some without doors, whose passengers and belongings spilled out at the sides. For a while, she was followed by a group of young children who pulled at her denim dress and clutched at the raffia bag slung over her shoulder. She smiled and kept shaking her head, declining the plastic camels and sprigs of jasmine they thrust at her until they gave up and looked for another tourist to pester.

She had signed on for this project because, at age twenty-four, she learned quickly that a degree in fine arts and courses in Egyptology qualified her for very little in the real world. But she could write and had a few magazine articles to her credit, and she had an amateur's interest in the stars, an enthusiasm her father had nurtured. The project director at the sponsoring museum in Toronto had viewed this odd combination of talents with cautious optimism. A plum assignment, he stressed, no doubt to soften the blow of the meagre remuneration. Alexandria, Cairo, modest expenses paid—surely a stepping stone for a permanent position down the road.

Nigel held up the "scope of work" dossier she gave him to look through when they had met for coffee after her interview, and read from it with affected reverence:

... a highly imaginative and far-reaching exploration, bringing new dimension to our understanding of the cosmological beliefs of the ancient Egyptians, "blah blah..." *multi-media exhibit will highlight their relationship with the night sky, how they interpreted the stars and the movements of the planets, how all this influenced their daily life, their art, their ...*

He flicked the dossier to the side. "I thought you were going to take that art criticism course I told you about. Of course, it's all filled up now but you should at least put your name down for next year."

As he launched into his usual lecture about the need to get serious and turn her love of art into a career, she sat back and admired his *Vanity Fair* ensemble, wondering how he always managed to look so elegant despite his generous paunch and florid skin. Perhaps it was because his partner, Philippe, was considerably younger. Nigel had once confided that looking good was "a daily ordeal." Today, a soft grey Italian knit sweater artfully draped over his shoulders, and dark linen pants with barely a crease. Bright red socks provided his trademark dash of flamboyance.

He waved his hand at her. "Are you listening?"

"I need the money, Nigel. I can barely afford my crappy apartment. I think I might give it up, find something when I get back. These people are working with the planetarium—didn't you see it on the news? All that business about the lack of funding for the arts? This is a big deal. Don't be such a cynic."

He peered at her over the rims of his half-moon glasses, scooped the froth off his mocha frappé and licked the long, thin spoon. "What do they want from you exactly?"

She filled him in on the assignment, the writing for the catalogue and brochures for the major exhibition next Spring, a few articles for the museum's newsletter, the various Egyptology experts whose perspectives she must seek.

He sipped the coffee as though it were a glass of wine. "Not the safest part of the world."

"I thought you'd be pleased for me." She gathered all the papers from the table and stuffed them into her bag. "You spent a whole year in that part of the world yourself."

"Many moons ago. Cairo, Marrakech, Tangiers. Heady days." He sighed and reached for a brown sugar cube to stir into his coffee. "You should look up a fellow I knew in Cairo. Not exactly knew, but...well, never mind. Karl something. He lectured on astronomy at the university and had some kind of store selling telescopes. Probably in his early thirties now. I doubt he'd be on any official list of experts. Swiss. Randow or von Randall, something like that —though I was always suspicious of the 'von.' No idea if he's what you need but he could read all that hieroglyphic business. Had quite the reputation. I'll see if Da'ud is still in touch with him."

Rachel had gone to see Da'ud not long after she arrived in Cairo. He was Nigel's "man in the Middle East," an antiques dealer near the Khan el-Khalili bazaar. He seemed apprehensive and could not or would not give her a phone number. "Nigel makes mistake sending you," he said, "this man is not answering telephones." Her contact at the Alexandria University was no further help when she called. She did learn some intriguing things about the work the man did but was told he had "dropped off the radar." In the end, she had to be content with the name and address that Da'ud scrawled on the scrap of paper.

After half an hour of walking deeper and deeper into unfamiliar Cairo neighbourhoods, she could not escape the fierce burn of the afternoon sun and realized she was totally unprepared —no sunscreen, nothing to cover her bare arms. She pulled her straw hat down further and made her way with less confidence through the complex maze of narrow streets. Sometimes her path was totally blocked by flat-bed carts piled high with fruit and vegetables, or by the afternoon delivery trucks unloading huge urns, trays of baked goods, water canisters, jugs of milk and bags of sugar. The *rubabikya* man passed in front of her, two tired donkeys pulling his wagon overflowing with rags, bottles, scraps of plastic and metal. She was caught in a cloud of dust that spun up behind the wheels and broke into a spell of coughing, glad that at least she had thought to bring a bottle of water.

Eventually, she found herself in a small square with several laneways running off it. She looked at the map, turning it this way and that. Two elderly women sitting in a doorway watched her with open curiosity. They called to a group of boys crouched in the gutter, playing a game with pebbles. One of the boys ran over.

"Where you going, Miss?" She showed him the scrap of paper with the address. "I am knowing this man. I take you."

The boy skipped ahead, and she began to wonder whether this had been a smart move, venturing into an unfamiliar part of a foreign city to meet a person she knew nothing about, one who may not even be there.

She had started the project with such confidence but her enthusiasm quickly dissipated at the university in Alexandria. The impressive credentials of the people she consulted and their thinly disguised condescension made her acutely aware of the superficiality of her knowledge. She couldn't wait to get to Cairo for the second phase of the work. After a week here in her modest apartment hotel on the Nile, she had organized the material from the university into different themes, sent off her draft outline, and begun to write in earnest. But she was not happy. Something was missing. That's when she decided to look up Nigel's contact.

The boy was almost out of sight and she had to walk quickly to catch up. She could feel the sweat around the waistband of her dress and loosened her belt, cursing herself for not taking a taxi. After a few minutes her little guide turned sharply to the left. She found him stopped in front of an old brown wooden door. He gestured proudly to the brass plate with the name: Herr Karl Gustav, and what she assumed was the Arabic version underneath.

"This is not him," she told the boy. "I am looking for Karl von Randow."

He pointed at her scrap of paper and again at the door. "Star reader man. His shop."

She gave him a few coins, too many from the way his eyes popped open in astonishment. He leapt up to ring the bell and ran off.

Through a small window at the side of the door, she could make out tall glass-fronted cabinets filled with telescopes. She rang the bell again and edged the door open. It was heavy and creaked loudly. A wooden staircase led from the centre of the store and, toward the back, a recessed alcove overflowed with Egyptian paraphernalia, from ornaments and bright jewellery to large busts and statues. There was the smell of leather and pungent cigarette smoke. Most of the larger windows were shuttered against the afternoon sun so it was dark and cool. She stood for a moment to catch her breath and let her eyes adjust, enjoying the respite from the stifling heat and noise outside. She fingered the pamphlets by the cash register, most concerning astronomical equipment, and listened for signs of life. A scrawny grey cat appeared from behind a display case and came to her side, weaving around her legs and flopping down at her feet. She put her sunglasses on one of the counters and bent down to stroke it, hoping she hadn't come all this way for nothing.

"What is it you want?"

The voice came from behind her. She was so startled that, as she turned, her bag slid from her shoulders to the floor, and the cat leapt away.

He was standing half-way down the stairs, one hand resting on the rail, a gold watch hanging loose at the wrist. His feet were bare and the cuffs of his khaki pants were rolled up as though he had been paddling in water. His straight blond hair, which looked slightly damp, fell well past his collar. In the dim light, his features were angular, his eyes deep-set and cold. There was no sense of welcome, none of the anticipation a store owner might be expected to feel with a new customer. He stood motionless, appraising her with undisguised irritation.

"Sorry. I did ring the bell." She picked up her bag and took a couple of steps towards him. "I am looking for Karl von Randow. It says Karl Gustav on the door. I wasn't sure."

"My last name is von Randow. I rarely use it." He descended to the foot of the stairs. "What is it you need?"

She was taken aback by his directness. Stammering like an anxious school girl, she gave him details of her work. "I'm looking for different perspectives on the ancient Egypt—"

He shook his head to interrupt her. "Who gave you my name?"

"A friend in Canada. He met you some time ago and works with Da'ud Karaoui. And the Alexandria University said you were once listed as a reference for work on the ancient—"

"I'm an astronomer, not a historian." He walked over to the counter and straightened the pamphlets she had moved, tapping them into a neat pile. "I can't help you."

"But it's the astronomy and astrology stuff I need for this project. Look, I have a letter of introduction." She rummaged in her bag.

"Astronomy and astrology *stuff*?" He raised his hands with mock drama. "You are talking of thousands of years of complex mythology. Dedicated students put in a decade of intense study before they even begin to understand."

Her cheeks flamed and she started to apologize, but his tone softened a little. He said he would give her the names of some people at the Council of Antiquities who might be willing to help and invited her to look around while he searched for their phone numbers.

A photograph of the moon was pinned to a cork board next to a display of telephoto lenses. She looked closely at it; it seemed familiar. A brief shiver seized her and she hugged her shoulders. Herr Gustav was over at the counter, writing names.

"Yesterday, the moon was nearly full, low on the horizon," she said. "Just like this." She paused, hesitating to risk his impatience with a question. "Is this last night's moon?"

"It is." There was a note of mild surprise in his voice.

After a moment or two, he came and stood at her side. She could smell a faint citrus scent, aftershave perhaps, and wondered if he'd just taken a shower and that's why he hadn't heard the doorbell.

"What made you notice it particularly?" he asked.

She looked straight ahead, unwilling to turn to him because he was so close. "I was at one of those restaurants by the pyramids. I walked out on the sand to look at the stars."

He pointed to a bright star close to the moon. The rolled cuff of his shirt sleeve brushed lightly against her hair. "Do you know the name of this one?"

She examined the pattern of the surrounding stars. She wanted to be right. The ticking of a brass clock on the wall in front of her grew louder in the cool silence. She felt the need to take a step to the side but couldn't move. "Antares? I know that's Scorpio." She circled the constellation with her finger. "The Goddess Serqet, I should say. I guess the Ancient Egyptians would claim it's a good time for new beginnings. Infinite lives, constant rebirth. A powerful place for the moon to..." She stopped. Would he think she was sounding superficial again?

He turned to look at her, his thumbs hooked into his belt. "You know your stars."

"My father was keen and he taught me a little. He had a telescope. Nothing like these of course." She gestured to the shelves of telescopic equipment. Under his steady gaze, she felt flustered and scanned the store, seeking a way to put some space between them. In a glass case in the centre of the room was a wooden contraption spanned by circular metal rings. She went over to look at it more closely.

"That's an orrery, a miniature," he said. "Perhaps you know this? It was used years ago to explain the orbits of the planets." Once more he came to her side. He slid open the glass door, removed the device and set it in motion with a small wind-up key. White spheres at the end of brass spikes began to move with a ratcheting noise, counter-clockwise around a central brass dome. "The sun is in the middle, of course. These spheres are Mercury, Venus and so on."

She glanced at his face as he leaned forward to point out the planets. In the fuller light his features were not as sharp. His eyes were a very clear grey.

"The device is not accurate," he said. "The earth is too large and its axis is 25° to the ecliptic. It should be 23.5°."

She caught his slight frown. "That bothers you, I think," she said, smiling at him.

He stopped the mechanism, replaced the key in the drawer and leaned back against the counter. From somewhere in the back of the store, the low hum of an old fridge switched to a noisy shudder and fell silent.

"I wonder, *Fräulein,*" he said, "how you can claim to know what bothers me?"

A deep blush crept up from her collar. She went quickly to the counter to retrieve her hat and sunglasses. "I'm sorry. It's just, well, this job is important to me ... I was told you had a certain reputation ... anyway, thanks for giving me these names." She picked up the piece of paper he had written them on.

"A certain reputation?" He walked to the door but, instead of opening it, turned the key in the lock. "Time to close," he said, a faint smile playing at the edge of his mouth. "And time I learned a little more about you."

Chapter 2

So many times in the years to come, Rachel would wonder how different her life might have been if she had not pressed her case, if she had walked out when he was so dismissive and taken the nearest taxi back to her hotel. He had obviously caught the brief flare of panic in her eyes when he locked the door. He pointed to the key still in the lock, making her feel foolish but relieved that she could leave any time she wished, and then nodded toward the stairs, telling her to make herself at home in his study and he'd bring them some jasmine tea. She couldn't quite believe she had so readily agreed to this. As she climbed the stairs, she tried to compose herself. After all, Nigel had recommended this man. Maybe he wasn't good at small talk.

Every square inch of his study was put to use. Bookcases climbed to the ceiling on all four walls, their shelves buckling with the weight of heavy-bound volumes whose spines were worn and cracked. Near the window was a wooden desk with neat stacks of paper on it, a decanter of what looked like whisky and a Tiffany-style lamp.

The window was ajar and she caught the smell of warm cinnamon and the sound of children laughing. There was a bakery opposite with a display board in front, pictures of flatbread, buns and sugary cakes. Three young boys, barefoot with sun-browned bodies, were bouncing a soccer ball off its walls, screaming and pushing at each other. The old baker came running out, his heavy hands and forearms floured over, his white *gallabiyya* flying out behind him. He pointed to his broken window, yelled at the boys and chased them off. As he turned to go back inside, his eyes drifted up to Rachel and he paused for a moment. She smiled but he looked away and hurried through the door.

She sat in one of two overstuffed brown leather chairs in the corner of the study. Many of the brass studs that kept the leather taut were missing so the seats bulged in the wrong places. In front of her, an engraved brass plate on a three-legged wooden base served as a coffee table. There was an ashtray on it and next to this an elaborately carved decorative case. She lifted the hinged lid to take a peek inside. It was packed with neat rows of slim, pastel-coloured Turkish cigarettes. She was making valiant efforts to stop smoking and snapped it shut.

She shifted position, trying to get comfortable, grateful for the modest draft from the overhead ceiling fan. In a small mirror on a shelf at her side, she caught her reflection and saw a band of sweat at her temples where her sunhat had pressed too close. She searched in her bag for a tissue. The grey cat jumped on the other chair and settled down to watch her, his paws stretched out before him.

When her host returned, he brushed the cat away and took its place, passing her a small cup of strongly scented tea. With the barest hesitation, she took the Turkish cigarette he offered and bent toward him as he reached over to light it. He took a deep drag of his own, blowing out the smoke in a slow exhale, and looked at her quizzically, saying nothing.

"What's your cat's name?" she asked.

"He is not my cat. He chooses to live here."

"And did he choose a name?" She caught only the glimmer of a smile from him.

"I call him Copernicus."

"The first to put the sun at the centre of the universe. That's appropriate. Cats believe *they* are the centre."

He raised his eyebrows. "Copernicus was not the first. He simply rediscovered what the Egyptians and the Mayans knew long before."

She resolved to stick to business. "This is my letter of reference. Please feel free to contact the museum if you have any questions." She placed the envelope on the table but he made no move to take it. He stretched his long legs in front of him and crossed his feet. She noticed he had put on sandals. They were dusty and well-worn, the leather fraying at the buckle.

He tilted his head back and blew a perfect smoke ring. "If you stand outside the Cairo museum for ten minutes," he said, "you will meet half a dozen local people with the qualifications you seek. Why go to the trouble to come here, to me?" His speech was clipped, precise, the 'w' sounding a little like 'v.'

"My friend mentioned your name. I thought it was a lucky coincidence that he had met you and knew you had the kind of experience I was looking for."

"There is no such thing as coincidence."

He stated this so categorically that Rachel felt there was no point in trying to challenge it.

She tried a different tack. "At the Alexandria University they said you used to take students on star-watching nights in the desert—to learn how the ancient Egyptians looked at the sky."

"Did they indeed?" The cat jumped onto his lap and he stroked it. "What else did they tell you in Alex?"

"That you could create Egyptian horoscopes." She hesitated, fiddling with the copper bracelets she had picked up the day before in a tourist bazaar. "Not the ones everyone reads in newspapers but the way the Ancient Egyptians would. The mythology I mean, the beliefs they had."

There was no acknowledgement in his face, just that hard stare. She wondered if she wasn't supposed to have known about the horoscopes. The woman who told her had been cagey.

He pulled a file from the shelf at his side and pointed to a large circle on one of the pages. It was covered in complex numbers and symbols. "I assume you know the planetary symbols. Can you read hieroglyphics?"

"I'm a bit rusty." She pointed to one of them. "This is *Djehuti* or *Hermes*, the Neter of Resonance, right?" She turned it to get a better look. "And this one next to it, I think is *Heru*."

"No, it is *Nebt-Het,* the 'lady of the house,' working through your unconscious mind—while you are sleeping, perhaps. Anything interesting about the position of the planets?"

"Two major planets in conjunction in the constellation Capricorn ......" she traced her finger across the glyphs, "...the Mercury-Saturn square. Mercury in retrograde." She looked up and realized he hadn't been following her tracings on the chart but was simply watching her.

He smiled fully for the first time and went over to his desk. "Let's see what the Ancient Egyptians would make of you." From the drawer, he took a piece of paper with a twelve-section circle on it and placed it neatly in front of him. "Where were you born?"

"Italy."

"Ho bisogno di sapere il luogo e l'ora precisi. Voi sapete questo?"

"I'm sorry?"

"Do you know the exact place and time?"

His use of Italian startled her. She had let the language of her birth grow rusty and was irritated that this was yet another reason to feel embarrassed. She answered in English and stood at the side of his desk to watch. He worked methodically, looking up information in two large, densely printed books and quickly plotting the data on the chart. His long hair fell forward as he wrote. He had a fine sloping script and she was impressed with his ability to draw the hieroglyphics so quickly. She noticed a scar at the base of the thumb on his left hand, a thin white line against his deep tan. He took a ruler and mapped in the trines and sextiles, the supporting and conflicting planetary alignments. She wished he would share his thoughts but he remained silent and, after a few minutes, she felt awkward standing beside him. There was a computer on his desk and she wondered why he didn't consult online sources. Surely there must be hundreds these days.

He stopped, his pen hovering over the page as though wondering if he might have miscalculated, then took another book from one of the shelves. "Sit down Rachel. This takes time." He motioned her back to her seat.

His use of her first name took her by surprise. "Ray-chelle," each letter pronounced, the "ch" hard, the "el" drawn out slightly. She took an English magazine from a pile by the table and began to leaf through it without registering anything. What the devil was he concluding about her, she wondered. This was not what she had in mind. It was easy to find people who knew a great deal about the ancient Egyptians. Even the casual tourist guides, as he himself suggested, were experts on the subject. But the museum had made it clear that they were looking for something that would give their exhibition an intriguing perspective. And there was certainly something intriguing about this man. She couldn't define it but felt a strong need to learn more about him.

Eventually the scratching of his pen and the rustling of paper stopped. He sat back, apparently finished. She couldn't read the look on his face. Curiosity? Irritation? Mockery? Could he silence a lecture hall full of students with that stare, she wondered? He came and put the finished chart face down on the table between them, settled back into his chair and lit another cigarette. The sun was now directly at the window. Rachel felt hot, sticky and increasingly uncomfortable.

"Anything I should know?" She pointed to the chart, wondering if she should call him Karl but feeling too self-conscious.

In one quick movement, he lifted the magazine from her lap, crouched in front of her and seized her wrists. She froze. "Close your eyes. Breathe deeply," he said. "What do you feel?"

Her voice was stuck in the back of her throat. She tried to wrestle her hands away, but he tightened his grip. "I don't feel anything. Please let me go."

"Nobody feels nothing. Do you feel you are in the right place, the place you are meant to be? Do you feel centred, grounded, aware only of this very moment? Clear your mind. Focus."

She could smell the citrus scent on his skin again and the perfumed smokiness of the Turkish cigarettes. Panic flooded through her. No wonder Da'ud had been uneasy about her visit. She thought about the locked door and the baker looking up at the window and wondered if she should scream.

"Please stop." She jerked herself free.

He stood up. "You don't trust your own instincts, Rachel. That's obvious from the reading. Your dominant element is air. It distracts you. Makes you try to rationalize everything. Don't be alarmed. I wanted only to show you what the Ancient Egyptians would claim. Beneath all the chatter of your mind, you are an old soul. Centred, anchored."

"I don't have any idea what you are talking about." She shook her head at him and wondered how she could get away.

He went to the window and leaned back against the sill, blocking the light. "There are things we can never truly know, but there are forces we can connect with, that we can feel." His eyes locked onto hers. "That is, if we work in harmony with the rhythms of the galaxy."

"I'm afraid I'm not following you." She gathered her things from the floor.

That thin smile again. "If I were to break your sentence in two—*I am afraid. I am not following you*—would that be closer to the truth, I wonder?"

"I think we're both wasting our time." She stood and walked toward the door.

"You are free to go, of course. But if you want to learn how the ancient Egyptians interpreted the stars, you will have to start to think differently. You must understand their concepts of cosmology, the way they physically and spiritually connected to the universe. For many, it's the study of a lifetime."

"I see. Well, I've only got a few weeks." She slung her bag over her shoulder, expecting him to see her out, but he made no effort to move.

"Then we must get to work immediately."

***

Later that night, as Rachel rode in a taxi back to her hotel, she was at a loss to remember exactly what had happened next, how she went from nearly walking out on him, to being seated once more in the leather chair, smoking far too many Turkish cigarettes, even eating with him. She had no memory of any discussion about food, only that at some point there was *aish baladi,* the dry wheat bread, *tahini,* nuts and fruit on the brass table and that she ate hungrily and drank the jasmine tea that was somehow constantly refreshed.

As Karl began to talk, the cadence of his voice and the clipped edges softened. He spoke of the ancient Egyptian *Book of the Dead,* the concept of "coming into light," about their belief in permanence and predictability, the rising and setting of the sun, the course of the stars, the flooding of the Nile, the idea that goodness would be rewarded and wrong-doing punished. He talked of their conviction that chaos was always there beneath the surface and that balance and harmony were critical to the natural order of the universe. Rachel felt she was listening to a long, long story, a story that stretched across thousands of years, a story that was a message, something she was meant to hear, and that somehow, she had a role in this story. She thought back to his strange behaviour earlier, when he took her hands and asked her what she felt. Perhaps he had tried to explain, but she was mesmerized by his words and could not follow every twist and turn.

She became aware of the changing of the light at the window and realized with a start, as though she had drifted into sleep and woken suddenly, that she had spent nearly three hours in his company. She stubbed out her cigarette and got to her feet, not sure what to say.

"I think I should be going."

"If you want to learn more, you must commit yourself." He began to re-arrange the papers on his desk. She felt he was waiting for some kind of response.

"I'm here on assignment," she said. "The sponsors would compensate you, of course."

"What a strange word. Compensation is for victims. It's not what I mean. I'm looking for someone, an assistant, to help me with the store and with other aspects of my work. You're here only for the rest of the summer, you said. That's not ideal, but we can make a start. We can help each other. And things change, especially if we really want them to. This will suit you?"

She could scarcely believe what she'd heard and was tempted to ask what had caused this change of heart but didn't want to try his patience. She told him she would be pleased to help and gave him more details about her project, but he continued to sort the papers on his desk and she could tell he was only half-listening.

***

Weeks later, he told her the truth of that day. He had no thoughts of looking for an assistant. In all his years of work, it had never entered his mind. But he had seen a rare psychic sympathy in the pattern of stars in her chart, a strong synergy to those in his own, and there was something in her eyes that he recognized, a chord of connection. He was certain it was linked to the strange energy and the jolt of premonition he had felt when he was out in the desert the night before, taking photographs of the Scorpion moon.

Chapter 3

The very mystery of Cairo was comforting to Rachel. Gradually, she became familiar with the narrow streets and made her way to Karl's home each morning with a light step, watching the day unfold. The local people began to recognize her and she would greet the merchants unlocking and sliding up the corrugated metal doors to their shops. Waiters setting up the tables outside their small cafés tried to coax her in for a mint tea or the thick, rich coffee she could smell brewing in their back kitchens.

Later she would look back and wonder why she hadn't been more curious about Karl's work, the lack of customers in the store, his dismissal of any concern about this, the long telephone calls, and his disappearance into the study to take them. But those first few weeks were a jumble of new sights and sounds, the delight that her work for the museum project would take on new relevance and meaning, and the first inkling of something deeper that she dared not acknowledge.

In the morning, Karl sometimes printed off night sky photographs and pinned them on the cork boards, writing different notations and observations beneath them. But usually he was up in his study. His lectures at the university were in the evenings, he told her, and she assumed he spent most mornings preparing for these. He rarely surfaced until mid-day. He liked classical music, and Rachmaninov's third piano concerto, a particular favourite of his, would often drift through the low ceiling. Years later, hearing a passage from that same concerto brought back the heat of those days, the smell of incense and old wood, the shafts of dust at the window, the competing noises of the muezzin and the street merchants—memories that spiraled into a twist of excitement in the pit of her stomach, a jolt of suffocated longing.

While he was occupied, he encouraged her to do her own work, or get to know the things in the store by rearranging them however she wanted. Clearly, he had no interest in this. She felt like a child on a treasure hunt, turning each item over in her hands, blowing off the dust and wiping it clean: astrolabes, globes, maps of the world, astronomy books in several languages, almanacs, ephemeris tables, charts of the heavens in both hemispheres in every season, complex diagrams of the ancient Egyptian *Neter-Khert* astral plane. She lingered over the shallow, glass-topped drawers filled with copper, silver and gold amulets, and systematically polished and rearranged these, standing back to admire her efforts.

At lunch, he would bring out Egyptian flat bread, two or three cheeses, nuts, fruit and jasmine tea. The closeness of him began to unsettle her and made her blush or stammer.

He was not good at idle chatter and would often read while he ate.

Ahmed was the first person he introduced her to. He was a young man, easy to recognize because he always wore a *tarbouche*. Later, Rachel learned this was for nostalgic reasons. He was Moroccan and his father used to earn his living making these red fez caps. But Ahmed resisted her attempts to get to know him. He brought what she assumed were papers for Karl to read or mark and the two of them usually retreated upstairs. They spoke to each other in Arabic. Rachel often heard raised voices, and Ahmed would leave in a hurry.

Sometime after lunch, Karl would signal to her to join him in the study to discuss her research and work with her on her project. He gave her reference material and pictures of ancient Egyptian carvings that featured the night sky, encouraged her to write her own interpretations, and helped her to expand on them.

Usually, in the afternoon, he would make tea and bring up a few *ghoraiba* cookies that she had become particularly fond of. Today, he poured the tea in silence and sat back in the leather chair, his hands pressed together in a steeple. He appeared to be thinking carefully about something. It was several moments before he leaned forward to pick up his tea.

"So, Rachel," he said, "I believe you can help me with some of the other work I do."

He told her he developed astrological interpretations, incorporating the beliefs of the ancient Egyptians, for clients:

businessmen, bankers, international government officials, some of them high-ranking, all of them fearful about their careers, their finances, their mistresses, all wanting reassurance and "answers."

"People are always anxious to learn their destiny," he said, "to believe that there is an explanation for the way things are turning out, a reason to hope that things might be better."

She was astonished that he was involved in what many would consider to be a questionable pursuit. She wondered if he needed the money. "So that's why you're called 'Star Reader,'" she said. "The little boy who helped me find you—that's what he said."

Karl smiled. "I can see you are struggling with this, Rachel. But the stars and planets have influenced so many old and highly intelligent civilizations. Why would they stop now?"

There was no logical answer to that.

He told her she could help him with the preparation work, the mapping of the skies, the ancient Egyptian beliefs and mythologies that he always referenced. And surely, he added, this would help bring a new and compelling angle to her research. Despite her misgivings, she was thrilled by his faith in her abilities and anxious to prove she was capable of helping him more.

But back in her hotel that night, she struggled to get to sleep. An old memory from her childhood came unexpectedly to mind. She had done well in a science test and was excited to show her father, who usually picked her up from school, that the teacher had written "excellent!" beside her mark. But it was her mother who came that day. She looked at the test. "Let's see if you can get those results for *every* subject," she said.

Now she wondered if being so pleased with Karl's confidence in her was a pitiful need for praise, something that often worried her but she was loathe to admit. She pushed this aside. She would take pleasure in helping him and she convinced herself there was nothing wrong with that.

***

Increasingly, she looked forward to the afternoon talks, checking the clock all morning and willing the time to pass quickly. At first, she made copious notes but eventually she would just stop and listen, letting her tea grow cold, letting Karl take her effortlessly through the scenery and language of the cosmic planes and pathways in a long-forgotten world. There was a stillness about him that she was drawn to, a sense of being in an elevated state of mind where everything around him was in its right place, contributing to his own particular harmony but assuming a greater significance simply because he was close by.

To prepare for the readings, she looked up information in his huge reference books, plotted the charts and tackled the initial interpretation. She asked if this information had not been digitized on the internet, readily available with a few clicks of the mouse. Karl told her that relying on these sources was lazy, that it was too easy to fall into sweeping generalizations, not something he ever wanted to be accused of.

She found herself enjoying this aspect of the work and was delighted when he leafed through her papers, nodding his head slowly. "You obviously have a knack for reading the stars," he said. "But I believe it is an intellectual fascination. Am I right?"

The question caught her off guard. "Yes. I mean... I'm enthralled by it. It's all so interesting."

"But you don't believe it."

"Believe? Well ... I'm not sure what I believe."

He smiled, but more to himself that than to her.

***

The cramped study soon began to feel like home. She was conscious of when the sun's light filled every corner and when it passed behind the jumbled buildings in the distance and threw her work into shadow. She often lingered by the open window and took in the warm vanilla smells that wafted up from the bakery. Young boys strolled beneath her, trays piled high with hot pita bread and crescent rolls balanced on their heads, delivering to the local cafés. They learned her name and called out to her in broken English as they passed. "Rachel-Rachel. You are to be having special good day, *in shaa Allah.*" Sometimes they took a furtive look both ways then tossed a sweet roll for her to catch. Her life in this city felt separate and complete, as though it existed on another dimension, like something Gulliver might have found on one of his travels.

She was eager to learn more about this man she worked with but felt he would resist direct questions ... like had he ever been married, was there a woman somewhere, what family did he have? She tried offering details of her own family as a hopeful conversation starter. She told him that her Canadian mother spent years in the London theatre, aspiring to be British, that her father was Italian and she was born and grew up in Calabria. After her father's death, her restless mother had moved her and her brother Robert back and forth from Canada to Europe. Robert eventually settled in England but she chose to stay in Canada to attend university because North America promised an openness and freedom she longed for. She found herself blurting these things out but would then stop, embarrassed by his silence. He listened politely but offered little in return, telling her only that he had come to Cairo several years before to do some lecturing for the university, and decided to stay.

He was obsessed with neatness and order. After she had tidied up at the end of their working sessions, he would always find something to rearrange, some book that had been put back in the wrong place, a stray pen that needed to be returned to a drawer. In the kitchen, cans were lined up like soldiers, their labels facing forwards. Nothing was haphazard.

One morning, looking at plates of engravings through a magnifying glass, she felt him watching her and turned to see him smiling. He asked how much she paid for her copper bracelets and, when she told him, said "Come, I'll teach you some Arabic and show you how to bargain."

As he guided her through the narrow alleyways away from his home, he made a conspicuous figure, she thought, with his clear grey eyes and that blond hair falling past his shoulders. His fairness was a curiosity to those who didn't know him; some would stare, then freeze in astonishment as he called out a greeting in fluent Arabic.

They went to the Khan al-Khalili, a teeming bazaar, where he surprised her by joking around with the merchants, who performed admirable imitations of outrage and hurt pride when he haggled for a lower price. She was amazed to see him grinning as he pretended to argue with great animation in this guttural, aspirate language. He made her repeat certain phrases: *Bikam hadha?* How much is this? *Hatha ghaliah ghidan.* That's too much. *Lust muhtalmsetm.* I'm not interested. She was aware of the looks the vendors were giving the two of them, eyes raised, rapid exchanges of Arabic, and wished she could understand what they were saying. Karl took a photograph from one of them, a new grandson, she gathered. His fingers were long and slim, neatly manicured, and the blond hairs on his arm were caught in a stray shaft of sunlight. His other hand was hooked into a well-worn leather belt, his thumb pulling it down at the waist, a habit she found strangely alluring.

She admired a pewter pendant with the hieroglyphic for wind. The merchant clasped his hands to his throat when Karl suggested a price but, with much fake anguish, he relented. Rachel reached for her purse but Karl insisted on paying. He removed her sunhat and slipped the pendant over her head. His eyes lingered on hers for a second and her breath stopped at the back of her throat. Maybe this little outing was his way of making a move.

But the next day he was curt and impatient. When the work was done and they said goodbye, she was left wondering if the previous afternoon had been a dream.

Chapter 4

One morning, Karl announced he'd be out for most of the day. He left some night-sky maps on the desk and suggested Rachel study them, plotting in the planetary aspects, the associated gods and other symbols, and interpreting them as the ancient Egyptians would. He left a list of questions for her to answer.

This was the first time she'd been there alone and she felt a guilty pleasure, like a child momentarily forgotten in a room that was usually off-limits. She was needed down in the store only once, to help a couple of students who were looking for telescope filters. When she went back upstairs, she noticed that the bedroom door was ajar. She tried to squeeze around it to peer inside but stopped herself and walked away. Then she stopped again, her sense of propriety warring with an intense desire to snoop. She went back and edged around the door. The room was stark—no pictures, no photographs, nothing to give any hint of a past or a personal life. The only relief to the bare, whitewashed walls was a faded map of the northern sky and, on the simple chest of drawers, an old globe showing a world long out-of-date. Her eyes lingered on the bed. It had black wrought iron head and footboards and was neatly made. There were iron lamps on the bedside tables and, on one of them, an ashtray. A chair and a large wardrobe stood against the far wall. With only a second's hesitation, she stepped toward the wardrobe and opened the door: a row of shirts on wooden hangers, a dark linen jacket, jeans, several pairs of sandals lined up on the floor, sweaters folded neatly on the shelf above. She thought how he would recoil if he saw the jumble of her own closets. She fingered the sleeve of the jacket and brought it close to her nose. A hint of Turkish cigarette smoke. Feeling a flush of shame, she dropped it, resolved to get over this infatuation, get on with her work, and go home. She left quickly, making sure the door was exactly the way she had found it.

The work he'd given her was difficult, and she grew restless. She gazed out over the thick haze of the city, through a break in the rooftops of the jumbled dwellings nearby, to the minarets of the Mosque of Al-Azhar outlined in the distance against the yellow sky. The high-pitched cry of verses from the Koran signalled *Salat-ul-Zuhr*, the call for the noon prayer. She had been dimly aware of the day taking shape outside the window but now she gave it a moment of full appraisal, letting the noises from the labyrinth of narrow streets fracture her thoughts. The hawkers were hustling, their reedy voices crying out their wares, the wheels of their carts, worn crooked on the uneven cobbles, creaking and rattling by.

She got up to stretch, moving to stand beneath the cooler air from the ceiling fan, and looked more closely at the books crammed on the sagging shelves. She recognized a biography of William Lilly, a 17th century astrologer, and leafed through the well-thumbed pages. Farther along were collections of Freud and Nietzsche, in the German, and Carl Jung's *Psychology and Alchemy* in English translation. *The Chaldean Oracles of Zoroaster, The Origins of Egyptian Culture;* some of these she knew, but most looked challenging, like so many closed doors to forbidden worlds. She pulled out one at random. *Secret Rituals from the Egyptian Book of the Dead.* Fanning the pages, she saw that several corners had been turned down and there were a great many notes in the margins.

It was nearly lunch time and she was getting hungry. Usually Karl made lunch. It would feel odd to muck about in his kitchen when he wasn't there. But then he couldn't expect her to go all day without eating. She had no idea when he'd be back.

She opened the fridge and found he had left a plate of vegetables and hummus and a few apricots, the pits removed, already sliced. The plates were covered with plastic wrap. Wow! That was decent of him. She put the kettle on for some mint tea and looked around. She had a craving for something sweet and wondered where he kept those addictive *ghoraiba* cookies. She contemplated going across to the bakery but thought better of it. The baker clearly didn't like her. A single man and woman working alone together was probably frowned upon or perhaps it was her bare arms and legs that provoked the shaking of the head and barked comments to his wife in the back on the rare occasions she ventured in. She resolved to be a little more discreet.

She opened a few cupboard doors. One of them appeared to be locked. She tugged on it unsuccessfully. All the doors had small keyholes underneath the handles but only this one wouldn't budge. She resigned herself to going without the cookies, made the tea and tried to remember where the tea canister belonged. On a shelf by the oven, she noticed a small wooden box, inlaid with mother-of-pearl. Inside was an iron key.

Leave it alone, she told herself. But the strong desire to pry, the same compulsion she felt earlier, took over. She looked over her shoulder. Copernicus was on one of the kitchen chairs watching her with his usual disdain. She slid the key in the locked cupboard. It opened easily.

The first thing she noticed was a piece of paper taped to the inside of the door. The words sloped forward. It was Karl's handwriting, all in German. It was a list of some sort, with measurements. It looked like a recipe. What on earth could that be and why was it locked up, she wondered. *Die Salbei Tinktur des Wahrsagers* was the heading. She found a piece of paper and pencil and copied those words down.

On the shelf inside was a canvas bag. She took this over to the kitchen table. It had different sized pockets around the outside, all with their own zipper. It was heavy. One by one she unzipped and lifted out the contents, each of them wrapped in white cloth. A small knife with a steel blade and ebony handle fell from the folds of one and clattered to the floor. Rachel jumped and Copernicus leapt from the chair. She unwrapped another item—a silver flask, beautifully carved with the four elemental genii: *Imset, Hapi, Duamutef, Qebehsenuef*—air, water, earth and fire. She tried to tell herself she had no business looking in here. But she couldn't stop. She found a pewter spoon with a deep bowl, a small glass bottle with a dropper and several plastic bags filled with what looked like herbs or dried leaves. She opened one of these and sniffed but couldn't tell what it was. She took the top off the silver flask. It smelled like green tea. She dipped her little finger inside and licked it. Very bitter. A car horn blasted outside the window and her heartbeat quickened. Anxious now, she gathered up the plastic bags, not realizing she hadn't sealed them properly. Some of their contents spilled to the floor. With growing panic, she scooped everything up as best she could, replaced it all in the canvas bag and put this back in the cupboard, trying to remember exactly how she had found it. She returned the key to its little box.

Back upstairs she made an attempt to reapply herself to the work, stopping frequently to drink the water and dab at the sweat on her temples. But she couldn't concentrate. The calculations required a good sense of geometry and arithmetic and she grew tired and made mistakes.

From the pocket of her jeans she took out the scrap of paper she'd written the recipe name on it and found the German-English dictionary she'd seen on one of the shelves. *Salbei*: sage. *Tinktur:* tincture. *Wahrsagers:* soothsayers. She scribbled the English words on a scrap of paper. "Sage tincture of the soothsayers." Well that didn't make any more sense, she thought.

She gave up on the work and dropped into her leather chair, lit a cigarette and inhaled deeply. *What are those things?* Except for the hieroglyphics on the flask, there was nothing connected to ancient Egypt. *And why are they under lock and key?* A more disturbing thought took root in her mind.

It was growing dark outside. She was hot and sweaty and the cigarette was making her dizzy. She wondered where the cat had gone. He rarely left the room when someone was in it. She felt a faint movement of air and twisted to look behind her. Karl was standing near the doorway, totally still, his feet planted apart, the air from the ceiling fan lifting the hair from his shoulders. He was holding Copernicus. Both were watching her. She let out a startled cry and grabbed the arms of the chair.

"What is the matter?" He reached over to switch on the lamp behind her. "Why are you sitting in the dark?"

She blinked in the yellowy light. "You frightened me, sneaking in like that."

He dropped the cat and walked round to face her. "This is my home. I'm not 'sneaking.' Did you finish the work?"

"I had to start a few calculations over. I'm not quite done."

He glanced at the waste basket of crumpled paper, shook his head, then sat at the desk to look at what she'd completed, flicking through the pages and tapping his pen in clearly suppressed irritation. After a minute or two, he reached for the decanter and poured himself a glass of whisky.

"Is it okay?" she asked.

He stacked the charts neatly and tidied up. "It will do for now."

A scrap of creased paper on the edge of the desk caught his attention. He looked at the words and froze. "What is this?"

Rachel's heart leapt to her throat. She groped for a plausible explanation. "I was looking for those cookies in the kitchen. I guess… I found a key to a locked cupboard. I'm sorry. I got curious. I thought it was a recipe. I was just messing around."

He looked at her in silence for several moments, then tore the scrap of paper in two. He spoke slowly, as though to a small child. "Please don't touch anything that doesn't concern you. There are things you won't understand."

"I'm sorry. I didn't mean any harm."

"Is there anything else you 'messed around' with?"

She thought about confessing to opening the canvas bag. God knows what he would think of her. Her mouth was dry. No words would come.

He gave her that cold stare again. "Ahmed's outside. He will take you back to your hotel."

She began moving past him towards the stairs. "I can walk. I do it every day."

He put his hand lightly on her shoulder to stop her. "Ahmed will drive you."

Downstairs, Karl exchanged a few brief words in Arabic with Ahmed and gave him an envelope which Ahmed slid quickly into the pocket of his jeans. With mock civility, Karl held open the car door with a slight bow of his head as she climbed in. She looked in the side mirror and saw him at the edge of the road, watching as they moved away.

Ahmed drove in silence and the car made slow progress, competing with donkeys and carts, bicycles precariously laden with baskets, street urchins proffering tourists tiny souvenirs —pyramid key chains, a miniature Sphinx, lucky charms. Her cheeks were flushed and she could feel Ahmed's eyes on her. He let her out at the entrance to her hotel and told her he would pick her up in the morning. He would call from the lobby at eight-thirty.

"Eight-thirty? But I usually start much earlier than that. And I enjoy the walk in the morning. Really."

"Karl has said." He waved goodbye and drove off.

For the rest of the evening, she went over and over the brief exchange with Karl and wondered why she felt so damned intimidated by him. *That infuriating tone of voice, the arrogance of the man!* She was angry with herself for getting all hot and bothered about him, hoping to get involved. And she thanked God he hadn't come home earlier and caught her at the kitchen table with those things from the cupboard.

Eventually, her own surroundings and the familiarity of her few possessions—her books, her clothes hanging in the closet, her shoes kicked under the table—made her feel better. In the bathroom, the shampoos, crèmes and lotions from home, little icons of an ordinary life, reassured her with their intimacy and their optimistic English names: *Herbal Essence, Dove, Intensive Care.* Obviously, she thought, he was fussy and no one appreciates meddlers. Tomorrow she would apologize and try to laugh it off. But after she went to bed the anxiety bubbled up and did not lift with the morning sun.

***

Eight-thirty came and went. For an hour, she stared through the window, trying to make out Ahmed's familiar red fez, but there was no sign of him.

The jangle of the telephone went through her like a jolt of electricity. "A change of plan. We won't work today." Karl's voice, crisp and cool. "Meet me at el Tahrir bridge at eight o'clock tonight. It will be an interesting evening."

Rachel wavered between relief and concern. "Wouldn't it be just as easy to meet here?" she said. "The bridge is only fifteen minutes away."

"Then it will be a leisurely walk. Enjoy your day."

The day was far from enjoyable. She wandered through the neighbourhoods, not at all sure how to fill her time, trying to fight off the little twists of fear.

She found herself at Fadoul's café. On a rare break from their work, Karl had introduced her to the owner, a grizzled old man with a permanent scowl and a few random teeth. He always ignored Rachel and would steer Karl to the back for whispered conversations. She was relieved to see his partner, Mustafa, a younger and friendlier man, attending to the tables outside. It was already hot and he sat her under the shade of an umbrella, the Fanta logos around its edges torn and faded.

She drank a lemonade, pulled out some postcards she'd bought and attempted to write one to her brother in England, giving him a few details of her project and suggesting it could lead to good opportunities later on. Her words sounded vague, but she hesitated to tell him more. She imagined her sister-in-law Melinda: "A postcard from Rachel, dear? Cairo! Oh, do tell!" "Some strange project or other," Robert might say. "God knows if she'll ever get a *real* job." Rachel ripped it up and instead wrote to Nigel, telling him she was making good progress with Karl's help and that she might stay on a little longer.

She looked around. She had the odd feeling someone was watching her, but she saw no one. When Mustafa brought the bill, she knocked over her glass and dropped several coins that he helped her retrieve from under the table.

Standing at el Tahrir bridge that evening, she doubted her common sense. She knew very little about Karl and no one, other than her sponsors in Canada, knew the substance of her agreement with him. Even they did not know his address. And here she was about to let herself in for "an interesting evening." She worried she wasn't even dressed right —the same jeans and strappy sandals she had worn all day. At the last minute she had thrown a loose cotton shirt over her sleeveless top, checked her hair and put on fresh lipstick. *Why, for God's sake?*

Within minutes, the car pulled up. Karl reached over and opened the passenger door.

Chapter 5

She could just make out the darker shapes of the pyramids in the distance. He steadied her arm as she stumbled in the loose sand.

She was barely able to keep up. Hanging over his shoulder was the canvas bag she had found in the kitchen cupboard. She felt the panic rising and pulled back. "Where are we going?"

"We've got a lot to discuss. This is the best place." He urged her forward.

"Let go of me, please." She jerked herself loose and began to run but couldn't gain any traction in the sand. He quickly caught her and held tightly to her wrist. A bolt of fear shot through her. She pushed at him wildly with her free hand. "You're scaring me. Let me go."

"Rachel! Calm down. You're hysterical. Listen to me." He let her go and she fell backwards into the sand. "What on earth has got into you?" He dropped the canvas bag and stood over her. "I want to explain something. That's all. Let me—" He reached out his hand to help her up but she swiped it away.

"Get away from me. What the hell do you think you're doing?" Her voice was shrill in the night air. She rubbed her wrist.

"What am I doing? I've been angry all day and night because you pried into things that don't concern you. And you lacked the courage to admit it," he said, "But now *you* have the nerve to yell at *me*. I'm sorry if I hurt you."

She pushed herself further away from him. "I knew something was wrong. I had a strange feeling all day. I should have left." She stopped, another dark thought fighting through. "Oh God. You followed me. Right? Or got someone else to follow me, more likely."

He didn't answer for a moment. All she could hear was her own shallow breathing.

"I will explain everything," he said finally.

"I'm right, aren't I?" she whispered. "Jesus Christ."

"I needed to know you were not going to run around talking to people. Doing more damage."

"You're sick. The stuff in that bag. I know what you're into. I want no part of it." She fought to stem the tears welling up behind her eyes. "Please. Let me go home."

She struggled to her feet and staggered away but the black vastness of the desert engulfed her. She had no idea which way to go. After a few steps she sunk down and covered her face with her hands. A repetitive click made her twist around. Through her fingers she watched him cup his hands to light a cigarette, take a deep drag and exhale slowly through pursed lips. Wispy clouds scudded across the gibbous moon, throwing him in and out of its pale light. In a while, he flicked the cigarette away, ground it into the sand with his heel and walked towards her.

"Stay the hell away from me." Her tears were spilling freely now. She hated herself for crying.

"I'm not going to hurt you." He knelt beside her and pried her fingers away from her eyes. "I brought you here because this is a special place. I want your full attention. When you disturbed those substances, you upset some careful preparation. I am going to explain." He took a tissue from his pocket and dabbed at her tears. She twisted away. "Rachel, look at me."

She met his gaze and felt the sinking heaviness of defeat, as though the blood were draining from her body. There was no way out. A light breeze picked up and scurried over the dunes, sending tiny showers of sand stinging around them.

"That work I left for you was not as it seemed. It was about you." He hesitated. "I wanted you to find out for yourself what I knew the day we met. How the Egyptians would have read your whole astral identity. Who you are. What you can be. I thought you'd be excited, asking lots of questions. But the information didn't register. You didn't see yourself in the charts. I came home to find you distracted, jumping like a scared rabbit, and then—" She heard the edge of irritation creep back in his voice. "You know the rest."

She thought back to the sky maps. She had approached them analytically, examining the angles, 'translating' the hieroglyphics. She hadn't let them tell their story. She turned away, her fear and anger now laced with humiliation.

He lay down full length on the sand and stared at the sky. "Look at all that, Rachel. Don't you feel its pull, its seduction? A thousand million worlds to discover."

She followed his gaze, trying to focus through her swollen eyes. The Milky Way arced down to the south, smearing the stars, blotting out the tail of the constellation Scorpio. Several minutes passed. She thought again about trying to run but even if she found where they'd left the car, she'd never get a cab out here at this time.

"There are things you must know," he said finally, sitting up to face her. "I was waiting for the right time. Now it has to be today." He pushed his hair back from his shoulders. "A little while ago, I was here, close to where we are now, studying the sky, taking photographs. But there was something strange about that night, a different kind of energy, almost palpable. The next day, you came." He leaned closer. "You were sent."

"*Sent?* What do you mean? Sent by whom? That's bullshit. I don't believe that stuff." Her voice broke, more tears bottling up at the edge of it.

"It's very clear. There's a lot you have to learn but this is what you must know. We were meant to meet. We were meant to work together." He pulled a cigarette from the pack in his shirt pocket, lit it and handed it to her. Her hand shook as she brought it to her lips. He took her other hand, squeezing her fingers lightly. She looked down at this, as though she were outside her own body, knowing she should pull away but having no strength to do so. "You have an old soul, Rachel. The four elements work beautifully through you here, in perfect harmony. In your other life, you were out of synch, never at peace with yourself or with the world around you. You belong here. You have come home."

She stared into the darkness. *How dare he assume to know how I feel, where I belong?* But he had touched a nerve, an old childhood anxiety that was fueled by her family's constant upheaval, and never having the chance to put down roots.

"It's something you feel but cannot describe," he said, as though reading her mind. "There's a universal energy around us, carried through the four elements. Most people walk through life half asleep, not even aware of these forces, much less able to identify them and use them. But *we* can. I will show you."

She scooped up some sand, scrunching it in her fingers, and tried again to steady her breathing. If she could play along and get through this night, tomorrow she would flee. "What do you mean, 'use' them?"

"Getting past the conscious mind, getting to an elevated state where the forces of the four elements can channel freely through you." There was an excitement in his voice that scared her more than his cold irritation. He put his hand on her shoulder. "There is no reason to be frightened, Rachel. This is what you came here to study, this higher consciousness is what the ancient Egyptians embraced long before our own civilization took its first breath. Why should we only read and write about it in research papers? Why should we not experience it first-hand?"

"That's not why I came here. You're talking about drugs. I know. That's what I found, didn't I?"

"Drugs! Ah Rachel, what a pedestrian way of classifying." He placed the canvas bag between them. "These items are symbols and instruments to summon the power of a much higher state of awareness. They are natural substances that must be carefully blended and measured to help with the transition, to get past the conscious mind, the rational, artificial boundaries. You spilled them and mixed them all up." He looked down and paused a few seconds, then reached for her hand. "I apologize for my anger."

She managed a weak smile, then couldn't believe she had done this. Was she under some kind of spell? Was he bewitching her right now?

"Tonight," he said, "I will show you what these things can do. They are not harmful. I promise you."

The anxiety welled up again and she edged away. "No. I want to go back now."

"Think about your own work. The Egyptians believed in the importance of ritual and symbolism and developed different kinds of stimulants to release the conscious mind. What I'm going to show you is how you can do this too, how you can tap into the deeper energy that flows through the very core of you, how you can channel the power of your imagination."

She shook her head, still trying to back away.

"Don't be scared, Rachel. Tonight, we will summon the elements: fire, earth, air and water. I'll show you how to respect them and work with them. You will feel wonderful."

The air had grown cooler and she shivered. She hadn't dressed for a Saharan night. He gave her the sweater that was tied loosely around his shoulders and sat cross-legged in front of her. The desert rolled away from them on all sides in total darkness. In the slender beam of his flashlight, he laid out all the items from the canvas bag and began to explain things that would change her life forever.

Her last coherent memory was sipping from the silver flask, holding the liquid under her tongue before swallowing it. The anxiety left her. There was no more reason to be afraid. All sensations collided with the full force of the four elements that coursed through her.

A fierce wind blew so strongly that she had to lean into it. It swept her hair back, it whipped up the sand around her legs, stinging her skin. It snatched the words from her mouth and flung them skyward. She was weightless. She lifted easily into the air, floating freely. He gave her things to hold. She looked down and saw them but did not feel them in her hands. Her hands belonged to someone else.

She stepped into a field of fire, yellow and red. The flames licked at her, she smelled the scorch of her clothes, she felt the heat course through her and rivers of sweat break out on her forehead. But she was not afraid. The fire engulfed her and she reached out and took whole flames of it into her hands. She embraced it, teased it, danced with it. It did not burn.

She was being dragged into the sand. The sand smelled of rich, dark earth, heavy and rain-soaked. Her limbs became long tap roots, twisting underground, pushing downwards to draw up all the goodness of the planet. The warm soil soothed her, filling her mouth, her ears, her eyes. But she could see and hear clearly and her breath carried its earthy fragrance.

She stepped into a pool and slid under the surface. The pool grew deeper and deeper, a bottomless abyss, dark blue. The water was cool silk on her skin. She swam down effortlessly, not needing to breathe. A soft peace flooded through her. Her hair swung gently around her face. She let herself hang, motionless in the water, then slowly rise, endlessly upwards. The surface was miles above but she had all the time in the world.

She heard Karl call her name but his voice was weak and distant as though in a dream. She tried to answer but she was still under the surface. His voice grew louder, insistent, and finally she could feel the full force of his presence. She felt his hand on her shoulder.

She was shivering uncontrollably. "What happened? Where are we?"

"You are here. With me. Everything that happened was under your control. *You* made it happen. It's okay. Breathe deeply."

She clutched his sweater to her body and tried to bring the images into focus. But they slid away.

He helped her to her feet. "Come, you are tired. You will sleep long and deeply tonight. Tomorrow you will feel as light as air, I promise."

Back in the car, dizzy and disoriented, she pulled down the visor and looked at herself in the mirror. "I thought my hair was wet." She touched it and rubbed her fingers. "I remember water. A lot of water."

He smiled and his eyes flared with excitement. He put the car into gear. "All in good time, *mein Schatz*, you will understand everything in time."

Chapter 6

There were so many opportunities to get away. He never made any attempt to restrain her. He dropped her at her hotel that night and she could have booked a flight the next morning. But already, even in those early days, before he turned her life inside out, some force, some dormant desire kept her captive.

The very next evening after the trip to the desert, they went to a restaurant on the Corniche on the banks of the Nile. Methodically, like a teacher with a new student, Karl explained the true nature of his work. People came to him with their problems, their deep desires, he said, not only because he was a 'star reader' but because he could help them channel their true energy, achieve a finer balance in their lives, work with the rhythms of the galaxy instead of fighting against them. He said all this matter-of-factly, stopping to reach for the salt, to refill her wine glass, to ask the waiter a question, as though he were talking about any ordinary day at the office. She was unsure whether the information itself or his unequivocal belief was more startling. These people paid him, of course. Sometimes they bought the various ingredients from him and worked alone but usually he stayed with them, helping them with stimulus and suggestion.

"Come on Karl," she said. "That all sounds very noble. But in the end, you're interpreting the stars for them and then selling them drugs to help them believe it." She was surprised by the candour of her own words. Somehow the busy environment of the restaurant, the sounds of horns outside on the road, the commotion of ordinary life gave her courage that she would not have felt at his home. "And whatever the impact," she continued "surely it's only temporary."

He took a sip of wine and looked at her over the rim of the glass. She felt the coolness of his gaze. "Ah, the handcuffs of conventional wisdom. If it isn't proven, it can't be true. But it is true. Wishing hard for something to happen is a very powerful tool. I'm saying 'wishing' because it's based on pure desire. Praying is different. Praying is rooted in desperation and therefore doomed to fail." He put the wine glass down and leaned forward. "Pure desire is at the root of what I'm doing, what we can do, for those who seek help. The ancient Egyptians believed the spirit body, the *Ka*, could leave the physical body, and they were able to envision whole new states of being. For them, ceremony and ritual played important roles, as you know. They intensify emotion, give it greater purpose and direction so the different reality you imagine has a greater chance of manifesting itself."

"That stuff I found, what I took out in the desert —it's hallucinogenic, isn't it? That's why I had all those weird sensations. Isn't it dangerous? Is it even legal?"

"Let's just say it would be frowned upon. Not a good thing for the authorities to discover. That's why I was concerned." He told her about *salvia divinorum, Die Salbei Tinktur des Wahrsagers* or "Diviner's Sage," how it was sometimes difficult to get, but Ahmed, who had a good source, took care of that. He explained how it releases you from the conscious mind but, because of the way you prepare yourself, you are not hallucinating, you are simply imagining—imagining a greater sense of peace, of control, of power, of harmony. He stressed that, used correctly, it was not dangerous. It was therapeutic, giving people a new sense of possibility, new resolve with which to tackle the challenges of their lives.

As he talked, she kept questioning her state of mind and why she was even listening to this. She imagined how she would react to someone else describing the same situation. Surely, she'd tell them this man was manipulative, dangerous. She wished there were someone she could confide in. Perhaps Janet, her old university friend. But Janet could be critical and bossy. Against the backdrop of the noise and laughter in the restaurant, she felt the old familiar ache of her childhood loneliness, the sense that she was always on the sidelines, irrelevant. She wasn't good at making and keeping friends. Nigel was her best bet. Dear Nigel. He was nearly twenty years her senior but, in many ways, the closest friend she had. They had met in the art section of a book store while she was still at university. She was flipping through a book on Vermeer. He bumped into her while trying to pass by, causing her to drop it. "If you're serious about Vermeer," he said, retrieving it for her, "there is only one book you should have and it's not here." He told her he had a copy at home and she could pick it up at his store if she cared to drop by the next day. And so, began the regular Saturday morning get-togethers over coffee. Sometimes Philippe would join them and she learned so much about art and the whole world of antiques. Nigel probably thought of her as a protégé. She wondered how much he knew about all this stuff Karl was into. She had only a vague idea of what Nigel himself was up to when he was in this part of the world. "Sex, drugs and rock and roll, my dear ... what else?" he had once told her with a wink. He had made her put her name down for that art criticism course. It was over a year away and she didn't understand why he was so insistent. It was as though he wanted to ensure she'd be home by then. But surely, she reasoned, he wouldn't have given her Karl's name if he thought the man was dangerous.

The evening air was still hot and clammy as Karl walked her back to her hotel. The heat never bothered him; no sweat stained his clothes or darkened his hair. He stepped into the road to make way for a man with a crippled leg who was valiantly pushing a cart laden with fruit and vegetables. Drivers veered around him, honking their horns.

They came to a section of the Corniche that widened out with tall palm trees and stood for a while, watching the boats plying their way up and down the Nile. Their shoulders were nearly touching. Rachel imagined what the feel of his blue cotton shirt on her bare arm would be like if they were just one inch closer.

"Everything I have told you is about staying in harmony with the rhythms of nature, the elements, the forces of destiny," he said. "We are giving people a respite from the trauma of their lives, helping them to get in touch with their deeper selves."

A bus pulled up close by and disgorged its cargo of noisy tourists clutching cameras, maps, sunhats, some announcing they'd be heading straight to bed, others claiming to be desperate for a cold shower or a beer. Karl watched them for a while, then turned back to look across the river.

"The ancient Egyptians were masters of this larger concept of the universe and, as long as the knowledge is in the hands of people who respect it, people like us, we can use it to help others."

He turned to her, his face so close to her own. She could smell the smokiness of his breath. She had no idea how to respond. She was dwelling only on "people like us" and trying to deal with the tight grip of anticipation as she met his gaze.

Chapter 7

There were more visitors to the store now. He had been postponing appointments until Rachel fully understood his work.

The customers were cautious around, her but Karl would laugh, reminding them that all alchemists worked with a female assistant. They smiled then, clearly more surprised by his laughter than by her presence. He took them off to his study and, later, asked Rachel to draw up new astral and elemental balance charts and think about the session they would run with these people, how to help them visualize new journeys for themselves.

Against all her rational belief, Rachel began to feel that maybe she *was* meant to be here. But the decision to step so willingly into his hands was simpler than that: he cared for something that she harboured deep inside; he reached into the core of her, knowing everything else was trapping or pretension. No one else had bothered to even scratch the surface.

She began to tread more even ground with him. They sat side by side at the desk with sky maps and photos spread before them, Chopin or Rachmaninov playing in the background. They would reach across to jot down margin notes on each other's work, finish each other's thoughts and discuss both hieroglyphic and astral interpretations in a more balanced partnership. He didn't mention the night in the desert and she began to wonder if she were just some kind of "experiment" for him. She was unsettled by his apparent desire to be close yet his lack of initiative in taking the relationship further. In the evenings, walking back to her hotel, she flew from one conclusion to another: he didn't find her attractive, he did but he wasn't interested, there was someone else, he had a problem, he was gay, he was waiting for something. *But what?* She settled on the last and fought to keep her feelings under control. Sometimes, if they leaned together over a book or brushed hands accidentally, his physical closeness overwhelmed her and she would keep still, waiting for the flush to subside. After a moment, she would glance at him with affected nonchalance and he would hold her gaze in silence, long enough to unsettle her again.

In bits and pieces, she learned he was born in Zurich, studied astronomy and ancient history, and spent six months as a volunteer on an archeological dig in Luxor which sparked his desire to specialize in Ancient Egypt. He had come to Cairo to lecture at the University but exactly what made him stay on, he never said. He told her he was no longer involved with the faculty ... just the occasional lecture. Once, he mentioned his father, now dead, she presumed, who had been an astronomy and astrophysics professor at Stockholm University. "I wondered if there was Scandinavian blood in you," she said, hoping to pry open a few more doors. He frowned. "And I wonder why you are wondering, why it could matter."

One afternoon she was reading from some marked pages in a book he had left for her while he went out on an errand. The coffee table was stacked with papers and charts but she noticed one in particular: a map of the northern sky. The date at the top was today's. She turned her head sideways to read some of the notes he had made, but, knowing better than to disturb anything, she gave up and went back to the book.

When unleashing the power of the imagination, success involves distancing the consciousness of the physical body and maintaining the link psycho-magnetically through the silver cord of connection.

She read this again but it wasn't sinking in. Copernicus rubbed against her legs, his tail curled in the air.

There were voices at the window. Karl was back, arguing with someone in the street, or at least it sounded that way. *"El taman ghaeli 'awi"* ... something about a price. She had picked up a few Arabic phrases but not enough to follow a conversation.

"I've made a fine deal with a friend of Ahmed's," he called from the stairs. He came into the study, tossed a small brown packet in the air and caught it with one hand. "The finest hashish this side of heaven. Nectar of the gods. It will make for some pleasant evenings."

She knew about the hashish ... there was enough evidence around, but he'd never referred to it before, and she wondered, with a tight squeeze in her stomach, what he had in mind. She continued working, worrying that her project for the museum would never be finished. Every time she came close to concluding a particular idea or theme, Karl offered new insights or asked her questions that made her feel she'd hardly covered the subject at all.

The sun crept over the rooftops and shone directly through the window, catching a thousand flecks of dust in a wide shaft of light. An hour passed in silence. Karl seemed restless. She was distracted by his mood and wondered with a tiny flare of jealousy what sparked it and whether he led a different kind of life when she wasn't here.

He got up to stretch. "Put the books away," he said, startling her. "It's getting dark and the skies are clear. A good night to initiate you in the Schmidt-Cassegrain telescope. It's catadioptric, lenses and mirrors, but not too heavy. We'll go south of Giza, down the Faiyum Desert Road. And we'll take this." He put the brown package in his pocket and took a hash pipe from one of the desk drawers.

It was a long drive and he said little. She was tired and hoped it wouldn't be a difficult, instructional evening but she had come to accept that she could not refuse him. She watched his hands on the steering wheel and let her imagination wander. He was always so focused on whatever it was he was doing, oblivious to the catapulting sensations she was constantly wrestling with. She shifted position and looked out of her window but there was little to see.

When they stepped away from the car and walked into the sandy barrenness of the desert, the darkness enveloped them. He lit their way with a flashlight and spent some time setting up the telescope. She sat on the blanket nearby and gazed at the stars, trying to convince herself that this was a lesson in astronomy and not a good reason for the quickening thud of her heart.

After a while, he called her over and showed her the mechanisms and what she must do.

"Remember the image is inverted." He made some final adjustments. "So. Now we find out how good you are without a sky map."

She couldn't believe what a different sky she was seeing and it took a while for her to adjust to the sheer number of stars that were normally not visible. The usual patterns of constellations were difficult to isolate. "Virgo's got to be up there somewhere but I can't place it," she said. "There's just too much."

"Look for Ursa Major, then find the handle of the Big Dipper. Follow it down to Arcturus. Now jump over to Spica."

"Got it." She peered closely, blinking and refocusing. "I think."

"Good. It's actually two stars but you can't distinguish them. One of its Arabic names is Azimech. 262 light years away. Magnitude of 0.98. The 15th brightest star in the sky."

She turned away from the telescope. "I don't believe it. How do you remember all that?"

He gave her an arch look and made more adjustments to the scope. She watched his long, slim fingers as they worked with the dials, the nails clean and straight-cut. At one point, he put his hand on her shoulder and guided her own fingers to teach her how to adjust the instruments. She was glad he could not see the blood rush to her face. She tried to concentrate on the phenomenal world on the other side of the glass.

"If you move it higher, you'll find Polaris," he said. "Try to trace Ursa Minor. The pole star is at its very tip."

"Amazing."

After a few minutes, she felt a slight chill and realized he was no longer behind her. She stretched and rubbed her neck, which was stiff from the angle she was holding her head, and looked around. For a while she could make out nothing but gradually her eyes got used to the dark and she saw him sitting on an outcrop of rock, a little way off. She could smell the hashish.

"Come and sit here," he called over. "I've got something for you."

He switched on his small flashlight and she clambered up the rock and sat at his side. She caught a glint of silver in his hand.

"It's been locked away for years." He shone the light on it. It was a ring, black, turquoise and silver, shaped with the symbol of the Eye of Horus. He took her right hand and slid it on the middle finger.

She tried to slow her breathing and hold her hand steady.

"Do you like it?"

"It's beautiful." Her voice was hoarse. She coughed and swallowed.

"And you see, it fits perfectly."

"It looks like it's really valuable."

"The Ancient Egyptians believed the Eye of Horus had special powers. You've already written about this. In the Pepi II pyramid ritual. Remember? It's magnetically charged, channelling planetary energies to protect you."

"Do I need protection?"

He paused for several seconds and she grew alarmed with the silence. "Let us hope not."

A jolt of certainty shot through her. She felt she had no reason to worry—she could trust him. "Why was it locked away?" she asked.

"Waiting for you."

He leaned back and scanned the heavens. She could not see the expression on his face and had no idea how to respond. He picked up the hash pipe, relit it and handed it to her. They smoked for a while, saying nothing. She was aware only of the leap and lurch of her heart and how different thoughts slid out from her head, bumping into each other, blending into the air, making no sense.

"Rachel." His voice came through the darkness. "Tell me you know what's happening."

She inhaled deeply and let out her breath slowly. The stars behind his head blurred and warped into strobes of light. "I think ..." Her throat was dry with the sand and dust that blew around them. She did not trust herself to say more.

"We were meant to be here together. I think you believe this now. We are like two rivers that have met and should now flow inseparably. As one."

There was a long pause. The sweet burn of the hashish filled her lungs and nose. The eye of the ring stared up at her, unblinking, omniscient.

"I think you saw the chart I left in the study," he said. "It as though the stars themselves are waiting. There is a beautiful ancient ritual I can take us through. It will be like nothing either of us has ever felt before." Each of his words was suspended in its own universe. "I think ... I hope you want this too."

She took another drag and handed the pipe back to him. On the far horizon, she could see a faint splatter of lights from the city. "A ritual? I... I don't know. I—"

He stood and pulled her to her feet. She was swaying and her knees began to buckle but he held on to her. In the moon's half-light, she could just make out his features and saw a new look in his eyes, something that hovered near the fine edge of madness.

"Are you afraid?"

She nodded, unable to speak.

"Don't be. The forces we tap will pick up negative energy like a high-strung horse will sense a nervous rider. They can turn against you." He tilted her chin up towards him and she fought the mounting swell of disorientation. She saw the muscles tense under his shirt, caught the glint of the silver *ankh* talisman that hung from his neck. "Can you imagine how potent these forces will be when they fuse together? Do you think I would let anything happen to us?"

Us. That tiny powerful word again.

She felt a wave of something near compassion pass through him. His taut body slackened and he pushed a damp lock of hair out of her eyes, his other hand still resting on her shoulder. She felt herself tipping towards him, aching to close the narrow gap between them. For a few moments they stood this way, joined with only the lightest of pressure from his fingertips.

Chapter 8

They did not return to his home until the rose hue of the sun was fingering the rooftops. She was exhausted, yet Karl walked with an easy grace as though he had slept long and soundly. He left the car outside the store and helped Rachel up the stairs to the bedroom.

"I'll go to the hotel and get your things, settle the account," he said.

She held onto his arm, reluctant to stand alone. "But I haven't packed."

"I'll bring it all. I won't be long." He squeezed her gently to his side and kissed her. Then he was gone, leaving her fighting to clear her head and sort reality from fantasy.

She took off her shawl, sank onto the bed and stared down at her hands. She could not lift them. On her left wrist was a square of bandage, tied tightly with papyrus twine. She tried to untie it but her fingers were too weak. After what seemed like a long time, she leaned down to unbuckle her sandals and caught sight of her reflection in the mirror on the open closet door. Her eyes wide with disbelief, she rose to look more closely. Her hair was tangled and matted with sweat and sand, her dress torn at the sides. A thin, dark line ran across her collarbone. She wrestled with the zipper, her hands trembling, and pulled the dress down to her waist. Scratches and fine abrasions covered her shoulders and breasts, some so deep they had bled and were still wet to the touch. As she moved, she felt a sticky moistness between her legs. She took quick, shallow breaths and held on to the closet door to steady herself, twisting slowly to see her back. The deep gouges of his fingernails were visible across her shoulders, and grains of sand stuck to her skin. Letting her dress slip to the floor, she ran her hands tentatively over her whole body. A bruise on her arm was beginning to darken.

She stood motionless in the shower, leaning against the tiled wall, letting the cool water rush over her, trying to breathe evenly, to stop the dull thud of her heart in her chest. She knew now that he had planned this from the beginning. He had always wanted her, he said, always imagined it this way, willing her to believe what he believed, wanting her to take these journeys with him, sharing everything, clawing their way into a whole new dimension where she didn't know herself, where she fought for more, where she screamed with need.

Through the jangle and clatter in her head, a persistent question struggled to the top. *How could you have been so scared but felt so good?*

***

Out in the desert, the bitterness of the liquid in the silver chalice had slid down her throat, filling her whole body, lifting her. The world drifted away, pieces of it floating in the air, and she felt herself flying, far above her body, the stars flashing and glittering around her.

So much, so quickly then: the lighting of the candle, the silver flask again at her lips, the ebony-handled dagger, the shock as she watched herself make a quick cut at the base of his thumb, the spike of pain as he did the same to her, rubbing their wrists together, letting their blood drip into a little glass vial. He told her to pour the mixture onto the flame of the candle. They watched it spark and sputter and die. He held her close. "Let go. Let it take us," he whispered.

The water came. A vast, churning cauldron of sea. It spat up a rebel wave that swelled and heaved, arching over at the top. She felt she would surely drown and tried to tell him but he held her tightly. "You will not outrun it," he whispered clearly above the roar. "It came because you called." The wave reared up and curled around them, carrying them out across the sea.

From over the horizon, through the canyons of darkness, she heard the sound of the wind. She ran with him to the end of the water, diving over the edge into nothingness, hanging, weightless, in her own element. The sky was black and the fierce light of Venus shot through like an arrow. A gust of wind sprang up beneath them, turning them around, growing stronger, beginning to swirl, gathering speed, changing to water, faster and faster, a liquid cyclone.

He picked her up, cradling her, braced against the wet wind, and carried her into the vortex. She felt the warmth of his breath on her face and the sweat running down his temples into her hair. She felt the weight of his hands, bringing her down, the push of his body against hers, spiraling inside the whirlwind, sucked down into the dark centre, the loud, tearing wind in their ears, the water lashing around them. Air and water, water and air, reeling to climax. They gripped together, moving in a violent rhythm, deeper and deeper into the core and when she cried out, twisting wildly, trying to breathe, he covered her mouth with his, clamping his hands on her wrists and pressing into her with the last of his strength until it was over. Finished. No sound. No light. No movement. Nothing at all. Stillness. Emptiness.

***

The water turned off abruptly and she woke with a start, slumped down against the tiled wall in the corner. Karl was kneeling by the open shower door, pulling her towards him, wrapping her in a towel. "My God." He helped her to her feet. "I shouldn't have left you." He steadied her through the door and into the bedroom.

"Karl." She found her voice with difficulty. "Look at me." She let the towel fall from her shoulders. The thin red scratches glistened under the wetness of her skin. She watched his eyes move over her body.

"Everything will heal. You mustn't worry."

"I don't understand." The words jumbled in her mouth. "Nothing hurts."

"It only hurts if you expect it to hurt." He moved towards her but she took a step back, feeling fragile, confused. She reached for the iron bed-post for support.

"Please. What happened? What did you do?"

"What did *I* do?" He unbuttoned his shirt and guided her hand around his back. His skin felt rough and sticky. When she pulled her hand back, there were faint smears of blood on it.

She stared at him, shaking her head. "Jesus."

One by one, he took her fingers and licked them clean, like a cat, smiling, looking all the while straight into her eyes. He helped her onto the bed and kissed her, stroking the hair from her face. She was dimly aware of him unpacking the suitcase and several boxes he had brought from her hotel, putting her things away alongside his, dismantling and rearranging her entire life.

As she drifted off to sleep, she remembered the candle. She had picked it up when they were leaving and it flickered to life again. In one swift movement, he took it from her and pinched the wick. For the rest of her life, her dreams were long and vivid and always at their very edges was the faint smell of burning.

***

It was nearly noon before she woke and some minutes before she realized where she was. There was little light in his bedroom. The small window was shuttered against the harsh morning sun. Every limb felt heavy as she struggled awake. She had only a dim memory of him beside her but saw that half the sheet was turned back and there was a cigarette butt in the ashtray and a mug with a spoon. It was empty but she smelled lemon and whisky. She pulled on her silk robe that he had placed on the chair for her, and went down to the kitchen.

"You slept well." Karl pulled out a chair and eased her into it as though she were an invalid, lightly kissing the top of her head. He had laid out a simple meal and made the Turkish coffee that she loved. "You must rest more," he said. "We won't work today."

He poured the coffee and sat beside her, piling her plate with fruit and cheese and nuts.

He reached for her left hand. She had forgotten the cut on her wrist. Blood had seeped through the cloth and dried hard. There was no dressing on his own wrist.

"So, did it all go the way you planned? This... ritual?" she asked.

He unraveled the papyrus twine and, with the sureness of his touch, a new wave of longing flushed through her. "Just a small thing, at the end," he said. He lifted a corner of the square of cloth. It was stuck to her skin so he poured a little water to moisten it. "The candle briefly flared again. Did you notice?"

She nodded.

"In the ancient rituals, it would have meant resistance. From the fire element. When the ritual is perfect, the flame is extinguished with the blood. But with you, air is a strong force. It can snuff a flame or fan a flame. Some flames aren't easily extinguished. There."

She looked at his face as he concentrated on tending to her wrist. Did he really believe all this stuff, she wondered? But then, last night, she herself could have believed anything.

He pulled the cloth away and examined the wound. "It's healed already." He tossed the cloth and string into the waste bin and sat across from her, pouring more coffee.

She looked around the kitchen, marveling that this was where she would live now, this was her home. She noticed an Arabic calendar hanging on a hook on the fridge.

"You know …." She wiped some of the crumbs off the table in front of her. "I'm supposed to go home in three weeks. I have to finish the work I came here to do."

He was leaning back, his thumbs hooked into his belt, and gave her that long, appraising look. "The work you came here to do will take much longer than three weeks."

She fingered the fruit on her plate, arranging it in a circle. "I mean the articles, the research. You know what I mean."

"And you know what I mean." He came round to her side of the table, took a piece of tangerine from her plate and squashed it between his thumb and forefinger, his eyes not leaving her face. He slid it into her mouth, letting his fingers linger on her lips, smearing the juice across her chin and down her neck. He dropped to his knees and put his face between her breasts, his hands sliding under her robe, his tongue snaking down her body. "Of course, you must finish," he said, tightening his grip at her waist, his voice barely above a whisper. "But not today." She arched her back and clutched at his hair. He half lifted, half pulled her from the chair which fell and clattered backwards against the wall.

Later, lying spent across the bed, his sleeping body heavy and still half astride her, she realized that the question of her leaving was left hanging. He knew she would not go.

Chapter 9

Rachel did not return to Canada when the work for her project was finished and she did not go to visit her brother in England at Christmas as she had done for several years. Cairo wrapped itself around her and she gave herself up to its embrace.

Some mornings, after urgent hours of love and the sleep of exhaustion that followed, she would wake to the sounds of the *Salat-ul-Fajr* from the local mosque and stumble in the darkness to the study to listen at the open window and wait for the sun to rise. The steep spiral turret in the near distance caught the first rays and she would watch the light climb slowly up the spire and wash over the roof in one broad stroke, as though from the brush of a skillful painter. She sat until the faithful returned from prayer, until the light filled the dark crevices of the roof-tops and morning truly began. There were new sounds now: corrugated metal doors rolling up, shutters banging open, tables and chairs being dragged to the sidewalks. She caught the smell of yeast and vanilla from the bakery and watched the merchants hustle about, calling to each other and wishing for the best of days, *in shaa Allah.*

She turned from this reverie at the window one morning and saw a tiny cup of Turkish coffee sitting on the desk beside her. Karl was in his leather chair in the corner, watching her. She had not heard him come in. There was a deep tenderness in his eyes. At that moment, she knew how much she mattered to him, that the change she had made to his life was as strange and exciting as the one he'd made to hers.

An artful alliance grew between them, a complicity of thought and gesture, an ability to read others with consummate ease. She did many of the readings on her own now and, although there was always an air of mastery about him, an underlying confidence in his knowledge and his opinion, she felt his growing respect and his deep pleasure in their symbiosis.

He was never clumsy and never wasted movement or energy. It seemed to her his every word and gesture were orchestrated, part of a grand choreography set to complex music that only he could hear. Sometimes she took his composure as a challenge. On a hot, humid morning, unable to sleep, she got up before him and sat in the study reading, fanning herself with a magazine. After a while, she heard through the wall the low hum of his razor, droning in even waves, and went to see if he wanted coffee. His hair, still wet from the shower, was combed straight back off his face and lay heavy on his bare shoulders. Through the mirror, he caught her eyes and held them as he moved the razor smoothly over the sharp line of his cheekbone, turning his head from side to side. She untied her robe and circled her arms around his waist, her breasts pressing against his wet back. He kept shaving, moving his chin up to reach across his throat, but his eyes did not leave hers. She loosened the knot in the drawstring of his pants and slid her hands inside, moving her fingers gently, rhythmically until she felt him take a deeper breath. She allowed herself a small, triumphant smile as, finally, he closed his eyes and, turning abruptly, put the razor down and pulled her back to bed.

He taught her how to make the tincture of "Diviner's Sage," a painstaking process, and instructed her in the arts of ritual and suggestion. They went to the desert to gaze at the stars, to make love fiercely and compulsively, to take flight into other realms of consciousness.

Sometimes, she lay awake at night and imagined trying to explain her life to her friends, to Nigel and Philippe, to Janet. "Rache, you're hallucinating," Janet would say. "That's all. And it's fucking dangerous. Get a grip."

"Hallucination is the convenient way to describe something few understand," Karl told her when she struggled with these thoughts. "We are simply travelling through different realms of imagination, as real as what we call 'real life.' It's just that they are usually hidden from us."

He came over and seized her hands. "Rachel, we are not like the people who come to us for help. We have the skill to let go completely, open the doors to many new worlds, stand on the thresholds and let the energies and elements flood through us, taking us higher and farther." She buried her face against him. She could not imagine wanting anything more than this.

***

Over time, Karl let her take a more central role in the readings they did for others, mostly men with the complications of business or of love. Sometimes they took these men to the desert, sometimes they worked at their homes. Through ritual and suggestion, they created a hypnotic state, helping people to concentrate, to imagine and reshape events, encouraging them to *will* their circumstances to change. At first Rachel was nervous, anxious to justify Karl's faith in her but worried about the sheer madness of what she was doing, whether it was honest and valid, whether it was grounded in something more than dreams.

"If you wish for something with all your heart, if you channel that desire through the four elements, it will happen." Karl said.

He insisted that her belief in herself was the only important factor.

There were many successes: a pregnancy, a sick child getting well, financial hardship lightened, a floundering business given new life. When she saw the results of what they did, the joy or gratefulness of those who sought their help, she was filled with new, exhilarating confidence and hope. The doubts slid away and, in their place, something potent and irresistible emerged, a sense of self she scarcely recognized or understood. They guarded their time jealously, carved out long stretches where they would see no one, leaving the door and the telephone unanswered. Some days, they barely rose from bed and then only to get food or wine or to change the music on the stereo. She gave herself up to him completely. As the light in the bedroom window faded, she would lie naked, splayed across the bed, her body slicked with sweat, his head on her breast, his arm thrown carelessly across her. She would smell the hashish, heavy and stale, turn and see their crumpled clothes scattered about, the overflowing ashtray, the empty wine bottle knocked on its side, the last of its contents staining the wooden floor. She would stare into the growing darkness and marvel at what she had become.

***

They often went to Fadoul's café for a break. It looked onto a small, jumbled market square and Rachel loved to sit at a table outside and watch the hustle of the day. Fadoul usually seized the opportunity to usher Karl into the back to discuss some pressing concern. If this took time, Rachel would wander over to chat with the friendlier of the merchants whose shops lined the square, helping them replenish the canvas sacks of nuts and spices or rearrange bright tablecloths, copper plates and ornaments on the trestle tables in front. Today, having found her at tiny carpet store, Karl brought her back to the café and ordered coffee. He gave a few coins to a young boy tugging at his sleeve who had found a German newspaper for him.

"Fadoul is worried about Mustafa," he said, pulling out a chair for her. "He was supposed to have a lot of friends who would bring new customers but this isn't happening."

"Is he going to let him go?"

"It's not that easy. There's a partnership agreement. He believes Mustafa is working against him, that somehow, he is being cheated. He wants us to do a reading for both of them, without Mustafa knowing. A reading, nothing more. No doubt he's hoping for some kind of 'magic' solution."

He opened the copy of *Die Zeit* and offered her a section but she wasn't up to taxing her limited schoolgirl German. She stirred her coffee and looked around the little square. A shaft of sunlight dipped into a narrow alley, making the copper urns outside a nearby store glint fiercely. Through the kitchen window of the café she could see Mustafa washing out a large coffee urn. She didn't like to think there were problems. He was a friendly, decent person, whereas Fadoul was sullen, always complaining. She still found it difficult to believe that people would pay them for readings or for a pretty potent drug to simply imagine the solution to their problems. *Surely, they aren't that naïve?*

"I almost forgot," Karl said, putting the paper down. "These came a few days ago." He pulled two pieces of mail from the pocket of his jacket, one a slim manila envelope, the other white, hand-written and teeming with lopsided stamps. He propped them against her coffee cup.

"A few days ago?"

"My apologies. We were busy."

A new rush of emotions seized her. *Almost forgot? He doesn't forget anything.* Why hadn't he left them on the counter in the store where he usually stacked the mail so neatly? But she concluded she was being paranoid—he could have put them in his jacket pocket, intending to give them to her, and perhaps it had simply slipped his mind.

The first was from the museum that had sponsored her trip, thanking her for her work and enclosing her final cheque. They were disappointed she had missed the exhibit and expressed interest in any further research she may want to share. She was pleased with this and it made her forget her concerns. She read it aloud to Karl.

"You see," he said. "You can accomplish anything when you set your mind to it."

She ripped open the other letter; it was from her friend Janet who wrote with a sprawling, breathless prose, the same way she talked.

SO! What's up with your email? Constant bounce-back. Hence snail mail. What ARE you up to? Got your address from Nigel. He's <u>very</u> worried. Living with mysterious man, he says —feels responsible for making the introduction. Said your brother had called him for "the low-down." Apparently dear brother Robert is pissed you didn't go at Christmas and you don't keep in touch—says you're irresponsible, ha-ha, I could vouch for that! Anyway, Paula and I are going to Egypt. Yeah! Pyramids, Tutenwhatsit and so on. Don't panic, we won't be a nuisance—one of these packages, you know, if that's the Sphinx, must be Tuesday. Now listen up. Aren't you coming home soon? Nigel said you're doing some art course or other in a couple of months. We've been instructed to nag you.

The letter continued with news from home and suggestions on how to make arrangements to meet. Rachel replaced it in the envelope and finished her coffee. She thought about the course. It had seemed such a long way off. Maybe she wouldn't go. God, Nigel would never forgive her. But she could take a short break. Come back here afterwards, of course.

The sun had pushed over the roof of the building across the little square and she fished in her bag for her sunglasses. Karl turned a page of the paper.

"Two of my friends are coming here on a tour. I'd like to meet up with them for a day. If that's okay with you."

He appeared not to have heard and continued reading. She waited. Now she was annoyed with herself for asking. It was such a normal thing. A visit from friends, a girlie catch-up day. Eventually, he put the paper down and looked directly at her. "Of course. We'll show them a little of Cairo in a way they wouldn't appreciate from one of those tours. When are they coming?"

"In three weeks, but," she cleared her throat. "I thought I might spend a little time with them alone. We'll be gossiping about people you don't know. You'd be bored."

"I doubt that. It would be a good break for me too." He went back to the newspaper.

What on earth can make him uneasy about me spending the day in the company of two female friends? Perhaps he's worried I would talk about what we are doing. She thought back to that day when she'd found all that drug paraphernalia. He'd had her followed. But surely everything had changed now? She'd never discuss what they did for fear of the ridicule or the interference of her friends. Should she protest? If he came, the visit wouldn't be the same; the three women wouldn't be able to share the same intimacy. But something in Karl's manner, his clear desire for inclusion, held her back from pushing too hard.

She looked down at Janet's letter and remembered her small, untidy flat in Riverdale, where they would sit until three in the morning in their university days, speculating about the men they'd met, listening to Leonard Cohen and drinking too much Grand Marnier. It would be good to see her, she thought. She felt the need to reach back into her old life to make sure she could still fit, that she would still be welcome.

"Anyway." She affected a matter-of-fact tone. "Don't feel you have to be with us all the time. I could spend an afternoon on the Nile with them. On one of the feluccas or something."

She watched a shopkeeper leaning heavily on his cane as he tried to direct two young men unloading merchandise from the trunk of a car: pots and pans, jugs, cheese-graters, salt and pepper shakers, brushes, cleaning fluids, shoe polish . All over the world, she thought, people are content to live ordinary lives. They grate cheese and polish their shoes and make a living in simple ways.

She jumped when Fadoul came to remove their empty cups.

Karl folded the newspaper. "There's no moon tonight. The stars will have the whole sky to themselves. Come, we must make the most of it." He pulled her gently to her feet.

As they walked home through the bazaar, she tried to match her stride to his. He was nearly a head taller and always walked with purpose, but she felt his guiding touch at her elbow as they wove through the noisy crowds, and found herself indulging his proprietary attitude.

The colourful tea dispenser moved into their path, his cups arranged on the tray that fitted round his waist. His body dipped and swayed as he poured the liquid from the complicated urn strapped to his back.

"Where you from, Miss?" he asked Rachel.

"Canada," she said, edging by him.

"Canada Dry!" he called out, delightedly.

As they approached the store, they could hear Abdul muttering away to himself, as usual, through the broken window of his bakery, but otherwise it was quieter here. The key made a heavy crunching sound in the lock and the big wooden door squeaked loudly when it was pushed open. The sun had reached the first window and a cloud of fine dust particles hung above the glass case in the centre, caught in its amber light. Rachel could smell leftover jasmine tea gone cold in the kitchen, and the incense they had burned last night. She breathed deeply and relaxed into it. It was the smell of home.

Chapter 10

They waited for Janet and Paula in the lobby of a modest tourist hotel. It was a blend of western and Egyptian style, with soft couches scattered about, several low tables with inlaid tiles of ancient Egyptian art, and giant potted plants whose dusty leaves rustled in the heavy air-conditioning. Vacationers filled the lobby. Rachel heard a lot of English, German, and what she thought was Dutch. Karl was hunched over the coffee table, engrossed in a copy of the Herald Tribune that someone had left behind. With his head bent, his hair fell almost down to the paper on the table. She wondered why his obvious physical differences, his stature, his fairness, his voice, seemed natural and integral to the old Cairo neighbourhood of his home and yet so out of place here, among these Europeans. Why was it so important for him to be with them today? Was he worried that her old life might claim her back? She weighed this thought, both savouring the possessiveness it suggested and chafing against the loss of freedom that came with it. Surely, he would be bored and condescending. She fretted about her friends' reactions and the lecture she would likely get from Janet about picking the wrong men.

She looked up and saw Janet swinging out of the elevator, Paula in tow, causing all eyes to turn their way. "*Rache*, oh my God, look how tanned you are! You've gone native!" Janet stopped a few feet from Rachel before extending her arms for a hug.

When the kisses and exclamations of delight were done, Rachel stood back to take stock of her old friends. They were dressed in khaki and white, braided belts, fresh lipstick, painted toenails. She took in Paula's cotton blouse knotted at the waist, Janet's designer sunglasses propped on her chestnut hair. Both of them already sported gold cartouche pendants, the imperative tourist buy. In her well-worn jeans and faded shirt, Rachel felt underdressed and poor. She turned to beckon Karl and braced for the look of strained tolerance she expected on his face. Instead, there he was, standing patiently, smiling. He stepped forward to grasp the women's hands, and kissed them both on the cheek.

"I'm pleased to meet you both," he said. "I hope you'll allow us to show you the real city of Cairo."

"Absolutely," said Paula, "we're in your hands, aren't we, Jan?" She pushed Janet forward and hooked her arm through Rachel's. "My God, sweetie," she whispered, nodding in Karl's direction, "how very exotic."

Karl was charming and accommodating. Surprised and relieved, Rachel let him take over, leading them through the bazaars, helping them buy souvenirs and trinkets at the best prices, astonishing her friends with his command of the language and his friendship with the merchants.

"So, you two," Janet said, as he drove them slowly through the narrow streets of the old part of the city. "Please explain what gives, here." She raised her voice to compete with the honking horns. "What's this work you're doing exactly? We average mortals don't get it. Nigel said your emails are very vague."

"One thing led to another," Karl said before Rachel could answer. He swerved deftly to avoid a young boy wobbling unsteadily on a bicycle. "I asked Rachel to help me with my own research and she agreed to stay awhile. Is there anything particular you'd like to see in the old part of the city?"

"Ah, one thing led to another," said Janet. Rachel felt a kick in the back of her seat and caught the stifled laughter.

They spent the better part of the afternoon in Masr al-Qadima, and Karl showed them some of the major tourist attractions: the Coptic Museum, the Monastery, the Church of St. George. He was attentive and tireless, chaperoning the three women like a seasoned tour guide, looking out for them as they crossed roads, steering them past street hustlers who persistently plagued the tourists. Rachel could not believe the man she was seeing and wondered what was motivating him to act this way. She could think of no good reason other than a desire to please her. She latched on to this and tried to stop her doubting inner voice. As the afternoon wore on, he took them farther afield, through the narrow alleys they would have been lost in, and eventually towards the Mosque of Amr ibn al-As.

"I can't take any more of this heat," Janet said, drawing Rachel over to a bench under one of the long-covered archways. She waved her hands at Paula. "You go and do your cultural immersion round the mosque with Karl. You can tell me all about it later."

Rachel caught the meaningful stare she gave to Paula and braced herself for the interrogation.

"So, fess up, Rache," she said when Karl and Paula had walked off. "What's all this? You've been here nearly a year. I mean are we serious, or what?"

Rachel was stuck for an answer. Did the whole business of relationships come down to these two distinctions? Serious or not serious. Were all those early sexual encounters just basic training, getting into practice for that final, triumphant serious thing? She remembered her mother fielding the eager enquiries of her friends. "Is this one serious, Dorothy?" "Oh yes, this is it," her mother would say, until the next one.

"I'm not sure what serious means, exactly."

Janet rolled her eyes. "It means love, marriage, kids, future, settling down, you know, the things normal people do."

Those normal people again.

"Well?" Janet persisted. "Don't give me this research crap. You're screwing each other's brains out. Written all over you."

"Just a fling maybe."

Janet let out a whoop of laughter. "You don't know how to have a fling, baby. You think too much. Do you really feel he's right for you?"

"Yes. I mean, we're drawn together because of the work. We both love the same things."

"Not the right answer."

"Well, it's a dumb question."

Janet took a deep inhale through her nose and blew it out with a big shrug. "Okay. He's charming, he's attractive, he's even chivalrous, for God's sake." She turned to face Rachel. "And I'm not buying it."

"I knew I'd get this. You never approve of the guys I like."

"I smell a rat. You're too thin, your eyes are shiny. Like, unnaturally shiny. Your hair's a mess. You've gone spacey."

"My hair is always a mess."

"Are you listening to me?"

Rachel turned away. That old sense of her life being out of synch had returned and made her feel off balance. Why was she finding it so hard to talk to her friend? With all their past relationships, all those passionate but fleeting college love affairs, they would quiz each other relentlessly, sharing every intimate anecdote, analyzing and then laughing over every nuance of feeling. And now, in this relationship that was more consuming, more intense than anything she'd ever felt before, she could summon no words to defend her feelings.

"He's different, Janet. I don't know what to tell you."

"Different. You can say that again. Now this ..." Janet pulled a big envelope from her bag. "... is about that course. The stuff you've got to do or read or whatever ahead of time. Nigel took the liberty of opening it. Don't look so offended. You got your mail forwarded to him. Of course, he's going to open it. You know what he's like."

She began shaking her head. "Look, tell Nigel I'm not—"

"Whoa. Don't even think about it. Because this ..." Janet pulled a sheet of paper from the envelope "... is a note from him. You can guess what it says. You should have been home by now. If you stay much longer, you'll get into all kinds of tax or health coverage problems or whatever. Are you short of money? He said he'd buy your ticket. He's dead serious."

Rachel was not ready for this. Janet and Nigel ganging up on her? Tax, health coverage. She never thought about these things. She had given up the tiny shoe-box apartment she'd lived in so she had "no fixed address." Her life here was so complete, so separate, so isolated that the daily concerns of her old life no longer entered her mind.

"Money's not an issue, Janet. But this course. Things have changed. I don't see the point."

"The point is that you've got a lot of talent you're not using. That's what Nigel says. He's pissed you missed the museum thing with all your work on show. All sorts of important people you should have met—you know how he goes on. Shit, Rache, this is just another relationship that could go south and then you've got nothing. The course is like two weeks. It's still a ways off. August, right? How can that be a problem? You can stay at my place. Coming home might help you get some perspective. You don't seem to have much right now."

"You don't understand, Janet." Rachel took the envelope and stuffed it into her own bag.

"No, I don't. Promise you'll think about it."

"I'll discuss it with Karl."

"What? Why? It's not his decision. And from what I can tell, he won't like the idea. It's your decision. Your future. He shouldn't ... well, what do you know, here he comes now." She pointed to Karl and Paula crossing the courtyard. "Can't leave you alone for more than five minutes I guess."

On the way back to the car, they stopped to buy ice cream from a young boy with an icebox under a big red umbrella. Paula called Rachel over for another photograph but Rachel felt an unexpected sting of tears behind her eyes and raised her hand in front of her face, shaking her head. She caught Paula's surprised look and began to feel angry as the two women spoke to each other in low voices.

"So, what about dinner tonight?" Janet said when they were back in the car. "We thought we'd give you a break, Karl, and treat Rachel. Lots of gossip to catch her up on. We'll make sure she gets back safe and sound."

"Where do you suggest Rache?" Paula added.

Paula's voice sounded staged, like they had rehearsed this little scene. Rachel looked over at Karl. He was focused on driving. She couldn't read his look. She turned to the back seat. "There are some good local places not far from your hotel. I could take a cab home afterwards."

They all waited for Karl's response.

"I don't think so," he said finally. "Those restaurants are not suitable for women alone. I thought we'd go to Sofira's. It's still the best restaurant in Cairo. In fact, I made a reservation." He looked in the rearview mirror. "Would you two like to go back to your hotel first?"

"You made a reservation?" Rachel said. "Why didn't you tell me?"

"I'm sure I did."

"Whatever you think is best," said Paula, hastily. "If we've got time I would love to swing by our hotel, get out of these sweaty clothes."

They fell silent for the rest of the journey. Rachel stared through the window, not registering anything on the outside. The resentment boiled up inside her. How dare he go ahead and assume control of this visit, how dare he not give her a moment's freedom? And how dare Janet and Paula try to orchestrate this private time just so they could give her hell and nag her about being here, about the course? She had half a mind to leap out of the moving car and leave them all to each other.

At dinner, Karl kept up the charm, getting Janet and Paula to talk about the past, to tell him about Rachel when she was younger, to share their own stories and news. Rachel tried hard to get over her fit of pique but the people and places her friends talked about passed before her like photographs in an old album, familiar yet distant, and the lives they held up for her comment were like the stuff of dreams. Her friends were from an alien world and the fragile roots she had once put down there were slipping easily from the soil.

At the end of the evening, Janet pulled her aside once again. She dropped her voice. "Goddamnit Rachel. He's a control freak. Come home. We love you." More loudly, she added, "And please send a long email to Nigel. He'll be all over me like a dirty shirt when I get back."

They parted with a flurry of kisses and hugs, promising to stay in touch.

That night, Rachel couldn't sleep. Karl got up and made her a night-cap of whiskey and herbs. He sat on the bed while she drank it.

"Did you enjoy their visit?"

"I don't know." She felt the tears again. "I don't understand how I feel."

He pulled her towards him and kissed her until she fought for breath.

Chapter 11

A few days later, Rachel broached the subject of the course. They were walking back from the local market, laden with vegetables and fruit, nuts, yogurt, jostling with the crowds on the narrow streets. It was a bright noisy day, and she slid the subject into the conversation in an off-hand way, as though she'd just thought about it.

"I've been thinking I should make the effort. I've always loved painting but I was never really good. This course, it's mostly art criticism. An introduction. You know, it gets into the role of the critic. They always have big name agents and collectors there, people who run art publications, so it's popular. I was lucky to get in." She glanced over to Karl. No sign of acknowledgement.

"Do you want to be an art critic?" he said finally.

"I thought I did. I mean at one point."

"And now?"

"Well, maybe for later. I don't have anything that would qualify me to earn a living. I mean if I was back there."

"But you're not back there." He smiled in a slightly indulgent way, as though she were a child telling him what she wanted to be when she grew up.

"Right, but … what we have here, what we do, I mean, it's not—"

"Real?"

Two emotions battled within her: Relief because she didn't want to go home anyway and she was ready to buckle with the slightest resistance from him. She was happy here. She had everything she wanted, everything she could imagine wanting. But also indignation. *Damn it, I am my own boss. How dare he be so condescending?*

She searched again for the right words. "I could drop in on the museum people and I need to check on things like my health coverage and income tax, stuff I've kind of left up in the air. And the course might help me one day—down the road I mean."

At that moment, a passer-by recognized Karl and they engaged in conversation in Arabic. The other man appeared to be sharing good news. Karl patted him on the back and shook his hand, smiling broadly. Rachel put her grocery bags down. They were heavy.

After the man moved on, they walked in silence for a while. She had such difficulty judging Karl's mood and was surprised when he switched the grocery bags to one hand and put his other arm around her shoulders, squeezing her tight. "Where does your heart lie, Rachel?"

"Here of course."

Here of course. She had not hesitated for a second when she said that. Somehow, she felt so connected here in this chaotic Middle Eastern city. She looked around and took in the exotic smells of the sidewalk food vendors, the overflowing stands of leather belts, purses and flip flop sandals. She stopped and took a deep breath. "You knew I'd say that."

"Yes. This is your home," he said. "The other place is simply the one you came from. You feel good here. You know who you are. Why would you risk inviting negative energy, disrupting the natural order of things. You don't need to be taking courses."

Rachel could hear Janet's voice in her ear: "Give me a break Rache. 'Inviting negative energy. Natural order of things.' The guy's a psycho. He's manipulating you." She resolved to take a firm stand.

Later that evening, working in the study, she pushed her papers aside and took a deep breath. "Look, Karl. The course. I've made up my mind about it. I've already paid the deposit and it seems a shame to waste the opportunity."

He was sitting in his leather chair reading some notes and did not look up. She waited.

"Karl—"

He flung the papers to one side and threw the pen he was using so hard that it bounced off the door frame and broke. "*Scheisse.* I thought we'd discussed this. That you'd decided. You said your heart lies here. Is that not so?"

She was so shocked by the loss of temper that she couldn't speak for a moment. He never swore, he never lost control. "We didn't discuss it, exactly. Of course, I want to stay here. But it's only two weeks. I wouldn't want to be away more than that anyway."

"So why are you going? I'll tell you why. Because you feel the need to please other people. Why are you trying so hard to win affection? Why don't you concentrate on your own happiness?"

Abruptly, he got up, left the room and went downstairs.

She braced for the sound of the door to the street and felt a wave of relief when she heard him in the kitchen, aggressively opening and slamming shut the cupboard doors. *Jesus. Where does all this come from?* "Trying to win affection" *Is that what he thinks?* She could feel the beginning of tears. She squeezed her eyes and blinked them away. *And is it true*? He had not said anything about his own feelings, that he would miss her, even for two weeks. *Is that what this is really about? And if so, why can't he say it?* There was silence downstairs now. She thought for a moment of going down to him but forced herself to stay put. She went back to her work on the desk but couldn't focus.

After fifteen minutes or so, he came back up. He had a bottle of wine and two glasses. He leaned over the desk and kissed her. "Email them. Tell them you're coming. Book your ticket." She struggled to speak but he put a finger to her lips. "You know the things I believe, the things I wish you'd embrace too. I want to be sure that you are doing this for yourself, not for others. Remember you are a free spirit, as light as air, but other people can suck that air right out of you. If you are sure this is for you, I will not stand in your way."

She pulled back and looked at his face. That steady gaze, the slight smile. Why did he unsettle her so much? Was he right to question her motivation? What was she going to do with the results of this course anyway, assuming she passed it or got the certificate or whatever? But then again, the future...

But all she could think of now was that he was no longer angry. She stood and put her arms around him and felt the catch of his breath and the tightening of his grip as he pulled her close. "Come," he said, pulling her towards the bedroom. "The wine can wait."

The next day, she confirmed her attendance and booked her flights. It was still two months away and she pushed it to the back of her mind.

They did the readings for Fadoul. Rachel plotted the planets and took a stab at the interpretation. Fadoul took over her leather chair in the study so she had to sit at the desk. He was gruff and dismissive, clearly preferring to deal with Karl alone. Most of the time he spoke Arabic, cutting her out. At one point he asked her to bring him some tea. She was about to throw a fit at this but Karl said he'd do it. He told Fadoul, in English, with a rueful smile, that he should change his attitude to women or he would most certainly regret it one day. Rachel wasn't sure how to feel about this but decided she liked the gesture. She went back to the charts, ignoring Fadoul until Karl returned.

"There's a troubled soul," Karl said when Fadoul had left. "He looks at everything in the darkest way. In the end he just wants Mustafa gone."

"How does he feel about your idea of trying to find a different role for him? It's pretty clear that's what Mustafa needs—even if you look at all the indications literally."

"There's a lot of conflict. Fadoul has little patience."

They talked for a while about the recommendations they had made. Rachel still had difficulty embracing the validity of what they were doing but pouring over the charts and delving into the interpretations of the ancient Egyptians was fascinating to her. *And if it helped people, well, what harm can it do?*

***

As the weeks went by, she ceased contact with most of her friends. Occasionally she attempted brief, cheerful emails but eventually the correspondence on both sides tapered off. Only Nigel wrote faithfully.

My dear, I'm getting tired of the silent treatment. Janet told me Herr Gustav is a most charming character, but she is clearly worried about him and fears you are "losing your grip"—whatever that means. He and I had only a passing acquaintance but "charming" does not spring to mind. Your increasingly fewer friends are worried about you—we need news. And you are obviously not thinking clearly about the future. Thank heavens you're coming home in August. We shall have to have a big "sit down" as I believe some of your former countrymen used to call it. And please write to your infernal brother. He claims you've gone off the radar and expects me to furnish information. I barely know the man, and he treats me like a concierge.

Rachel wondered what Janet had said to Nigel. When she wrote back, she took a light, breezy tone. She described the markets and wonderful antiques that he would surely lust after. She told him to stop fussing, and she'd catch him up on everything when she was home in August. She even gave him the flight information and asked him to pick her up at the airport. That might mollify him for a while.

The relationship with Karl was all that mattered to her now, and she burrowed even deeper into her new life. They spent many hours making variations of the "Diviner's Sage," combinations of *salvia divinorum* and blue lotus extract to go into the silver flask. But salvia leaves were difficult to obtain and it was a long process of drying, soaking and boiling. Usually Ahmed would bring the ready-made tincture and they would dilute it. For weeks, Rachel had felt a growing dependency on the drug. She had trouble distinguishing day from night, what was a dream, what was a self-induced dreamlike journey, what was reality. She told Karl she was worried about addiction and the physical toll, that she was losing weight and had trouble sleeping. But he made light of her anxiety.

"These are natural substances. They get us past the ordinary physical senses, let our minds travel. And why should these other experiences be any less valid than what we call 'real' life?" He pulled her close. "We can travel through the stars to the far reaches of the universe, meet the sun-god Ra and sail in his boat up the Great River." His words mesmerized her and made her forget her concerns. She would fold into his arms and feel the power of his energy.

Sometimes, Janet's "serious or what?" question haunted her and an inner voice made her question her feelings. Was this a healthy kind of love, she asked herself. But she didn't care, couldn't stop, didn't want to. Whether it was love or lust or infatuation, she had never felt so vital, so energized, almost omnipotent. And what about him, the inner voice would persist, his possessiveness, his intense need to control? She clamped her eyes shut. No. It was not that. He had recognized something sleeping deep inside her and coaxed it beautifully to life, and she wanted more and more. And so did he. If sometimes the chaos of their dark journeys left her confused, scared, exhausted, she knew she was safe. He was always there, bathing her forehead in cold water, urging her to drink the tea he held to her lips, kissing away her concerns.

The focus of their days began to shift. They spent more time alone and would often pack up the telescope and go out to the desert. He taught her to recognize all the constellations and pick out the planets in every season, and she never failed to feel a sense of awe and humility. When she brought the night sky into focus, she felt a tacit understanding between herself and the multitude of stars. With Karl at her side, his arms around her, his voice guiding her, she learned to let herself melt into the night and go with these stars as they cruised along the elliptic. She understood more profoundly than ever why, thousands of years ago, ancient and certainly wiser people felt their influence and identified so strongly with their power.

As they lay on the blanket on the sand and stared at the great tapestry of the night sky, he would read by flashlight from the Egyptian Book of the Dead or recite passages from memory. Air and water, the elements that ruled their own nativities, these, he said, should be celebrated the most. He showed her how to track the constellations which represented these, focusing on them star by star. "Are you ready?" he would whisper. He'd sip from the silver flask and pass it to her. She would hold the liquid under her tongue, then cling to him, waiting for it all to begin.

She gave herself over to the euphoric release of tension, the extravagance of sound and colour, the vast, kaleidoscopic vistas, the loss of gravity, the furious pump of blood in her veins. He was always beside her gripping her hand and spinning her round to see what he saw. They watched Castor and Pollux, locked forever together, soaring across the universe, the great bull Taurus charging ahead of them, his red eye blazing through the darkness. When Karl spoke, the words spilled from his mouth and fractured into tiny crystals, hanging in the black night like diamonds. When they made love, she felt the whole world flashing and glittering around them. It was the only world she wanted.

***

When Rachel came back from an errand one morning, she found Ahmed in the store in a heated discussion with Karl. They retreated upstairs. Their voices were raised but she couldn't understand what they said. She had worked hard at conversational Arabic but had trouble with the Cairene slang. In the kitchen, she prepared some lunch. The voices stopped suddenly and she heard Ahmed leave.

"What's the matter with him?" she asked, when Karl joined her.

He scooped fresh hummus from the dish with a torn piece of flat bread and popped a stuffed green olive into his mouth. He chewed, taking his time. "Ahmed is trapped in the wrong body. He's an old woman, worrying for nothing."

Rachel watched him concentrate on his food. She sipped her tea and watched his long fingers move deftly among the *baba ghanoush*, the celery and olives, white cheese and thin slices of tomato. He put back his head to drain a plastic bottle of water and she could see the movement of his muscles as the water slid down his throat. The talisman he wore glinted in the sun from the kitchen's narrow window. She wanted to touch it, to feel the coarse hairs on his chest beneath it and the slight dampness of sweat under his collar.

She got up and went into the store. A number of packages of telescopic equipment had arrived yesterday and she was anxious to open them so Karl could put them away. There was paperwork to deal with too. She was leaving for Canada tomorrow. Karl had said nothing more about her impending departure. She wondered, after that outburst several weeks ago, if he had resolved not to bring it up again. He even helped her with the temperamental internet connection so she could print the boarding pass and other papers she needed. *Would he even miss me?*

She was leaning over the boxes on the floor, tearing at the cardboard, when he came up behind her, startling her. "Leave all that," he whispered, kissing the back of her head. He turned her around and pushed her back against the counter, his hands moving roughly over her body. She clutched at his hair, pulling his head back. She buried her face in his chest, tasting his sweat on her lips, feeling his breathing quicken as he slid the belt from her jeans and tugged at the zipper. Half undressed, they groped and stumbled blindly up the stairs.

***

The light at the bedroom window turned to the burnt orange of sunset. Rachel struggled to a sitting position, her breasts sore from the grip of his hands, and maneuvered the pillow to support herself. He was in the bathroom. She heard the splash of water and imagined him leaning on the sink, his breathing still heavy. Through half-closed eyes, she watched him come back in, flattening his damp hair behind his ears, pulling on his khaki pants that lay crumpled on the floor. He found a hash pipe in the drawer and took his time to fill and light it, sucking gently at the stem until it glowed and a thin coil of smoke spiraled up. He handed it to her.

She would remember that moment forever, the way he sat on the side of the bed, looking at her with great tenderness, pushing a strand of her hair behind her ear. She remembered the damp white towel draped round his neck, the delicate curve of the glass pipe she took from him, its surprising weight in her hand. She took a deep drag and held her breath. She could see the tiny veins of the jasmine leaves in her glass of tea, smell the cinnamon and vanilla from the bakery through the open bedroom window and hear the timbre and cadence of voices in the streets below. She blew the smoke out slowly, letting the sounds, colours and smells recede, letting her mind fill with lightness.

If she could stop time, that is when she would have flicked the switch.

Chapter 12

It was the fourth day of the art criticism course at Devlin's Point on Lake Simcoe and Rachel had been on her way to meet Nigel. She had taken a room at the conference centre like most of the participants. Although it was less than an hour from the city, it was still too far to drive there and back every day.

The course was interesting but the people taking it were already getting on her nerves. So into themselves, so breathless and sycophantic around the well-known artists, critics, gallerists, publishers. In the evenings, most went out in small groups to eat locally. She was not included and realized that, as usual, she was giving off anti-social vibes. They probably thought her stuck up. She had trouble sleeping, partly because of the jet lag, partly because she was already missing everything about her life in Egypt. She kept checking messages but Karl had not been in touch and she hesitated to reach out for fear of looking needy. She had brought with her a tiny vial of *salvia divinorum* and each night she put a couple of drops on her tongue. To help her sleep, she reasoned. But the visions and images that ricocheted through her brain were the stuff of nightmares. She wondered if it was too strong, or perhaps she had got mixed up with all the different tincture bottles and taken something else.

Today, the sessions had ended early. Some of the presenters hurried out to play golf, probably to avoid the schmooze-fest. Others gathered at the pool. Rachel went to the lounge and pretended to be immersed in her notes. After two glasses of wine she was feeling light-headed and miserable. In desperation, she phoned Nigel and asked if he'd meet her for dinner at a restaurant about half way back toward the city. She needed to get away.

She had borrowed Janet's car, having sold her own before leaving for Egypt. Janet lived near the subway and assured her she could do without it for a while. But Rachel found the car cramped and complicated, with lots of gadgets she was unfamiliar with. It had been a long time since she'd driven as she didn't have a license in Egypt and anyway, there was no need. She pressed a few buttons on the panel. Janet had tried to show her the navigation system that she was all excited about, but Rachel couldn't get the hang of it. Clearly, she thought, the whole world had moved ahead without her.

The country roads were relatively free of traffic. It had rained earlier and the farms and cottages she drove by looked bright and shiny in the late afternoon light.

She turned onto a stretch of road that climbed upwards into a heavily wooded area. Some distance ahead she saw a van pulled over to the side of the road and a man standing beside it, talking to the driver. She slowed down a little. The guy on the road looked angry. He raised his hands in the air. He tried to open the door and then, in obvious frustration, he punched it. Oh God, she thought—road rage or something. But there was no other vehicle. She was getting closer when the van abruptly pulled out ahead of her, and she had to brake hard. She turned to look at the man who was left stranded. She gave him a wide berth but was aware of him turning to look at her as she passed. The road climbed steeply up and there was a warning sign that several hairpin bends were coming. The van was going slowly but there was no way she could pass him on these curves.

What happened next would be forever muddled and confused in her mind. Every time she tried to replay the details, step by step, they would change or get mixed up or she'd forget one part and it would come back to her much later, totally out of context, and she wouldn't know where it fit. Only the first part was clear: a giant stag leapt from a stand of trees at the side of the road. He was magnificent, stretched out to his full length, his front hooves easily clearing the dense undergrowth, his head held high, his antlers a majestic crown. The van in front of her braked and swerved in a wide arc, its back tires squealing on the wet road. The stag seemed to freeze in the air. His huge head and those terrified eyes turned to stare at Rachel as she got closer and closer. He stumbled. Was it the van that was spinning or was it her? It was behind her now. She twisted her steering wheel as hard as she could. She caught a flash of the stag bolting down the road and into the trees on the other side. But now here was the van. Closer and closer. A bright metallic blue. Toyota. It was beaten up, lots of dirt splashed up the sides. The windows were dark. There was a fading Maple Leafs sticker on the back. She noted all these things even as she tried to twist her steering wheel still farther and press her foot harder to the floor. A sickening crunch whipped her forwards and back again. For a long moment, there was silence. And then the mad snapping and splintering of branches.

She had come to rest on the gravel shoulder. She groped for the seatbelt release button and stumbled out to the road. She leaned against the car until the pounding of her heart grew quiet.

There was no sign of the van.

Holding onto the car, she worked her way round to the back. There was a big dent in the right rear bumper, the tail light smashed, shattered pieces of it lying in the road. She scraped at these with her foot and pushed them into the bushes. She peered over the verge: a steep slope heavy with trees, lots of broken branches. And tire tracks.

She got back in the car and pulled out her cell phone. 911. *I must call. The van has gone over. Hasn't it? I saw the tracks. But maybe they are old. Has it somehow righted itself and carried on down the road, out of sight? But surely it would have stopped a bit farther on, in shock, just like me.* Her finger hovered over the digits. *Christ. I had two glasses of wine. Eight ounces. I could be charged. And the drug. But maybe it's no longer in my system. Janet's car. Could she be charged? Will the insurance cover third party? Shit.* She looked down at her hands. They were trembling.

At that moment her phone pinged making her jump. SMS. Nigel. "Traffic bloody awful. ETA 6.15."

She dialled his number.

"You'd better not be calling to cancel."

"No. I ... Nigel I've had an accident."

"WHAT! Where? What happened? Are you all right?"

"I'm okay. There was a deer. In the road. I swerved to avoid it. I hit something."

"Good God, Rachel. Hit what? Is anyone hurt?"

"I.... no."

"Any damage?"

"A big dent in the back. The tail light's gone. I think it must have been a post. That I hit. A sign post." *What an earth made me say that? It's surely another voice, another person saying it.* But even as the words left her mouth, she saw in the rear-view mirror a sign post on the side of the road. *Maybe it is one of those warnings about the curves. The pole is steel. I could so easily have hit that.*

"Well thank heavens it's not worse than that. Although I'm sure Janet will be thrilled. You sound shaky. Did the airbag inflate? Are you all right to drive?"

What about the call? You have to make the call. The driver could still be alive.

"No. No airbag. Listen, Nigel, I—"

"Where are you now? Would it be better if you stayed there and I drive up to meet you?"

"I think I'm okay."

"Drive slowly. I'll see you in about twenty minutes."

She started up the ignition and moved on. Then she pulled over, then changed her mind again and drove back into the lane. A car passed her, honking loudly.

There was little traffic so, after a few minutes, the deafening blare and sudden appearance of a fire engine coming the other way made her brake in panic. She kept both hands on the wheel and tried to breathe slowly. *Okay. This is good. Maybe the person in the van called 911 themselves. They'd be pulled out. They'd be fine. But oh God, they would remember me, they would remember being hit. Wouldn't they? Or maybe they'd think I'd gone over too. What kind of dent would be on the van? But there would be tons of dents ——it broke all those branches, banged into all those trees. Maybe that fire engine has nothing to do with this.*

She resolved to talk to Nigel, tell him everything. He would know what to do.

He was waiting in the parking lot of the restaurant. He looked at the car and professed great consternation but more because of the potential cost of repair than the damage itself. He said Janet would probably not want to get the insurance involved, and who could blame her. Two thousand dollars, give or take. Rachel had blanched at this and Nigel said he'd cover it but would hold it over her head for many years. And not to worry, he'd call Janet and tell her. He'd given her a hug then and Rachel found herself close to breaking down. *Okay, he had tons of money but still, he is always so generous.* She leaned into his shoulder.

The dinner made her feel better. A glass of wine helped. She sipped it slowly, telling herself that by the time she drove home she'd be all right. She wouldn't have another one. At one point Nigel reached over to hold her hand. He said it was shaking. She opened her mouth to explain but he started to tell her it was no big deal, and she mustn't get so upset about a minor accident. It wasn't her fault, it was the deer. He made a lame joke about deer in headlights, and aren't they supposed to stand still, not leap about all over the road, and no wonder she swerved. The more he talked, the more the truth receded into the shadows, like a bad dream, something she was involved in, but not really. It wasn't dangerous driving, she reasoned. She had done everything in her power to avoid the stag, to steer clear of the van. And if she made the call, she might be charged. Even if the other guy would have gone over anyway, she'd never be able to prove that. They'd see the dent on Janet's car, the smashed tail light. It was a serious crunch. But it was an accident. But what if they didn't believe her about the deer? They'd say she was DUI. She'd go to jail. She couldn't go back to Egypt.

Nigel had moved on. He was talking about his business and how, when she finally came to her senses and left Egypt for good, he would introduce her to the right kind of people, get her started on her real vocation. Of course, he wanted to know about Karl. Janet had told him Karl was a control freak. Rachel protested this and reassured him she was happy and this was a passionate fling and everyone should relax and let her have some fun. Nigel peered at her over his half moon glasses, something he always did when he wasn't buying a particular story. "Be careful. I don't know what you're taking over there but I'll bet it's dangerous. Believe me, I know. Aren't there better ways of getting good sex, for heaven's sake? And don't give me that look. It's clearly your primary motivation, never mind all this Egyptology gobbledygook."

As they walked back to the car park, Rachel knew that if she said nothing by the time she got to the car, she would need to stay silent forever. She hesitated, her hand hovering over the door handle. She took a deep breath. Nigel looked at her expectantly. But her courage failed her. She got in the car, blew Nigel a kiss through the window and left.

She drove back to the conference centre by a slightly different route, drank two or three more glasses of wine from the mini bar and fell into a fitful sleep.

***

Farmer reported spotting fire on section of the ravine bordering his property... plummeted off the side of Cedar Grove Pass and subsequently caught fire ...

Rachel had escaped to the bathroom off the main conference hall and was clutching a local paper, trying to focus on the lead article. She had caught a snippet of a whispered conversation between two people at the break that morning, the words "accident" and "sharp curves." The papers, not more than a couple of folded pages per issue, were lying on the counter at reception. One of the Receptionists and a bell boy were each holding a copy, exclaiming, hands to their throats. She saw only *ravine* and *fatal* in the main headline. Now, in a total sweat, she tried to read on. *Cedar Grove.* Where was that? *Subsequently caught fire.* That fire engine.

... pronounced dead at the scene... police investigating.... name withheld until next of kin...

She was back in the car. She took a different route to the city, worried there might be some kind of bulletin, an alert to keep an eye out for a car with damaged tail light. She looked in the rear-view mirror. Her clothes and binders and notes and laptop were all in her bags in the trunk and on the back seat. She had no memory of packing them. She wanted to get away before anyone at the conference noticed the damage on her car. She put the radio on. Classical. If she was stopped, it would make her seem calm, unbothered.

Somehow, she made it to Janet's. She backed the car against a wall in the far corner of the lot. In the lobby of the building, she dialled the code and prayed Janet would be home. After a lot of screeching in disbelief through the intercom, Janet buzzed her through. She was already waiting at the open door when Rachel got off the elevator.

"What the—"

"For God's sake, Janet. No drama. Let me in. Get me a coffee."

While Janet got the coffee going, Rachel went to the bathroom. She hardly recognized the woman in the mirror. Her face was flushed, her eyes tired, her make-up smudged. She splashed cold water on her face and dragged a comb through her hair.

"You look like shit," Janet said, setting two mugs down on the coffee table with a thunk.

Rachel threw herself onto the couch. "I guess the accident upset me. I'm so sorry. Such a pain for you. It got me all wound up. I couldn't concentrate."

"Rachel you swung into a fucking post. Haven't we all? WHAT is the big deal? And Nigel told me he'd pay for it. Relax already."

She wondered if Janet would be a better confidante than Nigel but thought no, she'd get hysterical—and once it was out, there'd be no way of taking it back.

"I didn't really like the course. It's not for me. I'll do another one some time. Don't tell Nigel I quit. Please Janet. I can't deal with it. I'll tell him tomorrow. Let's take the car in right now and get it done. I'd feel better."

"Whoa. Slow down. No rush for that. It's still driveable."

Rachel hoped the panic she felt didn't show in her eyes. "Indulge me. I feel so bad about it. It'll make me sleep better if I know it's getting fixed."

"Okay, okay. Let me call Paula first and we'll arrange dinner. Saturday, maybe."

Rachel watched her friend look for her purse and pull out her phone. She imagined the dinner with Paula. She imagined them picking her up and driving to an outdoor café, probably somewhere mid-town. She imagined ordering the meal and drinking wine and listening to the chatter, defending her decision to quit the course, answering their probing questions. She imagined the other patrons sitting at wrought iron tables under red umbrellas, all relaxed and happy in the August sunshine, talking about their busy lives, their families, their day-to-day concerns. And she knew she would not be there.

She began to cry, with fast shallow gulps, unable to catch a real breath. She reached over and seized Janet's hand holding the phone.

Janet began shaking her head slowly from side to side. "Rache—"

"I'm sorry, Jan. I should never have come back here. I'm going home."

Chapter 13

Rachel roamed in and out of sleep, the sheets twisted around her, wet with her sweat. When she finally woke to full consciousness, her stomach heaved. She leaned over the side of the bed and tried to vomit, grabbing the plastic bowl from the floor, not stopping to wonder how it got there. Outside, she heard the stuttering of wheels on the cobbled road. The blind was drawn but bright light shone in a thin line down its edge. Daylight. *"Hayya alas salah, Hayya alas salah,"* the muezzin called. What time was it? Which prayer? *Dhuhr? Asr*? She looked for the clock but it had disappeared.

It took so long to pull the sheet back, to ease her feet to the floor, to stand. She tried to raise the window blind but it was tied down. She couldn't cope with the tight knots in the cord.

She went into the bathroom, holding the walls for support. Her stomach heaved again and she retched into the toilet.

She stood on the landing, disoriented, holding the banister. The way down was blocked. A heavy cabinet that was usually against the wall had been moved across the top of the stairs. She tried to push it, straining hard, but it wouldn't budge. She made her way to the study but Karl was not there. She called out to him, her voice weak, and strained to hear him moving about in the store. But there was no sound.

Back in bed, the tears ran down her face. She watched the thin line of light at the window change from bright white to warm yellow, then dim.

A soft thud, a scratching by the door. Copernicus. She knew then that Karl was home. Eventually she heard his steps on the stairs and the scraping sound of the cabinet as he dragged it back. Then there he was, filling the doorway, looking at her with that cool gaze. He held a tray of jasmine tea. She said nothing, the tears still hot on her face.

He eased her to a sitting position. "You have not been well since you came home." He nodded towards the cabinet outside the door. "I didn't want you to fall on the stairs when I was out."

"And the blind?" she managed to ask.

"Darkness has healing powers."

She took the glass of tea, cupping it in both her hands. "What day is it?"

"Sunday evening. You must try to get up now, eat something."

"Sunday!" *When did I come back? Friday, surely. What the hell is the matter with me?* She coughed and drank more tea.

He helped her get out of bed. "Come downstairs. I'll make supper."

She could smell soap and the lemon tang of his aftershave and wondered when he would have showered and shaved and why she hadn't heard him. A deep and heavy tiredness filled her whole body and she wanted only to crawl back into bed and sleep. But she knew this was not a physical ailment, only the desire to escape, the inability to face up to what she had done.

***

For a few days, she slept late and ate little, giving in to the cough and cold that sapped her strength, and allowing herself to wallow in both regret and self-pity. One morning, feeling better, she walked into the study with new resolve, anxious to feel connected again. She picked up some of her files, the ones she had been working on before she left. On the desk, she noticed a densely printed sheet, one of its paragraphs highlighted in yellow.

The propensity to label things as good or bad luck is a way to come to terms with events that defy rational analysis. But there is a grander scheme that influences everything. When a person respects the harmony of nature, the natural unfolding of destiny, this will be rewarded; when a person thinks ill or upsets the order and balance, they must right the wrong, restore the harmony. Otherwise it is left to Fate to mete out its own form of penance.

She looked up. Karl was on the threshold, watching her. He came over and took the files from her hands. "It's good that you feel better. We must talk about what happened."

"I want to forget it."

He straightened some papers on the coffee table, tapping them at the sides until they lay in a neat pile, and sat in his leather chair. "Someone died, Rachel. That will not be easy to forget."

She slumped down in her own chair. "I should never have gone back. You were right,"

"Perhaps something stronger than you was pulling you away from here, from me. You tried to convince me you were taking the course for your own sake but I always doubted that." He brought his fingers together in a steeple, pressing and releasing the tips. "The sun was in Leo. The ancient Egyptians would say you have upset *Sekhmet*, the lion-headed goddess, the protector of *Ma'at*." He brushed a speck of lint from his shirt. "Don't you think you should confess?"

She put her head in her hands. "For God's sake, Karl. There are no ancient Egyptians around. I can't do it. If I do, everything will change. They'll charge me. I might go to jail. I might not be able to come back." She wondered how he could so calmly tell her to confess when it might mean he would never see her again. "It was an accident. And I don't know that it was me who sent him over the edge or if he'd have gone over anyway." She wondered if there was an extradition treaty with Egypt. But not for a car accident. Surely.

"In the end, cowardice may be more of a challenge than courage. You can't hide from fate, Rachel. It will always find you."

"*Madonna.* That's what that paper on your desk is about, right? That yellow paragraph? I hoped you'd be understanding and here you are talking about fate and punishment and the Goddess *Sekhmet*." She felt a tightness in her chest and got up to open the window. The sounds of the street floated through, fragments of laughter, a clatter of pans from the bakery across the road, the distant blare of horns. Comforting sounds. But it was too hot outside. Reluctantly she closed the window and came back to her chair.

"Believe me, it's not what I want to talk about," Karl said. "But think about it: too much air to fan the fire, no water to drench it, a person claimed by the earth." He took a cigarette from the box and leaned towards her, his hair falling forward. "The elements out of harmony. Remember the candle that sprang to life again on our first night together. Fire will always be a threat."

She stared at him, trying to gauge if he truly believed all this. Candles can smoulder for a long time. There must have been a breeze and it breathed new life into the flame. "Come on. Please. The candle and the accident? Those two things are so far removed from each other. At most it's a coincidence."

"You know what I'm going to say now."

"You're scaring me, Karl." She wanted him to tell her none of this was her fault. Was there any compassion behind that hard look he was giving her, she wondered?

"You've read about it. You've studied it. Why do you find it so hard to believe? There is a negative energy in motion. Look how ill it has already made you."

"I caught a bug! Probably on the flight, everyone was coughing and sneezing."

He pulled her out of her chair and tucked her beside him on his own, cradling her with one arm. Something made her leave, he said, something made her take another path. She could make things right but, if she chose not to, one day it would catch up to her.

As she sat there listening to him, she thought about how his whole life, his whole philosophy on how to live, was modelled on ancient beliefs. Some of them from the Egyptians, some from the Hermetics, the Rosicrucians, some from the Far East. At first, she had thought it was a vocation of sorts, the result of his studies and his work at the university—more or less an intellectual pursuit. But the more she knew him, the more she realized that he was immersed in these beliefs, particularly those that guided the ancient Egyptians. To him, what most people called "real life" was irrelevant. She wondered what it was that shaped that rarefied state of consciousness and, stripping aside all the mythology, whether the essence of what he believed could possibly be true. But the whole idea that fate would track her down and punish her? Surely that was far beyond reason. People who had done so much worse had walked free.

She curled up even closer to him. Even though his words brought little comfort, she wanted to stay sitting beside him forever while he stroked her arm and kissed her hair.

***

The next morning, the phone rang while Karl was out to pick up some supplies from Ahmed. There was a pause when she answered, then a man's voice. "You are Rachel? I'm Osman." He explained he was a friend of Karl's from "many long years ago." He sounded like an older man. He had a heavy Egyptian accent but his English was excellent. He said he had learned about her and how special she was and hoped to meet her one day. Rachel felt a small thrill that Karl would talk to a friend about her and wondered why he had never mentioned this man. "He sent word that he would like to talk to me," Osman said. "Please tell him I am staying with my sister this week." He gave her a number to pass on. Now she felt a pinch of discomfort.

When Karl returned, he looked distracted and went straight to the kitchen. She followed him. He began to sort through the packages from Ahmed.

She told him about Osman's call, then hesitated, always reluctant to ask direct questions and spark his irritation. "Why were you calling him?"

He continued to take packages from the bag, examining each. "It was Osman who started me on my own journey," he said eventually. "He is a master, my mentor. I wanted his advice."

Mentor? He had never mentioned such a person. *And needing his advice?* She couldn't imagine Karl needing anyone's advice on anything.

"Are you concerned about something?"

Again, he didn't answer immediately, just kept checking the packages, emptying them into their containers, locking the cupboard and replacing the key in the box. "It is always important to listen and to learn, Rachel. But now, we have work to do."

***

They had been working for about an hour up in the study when he said "Mustafa will be out of commission for a while."

"Mustafa? What happened?"

"Ahmed said he was taken ill. At a restaurant near his family's home." He began to flick through the papers on his desk. "I wonder if Fadoul will have the nerve to be pleased. It's more than he bargained for."

Rachel put her pen and papers down on the coffee table. "How bad is it?"

"He's in the hospital. Food poisoning, I believe. I don't know the details." He went back to his writing. "We must do the reading for this client," he said, as though the previous conversation were now over. "He wants to get involved in that other business. Not complicated. You'll need these." He pushed some charts towards her.

She made no move to get them.

"Rachel," Karl said, putting the pen down with an irritated sigh. "What's the matter?"

"Nothing. I'm thinking."

"Don't answer 'nothing' when it's obviously something."

"I don't trust Fadoul. Could he have taken the readings too literally?" She felt a sudden shortness of breath. "This doesn't feel right."

"Neither Fadoul nor Mustafa are our responsibility, Rachel."

Did she see the briefest flash of anxiety in his eyes before he turned away?

***

A few nights later, she woke from a fitful sleep to the sound of voices in the store below. She fumbled for the light to see the time. Two fifteen. Karl was not beside her. She rose and tiptoed to listen at the door. There were several voices, all speaking Arabic. She thought she recognized Ahmed's. She crept to the top of the stairs and saw police, two of them, talking to Karl. Ahmed was standing off to the side, clutching at his hair, his red fez knocked askew. She shrank back against the wall. She caught the names Mustafa and Fadoul. One of the officers was doing the talking. Karl seemed to be calm and polite. Ahmed fingered the amulet at his neck.

A soft pad on the stairs made her look down. Copernicus. The cat stopped when he saw her and mewed in surprise. All eyes turned upwards.

Ahmed came to life. He bolted up the stairs and seized her arm, his voice a fierce whisper. "The star reading. Everyone is frightened. Please, you will explain, you are a young woman. Canada. They will believe."

"Ahmed," she said. "What are you saying? I don't understand."

But Karl was at their side, pulling him away. "Leave Rachel alone, Ahmed. You're confused. This is a routine enquiry and we must cooperate." He guided Rachel farther along the landing. "The police are suspicious about what happened to Mustafa," he whispered, out of earshot of the others. "They're following up with people Fadoul knows. I'm sure Ahmed's worried about what he gets for us—that they will find out. Right now, they think he's hysterical. There's nothing to worry about. Please go back to bed."

He left her and went downstairs to the others but Rachel stood where she was, not wanting to move away. She peered down through the railing.

Ahmed began to moan softly. Karl was shaking his head and speaking to the officers. Rachel saw one of them smile and shrug. They maneuvered Ahmed towards the door. He twisted his head around. "Rachel," he cried, staring up at the bedroom doorway where she shrank back. "*Allah Karim.*" Allah is merciful.

Chapter 14

On September 11, the whole world changed. Nigel had wrested Karl's telephone number from Da'ud and called the next day in a panic.

"Do you have ANY idea what is happening in the real world, Rachel? I'm still reeling from your abrupt departure but now I'm seriously worried about your mental health. They flew planes into the twin towers. Are you aware of that? Do you know what's going on, how completely paranoid everyone is? And for good reason."

"It's nothing to do with Egypt."

"The whole Arab world is a hot bed. And you're in the middle of it. You should NOT be there."

"I love this country, Nigel. I'm happy and I'm safe."

"The good Dr. Strangelove must be feeding you some highly questionable hallucinogens. I had hoped to engage him in constructive discussion about the situation but had barely uttered my concern before he handed the phone over to you. You are both clearly on a totally different planet."

Somehow, she managed to calm him down and promised to email regularly.

But she did not feel well. She began to wonder if the bug she caught on her trip had returned or if it wasn't something more serious. Every night she slept fitfully, feeling that the whole world was now breaking into pieces around her, the memory of the accident playing and replaying in her head, the details changing, the trees life-like and threatening, the sky black, the wind roaring, the sound of cracking branches like gun shots that made her jolt awake, clutching her chest. Karl would gather her to him and hold her until her heartbeat quietened and she fell once more into troubled sleep.

Was her illness psychosomatic, she wondered, all the mental stress working its way through her body. When she suggested this to Karl, he took her hand and held it for a while against his lips. "You must try to sleep more," was all he said. She had noticed a change in him since her illness and often caught him watching her with a worried look. She took comfort in his concern. Somehow, he made everything feel safe and right.

***

When she was well enough to venture out, they went to Fadoul's café and Karl was immediately summoned inside.

One of the merchants Rachel had befriended, Rashid, beckoned her over to his store to help him. He emptied two big bags of linen items on the trestle table on the sidewalk. Grateful for the distraction, Rachel folded and stacked the bright cotton tablecloths, runners and place-mats with their crude renderings of Tutankhamen, Ramses and the Sphinx, or "Spinkies," as many called it, unable to manage the English pronunciation. She asked how he stayed so cheerful when there was so little business now. "Allah will make a way out," he told her. She admired his unshakeable faith.

"Truly, I am not afraid of you." Rashid shook his head with exaggerated vehemence. "Many people are afraid. They say you know where Ahmed is. Ignorant people. I am educated in good school." He tapped his head with a serious nod and gave her another pile to sort.

She stepped back, clutching the linens to her chest. She had no idea she was being talked about and this made her feel vulnerable. "That's crazy. I don't know where Ahmed is."

"*Madu*," Rashid jerked his thumb toward the store next door, "he says you bring bad luck. You cannot be helping him now."

A short, plump woman in a black abaya beckoned to Rashid, not even glancing at Rachel. Rashid followed her inside the store.

"Mother," he explained when he re-emerged, "thinks you are a sinful woman. She says that you are pregnant. She can tell this. She says truly this is a bad thing, a sign."

Rachel felt she had been punched in the chest. "That's nonsense."

He patted his stomach suggestively then offered her one of the sticky pastries that were always on hand to sweeten up the tourists.

Pregnant! Walking back to Fadoul's, she realized she always pushed this possibility from her mind. She'd been taking the pill. She stopped for a moment, trying to remember how disciplined she had been about this. Sometimes, she could barely tell night from day.

Their table at Fadoul's was still empty, but Karl's newspaper and jacket were on one of the chairs. A waiter pointed towards the room at the back. She hesitated a moment, hearing raised voices, then tapped on the door. It flew open. Fadoul filled the doorway with his large frame. "How long you have been there?" he asked.

"I just got here." She was indignant with the implication that she'd been eavesdropping. "Is Karl with you?"

Fadoul scowled and went back in. When Karl came out, he took a moment to straighten a cheap picture of Mecca that Fadoul had dislodged in his haste, standing back to make sure it was level, then steered Rachel away. "Bring us a coffee," he called over his shoulder.

He moved her chair into the shade. "You must be careful about the sun."

"I don't know why. I look so pale. I look awful."

"You do know why."

With a curt nod to Karl, Fadoul brought two coffees to their table and turned away.

"He's in no better humour, despite Mustafa's absence," said Rachel.

Karl watched him retreat. "Mustafa is dead."

Rachel stopped the cup half way to her lips. "What?" Her voice came out as a muffled squeal. "When?"

"A week ago. He went back to hospital. Complications."

She put the cup down and covered her face with her hands. "Ahmed knew, didn't he? He knew Fadoul wanted Mustafa out of the way. The police. Why did they come to us?" She peered at Karl through her fingers. "Oh God, did Fadoul do something awful?"

"Fadoul has had trouble with the law in the past. Mustafa's death looked convenient. The police started to ask questions in the neighbourhood and there was loose talk about us and what we do." He pried her hands from her face and brought them to the table.

"What happened to Ahmed?" She kept her voice low. "Where is he?"

"He has taken off. Never mind that. What's important is that he tried to implicate you."

"In what?"

"Mustafa's death. He knew we'd done readings for Fadoul. He said you were an 'evil' influence."

The chairs and tables around her began to blur. "And the police? What do they think?"

"They think he's superstitious or delirious. Or worse." He brushed his fingers against her cheek. "So, you see, Rachel, you are not to worry for another moment about where he has gone."

The sharp features of his face lost definition and the market crowded in: the breathy, guttural rat-a-tat of the Arab tongue all around her, the melancholy pitch of a *muzmar dakar* pipe, the cries of children running barefoot among the stalls hoping for a few coins and, from almost every store, quavering female voices singing through cheap transistor radios. She could smell cinnamon and jasmine, cloves and lotus oil, and felt the heat of the sun pushing her out of the shade.

Chapter 15

After 9/11, the mood in the city was sad and confused and the once friendly merchants were cagey when Rachel tried to engage them in conversation. The life she had come to love began to lose its lustre.

She lost her appetite and felt lethargic and shivery, as though coming down with the flu. Little jabs of fear shot up unexpectedly, taking her off guard. Karl gave her books and articles to read and took her on simple, meditative journeys to try to clear her mind. He sat beside her on the bed one night and told her the story of the ancient Egyptian *Ritual of Am Tuat* in an attempt to guide her into a peaceful sleep.

"You will sail in the boat of the Sun God *Ra* through the twelve hours of darkness. Close your eyes. He'll take care of you."

She smelled the camphor and eucalyptus oil on the cold compress he held to her forehead. She lay against his shoulder and smelled the cotton of his shirt and the damp saltiness of his skin. He stroked her hair and spoke slowly, his voice spinning from his mouth like silk. She saw the red and white crowned serpents, the sphinx-like gods lining the banks of the Great River, the black hawk, the five Pits of Fire.

"...the Star Goddess who strengthens the heart against enslavement, the Lady of the Boat who shuts the Door of Death." Through the landscape of the hours, she drifted onwards in the boat, his words like the lapping of water at its sides.

The next morning, she woke suddenly, in severe pain, and barely made it to the bathroom before the blood gushed. She sat on the toilet, her arms clutched around her waist, doubled over with paralyzing stomach cramps. When she stood to splash water on her face, heavy black clots dropped from between her legs. She called out to Karl but her voice had no strength. She knelt on the bathroom floor and tried to mop up the blood with toilet paper and towels. She was sweating profusely and her body flushed hot and cold. She tried to stand again but the pain came in waves and she had to hold the sink for support.

In the mirror she saw the bathroom door behind her open. Karl stood for a moment on the threshold. His face was filled with sadness. He gathered her in his arms.

He had known, when she herself was ignorant. Her illness disguised her condition, he said, and the anxiety of the accident was still consuming her. He told her there were only so many things she could notice and deal with. "Of course, I wasn't sure," he said. He stared into his coffee cup for a long time. "I should have asked, but I wanted you to get well, to realize on your own."

She thought she heard a catch of real distress in his voice, but perhaps she only wanted to hear it. He helped her back to bed. She was still going hot and cold, the tears welling up and breaking through as it all sank in.

"You must go to a doctor," Karl said.

"Why? A doctor can't change anything."

"Please. There is an American doctor in the embassy district. Let me call him."

She pulled the sheets over her shoulders and surrendered to the bittersweet deliverance of irrational grief. She cried from the pure frustration of confusion, from sadness, from relief, from not knowing how Karl really felt, not knowing how she wanted him to feel, not understanding how she came to be in this strange life with a man who had such a mesmerizing hold on her, who made her feel so loved and needed … and so scared.

A little later, he brought her fresh towels, wrapped her in his own bathrobe, and urged her to drink the tea he had made. "Angelica and black cohosh roots," he said. "I went to the herb store. The woman there said it's exactly what you need."

She was touched that he would make this effort. She looked at his face, the frown of concern, the shadow of shared pain. She had never seen him reveal this kind of emotion, never seen him sad. It made her own grief more bearable.

He reached for her hand. "I can't think of this as a life forever gone. If a new life is meant to be, it will come again."

She put down the tea and sobbed against his shoulder.

That night, the smell of burning woke her and she sat up abruptly before realizing it was part of her dream. Karl was asleep, his arm draped across her waist. She stared at the ceiling, trying to imagine the two of them like any other couple raising a child: buying clothes and baby food, getting up in the night to feed and soothe. But the images lacked definition and slid away. She looked at the waning Virgo moon in the window. Everything is going wrong, she thought. Even the moon is turning its back. Was it her fault, just as Ahmed said? Did she really harbour negative energy after what she did? And if so, what more damage could she do?

For the first time, she thought about leaving for good.

***

She wrestled with the decision for many weeks. When she felt better, they went to the desert again to gaze at the stars. She lingered on the dog star Sirius, outshining all the others.

"The doorway to the afterlife," Karl said. "The Nile floods every year when it rises."

She wanted to gather in the blanket and wrap it around them, protect them forever from the judgement of the Goddess *Ma'at* or whatever it was he claimed was now at work. Everything was ending in tragedy, she thought. The man in the blue van. Mustafa. The betrayal of Ahmed. And their child, obliterated before it even took shape rather than be delivered screaming into this labyrinth. The wrong place, the wrong time. She felt the voices of the future shouting at her through the stars, singling her out for recrimination as though she no longer had any right to gaze on the mystery of those worlds she had grown to love.

Karl brushed the hair from her face and kissed the sweat from her temples. "I know, Rachel. I know what you are thinking."

***

This time, he made no effort to stop her. He said everything quietly and matter-of-factly as though he were resigned to her departure but there were things she needed to know. The last time she left, she upset the harmony of her own life and that of others. She was vulnerable to the whims of fate. She must take care. One day she would have no doubt that she belonged here, in Egypt, in the desert, with him, all the magic of the land beneath their feet, all the wonder of the skies above. She closed her eyes and shook her head slowly from side to side. She had no words to challenge this.

Would she confess, he asked her. She shook her head. Surely, she thought, it was too late. He said nothing, just looked away.

If he harboured deeper feelings, he revealed none of them. But once she came on him unexpectedly in the kitchen. He was leaning forward, his head against one of the cupboards, his body rigid. He slammed his fists on the counter. *"Aber warum?"* she heard him say under his breath. "*Mein Gott, mein Gott. Warum*?" She backed away.

***

He helped her to go through her files and organize what she wanted to take. On the day of her departure, she sat on the edge of her chair in the study. He came in, stepping around the bags she had packed, lined up near the door, and walked past her to look through the window. "Mercury moves into Sagittarius today. The sign of the truth-seeker," he said. "A restless time. But perhaps a good time for a journey."

What had she been hoping for, she asked herself? That he would tell her their life, their work could be different now, that he loved her too much to let her go? She stared at his back, his thumbs hooked into his belt. If he turned around right now and said those things, she could never leave. She loved him still, a love that thrilled and frightened her.

Gritting her teeth, she removed the Eye of Horus ring and placed it on the copper table.

It went quickly after that. They were at the airport, swallowed up in the agitation of travel. She told him she would call when she'd settled in. She waited for a hand on her arm, a break in his voice. "No, stay." But he was staring over her shoulder, scanning the flight departure board.

They stood in line at one of the security checks. People pushed by. Announcements in several languages intoned through the speaker and echoed over each other, unintelligible. A family next to them surrounded a clearly embarrassed young man and hugged him, one by one, the older women crying and clutching his arm. He finally broke loose, waved and hurried away.

Karl looked directly at Rachel. He put his hand against her cheek. "All paths eventually return to the one that was destined," he said.

She saw nothing in his eyes, even as he handed over her bag and kissed her. She turned to show her passport and get her papers stamped again. When she looked back, he was gone.

PART 2: THE WRATH OF SEKHMET

Chapter 16

At first, Rachel couldn't relax with all the showiness and comfort of the new world —tall buildings that shut out the sky, acres of parking lots, air-conditioning, doors that opened automatically, shelves piled high with the latest of everything. Walking along the mid-town shopping streets in Toronto, she was struck by the absence of smell: the spices, the rich coffee, the smoky, flame-grilled *kofta* and *kebab* and she missed the mournful descant of the calls to prayer.

But gradually, the colour and clamour of her old life, and the acute longing for the love that once overwhelmed her, faded. Over the next ten years, she swept the memories into the darkest corners of her mind. Her days became simple and predictable. She worked diligently at her career as an art critic, bought a small town house, loved and lost and cried in the same way as other people.

Sometimes, in the early hours when she woke and could not get to sleep again, the memory of the accident reared up in her mind and she would check and re-check old news sites. As far as she could tell, there was no criminal investigation, no follow up at all. Gradually she grew to believe that the passage of time and the lack of any repercussions had somehow exonerated her.

But everything changed one evening in October when she was asked to review the work of a painter who was beginning to gain critical recognition.

***

A woman was sitting beside her on a bench. She had her arm around her. "Did you hit your head? Can you tell me your name?" she asked.

"Rachel. What happened? Where am I?"

"It's okay, Rachel. You're in an art gallery. You fainted. You were looking at this painting over here. My husband managed to catch you. Just drink this water and rest a while."

It all came back then. The paintings. The two chairs, the man on the road, the deer. "Thank you," she managed. "It's very kind of you.

I'm sure I'll be fine now. So stuffy in here." She looked about for the washroom, anxious to get away from the curious little crowd that had gathered and relieved that Nigel and Philippe had not seen her fainting spell. She'd never live it down.

Thankfully, there was no one in the washroom. She sat on a stool by the mirror and put her head between her legs, waiting for the dizzy feeling to go and wondering what on earth had caused this strange feeling. Reviews, articles, promotional brochures and prints raced through her mind, but she'd never heard of this painter until Nigel mentioned him and she was asked to do a five-hundred-word critique for his show. Nothing logical struck her, nothing to make her snap her fingers with its sudden, beautiful sense. That painting of the deer. That had really freaked her out. All those memories of the accident she thought she'd buried long ago. A swell of panic rolled through her and she felt the deft hand of precognition tugging at her sleeve.

She left the bathroom and headed for the back stairs. They led to a small outside garden, lit by a few electric lanterns in the trees and sheltered from the wind. She made for the stone bench against the wall and tried to calm herself.

Maybe, she thought, it was the pressure of work. She'd taken on too much, but she had no choice. Money was tight. Her mother had died unexpectedly a year earlier, leaving more than Rachel realized she had, but the estate was still not settled. That was another anxiety: humiliating conversations with her deep-sighing brother, Robert, in England. "Please, Rachel. Talk to your financial advisor and have him ring me." No point telling Robert that she'd never dreamed of needing a financial advisor. She imagined him pointing to the phone and mouthing her name to his wife Melinda with a sad shake of his head. He claimed their mother had died the same way she lived —in a mess. The latest "beau," as her mother called them all, had arranged a funeral in Corsica where they had lived for the last two years. No family had been invited. Rachel had listened, cradling the phone on her shoulder, and saying "uh-huh" and "yes, of course." Later, she lay on her bed and tried out different emotions. Sorrow, nostalgia, regret, anger. Nothing fit.

When the money did come through, she could relax a little, decline a few projects.

A lull in the noise at the open window to the gallery made her realize the guests must be departing. She got up to go back inside. As she searched in her bag for her car keys, she sensed once again a familiar presence. The painter was standing in the doorway.

"I see someone else needs fresh air," he said.

"It is hot in there, yes." Her chest tightened. That trapped feeling again. She found her keys, swung the bag over her shoulder and walked towards the door. He was blocking the exit.

He gave her a tentative smile. "Am I allowed to ask?"

"I don't write reviews on the spot." She tried to find the right way to say goodnight but all she could come up with was "It was well attended tonight. You must be pleased."

He bowed his head as she moved awkwardly past him.

***

That night, Rachel gave up trying to sleep. At four in the morning, she got up, made coffee and camped down in her study to write the review. Feeling unaccountably vulnerable, she kept glancing out the window, startled by her own reflection. When she finally settled down, she typed quickly and single-mindedly, finished the review in under an hour and emailed it to the magazine before giving herself a chance to rethink any part of it. Exorcism.

She got dressed, threw on a warm jacket and went out. It was raining softly and piles of autumn leaves lay heavy and wet on the ground. The air felt good after the restless night. She took long strides and breathed deeply, turning her face up to the rain. She walked until she was very tired and the old memories had gone quiet.

The critique appeared ten days later. Although she rarely read her own work once it was published, she waited eagerly for the advance copy email, wanting to see Steven's name and feel he was incidental to her life, not some unaccountable premonition.

Twilight Zone: The paintings of Steven Farrow, Steinmann Gallery, Toronto.

Gallerist George Steinmann certainly stepped out on the limb this time. There is enough torment in the soul of Steven Farrow to fuel a whole generation of unsung talent. But are we to look for the art behind the anguish or the anguish behind the art? Welcome to the Twilight Zone, that ambiguous place between artistic bravery and creative cowardice. The calm side of the work, mostly oils and ranging from small personal studies to vast, generous landscapes, is exceptionally well-crafted. But a closer look reveals there is something missing. For Mr. Farrow paints with contrivance, as though he is privy to a secret but has no intention of letting us in on it. The cedar chairs ('The News'), for example, are painted with layer on layer of stunning colour but the brushwork lacks final definition and the painting leaves us feeling robbed and strangely empty...

She noted with detached curiosity that her hand, hovering over the mouse, was shaking.

In his large-canvas symbolic work, Mr. Farrow has unleashed something more powerful, even menacing. This style is so free-form and fluid it seems ...

Her editor had blue-penciled a couple of sentences here and it didn't read the way she intended. Damn it. She scrolled down and skipped to the end.

It is as though the painter is scared by the strength of his feelings and, at the last moment, holds back and twists the work in on itself. This is a great pity. When Mr. Farrow ceases to be afraid of artistic freedom, he may be a great artist.

There he was, this person she somehow knew, right there on the screen in front of her, brought all the more to life, and by her own hand.

***

The boxes in her basement were white with dust. One by one, she opened the lids and pulled out the old books, the folders bulging with charts, maps and tables, some of them yellow with age. She took out a handful of files from one of the cartons and thumbed through until she found the one she was seeking: *Interpretations of the Egyptian Book of the Dead, the principles of Ma'at*. Beneath the dim light of one bare electric bulb, she began to read, crouched on the shabby carpet in the storage room until she got cramps in her legs.

Several times, she stopped to ask herself what she was doing, what it was about Steven Farrow's paintings that made her want to revisit a time, a relationship she had tried so hard to put behind her. *That damned stag. That memory. That's it.* But beneath that, there was a deeper gnawing feeling, one she could barely bring herself to articulate. *All those things that Karl believed—what if he is right?*

When she looked at her watch it was close to midnight. She stuffed the papers back and hauled several boxes upstairs to the study, clearing off shelves and pushing her work to the side to make room. It was almost ten years since she had looked at any of this but in the next few hours the past bolted up towards her, clamped its hands on her shoulders and stared her down. She ached and felt shivery. When she finally dragged herself to bed it was nearly dawn.

For the next few days, she left her laptop and phone turned off and went steadily through the files. As she stared at the planetary charts with their dense hieroglyphic notations, she felt her old fascination rekindling, the old questions filling her head. In one of the folders, she found the series of articles that were published as a result of her project in Cairo. She lingered over these, a little embarrassed by the writing style, the younger, less confident self they revealed. And she felt the gaze of her former lover as though he were sitting on the chair beside her, observing her interest with satisfaction. "You can't hide from fate, Rachel." She fought the urge to toss the whole lot into the fireplace.

***

The sound of rain beating at her bedroom window woke her early the next morning. Down in the kitchen, she put on the radio. Ordinary life: an overtime win in hockey, a highway accident, a tax protest. She stood at her kitchen doorway, clutching a strong coffee, and surveyed her tiny garden. The leaves lay in soggy piles, the chrysanthemums were quite dead, the big pot of begonias near the door was lying on its side, broken, dirt spilling out. A raccoon, probably. She should have raked the leaves, trimmed the perennials, started planning for Christmas, she thought—and now she must get her work done. Taking the pot of coffee and a stale cranberry muffin to her study, she switched on the laptop and phone and waited for several days of texts, email and voicemail to load. With a sigh, she reached for a pad and pencil. Friends, colleagues, her editor. She scribbled down some notes and numbers.

Finally, the message from Nigel she knew would come. She gritted her teeth.

"Rachel, are you quite mad? I very nearly choked on my cornflakes this morning. 'That convenient place between artistic bravery and creative cowardice.' How bloody pretentious." His plummy English accent was at full pitch. "'A wide range of profound emotions, strikingly rendered,' but...let me see here... 'inconsistent, marred by startling flashes of dishonesty, and retreating to the safety of ambiguity.' What on earth can have prompted such sophistry? With all your interest in new expression, I thought he'd be right up your alley. This is a rare talent and you know it. And now your dratted phone is beeping at me. Have the decency to call, if you —" The beep squealed and cut him off.

She punched the boys' number, took a swig of coffee and hoped for voicemail. Silence, and then Nigel: "What can you possibly say to excuse yourself? I'm all ears."

"He lacks courage." She turned and looked through the window. "He's held back by something."

"Held back? He's been painting for years. He's only just being noticed. A most impressive style range."

"There's a lack of resolve. To me it's clear."

"I suppose you've read Baxter. And the piece in *The Gazette*. You were quite rude to those people at the gallery. What have they done to upset you?"

"All those airy kisses, treating everyone like long-lost friends. What did they say?"

"Even long-lost friends from *The Gazette* might look good to you one day. Let me see, I've got it here. Jean-Claude, I believe, fairly yodeling with admiration. Nigel cleared his throat. 'Mr. Farrow has something important to tell us: the world is a deceptive and brutal place and we are slaves to its conventions. The fact that this brutality can be captured in such a beautiful and provocative way is a tribute to the triumph of the artistic spirit.'"

"Slaves to convention. Triumph of the artistic spirit. What a bunch of bullshit clichés. Anyway, I'm sure Mr. Farrow will get over my lack of enthusiasm. Has he even read the review? I mean, have you spoken to him?"

"What are you hoping for, may I ask? Gratitude?"

She had no answer.

"He was at our home the other night. One of Philippe's *soirées*. Naturally, you were to be invited but you were incommunicado. Thank God, in retrospect."

"Is he married?" Rachel instantly regretted the question.

"Well, well, well. If you are interested in the poor man, why such a ruthless review?"

"I stand by every word." She drummed her fingers on the desk.

"Suit yourself, my dear. He's divorced. Nasty business. A child who won't talk to him." She heard Philippe's voice in the background. "Philippe says we miss you, despite your appalling behaviour. And he insists you stay in circulation or he'll camp on your doorstep."

Staying in circulation was the last thing she wanted to do. The old books and charts claimed every idle moment and, at night, the old memories kept her awake.

She closed Carl Jung's book, *Synchronicity: An Acausal Connecting Principle,* and looked at the gathering darkness outside. What would Jung say now, she wondered, what beautiful and wise conjecture might he offer if he were sitting here in her living room. If she explained what she feared, would he make sense of it all or would he chide her for too vivid an imagination and tell her some things were better left the stuff of dreams?

***

On a chilly, windy afternoon in November she worked outside, sweeping leaves and clearing up her small backyard, chopping back the perennials, putting the terracotta pots in the shed before the first frost. Two squirrels busied themselves at the far end, digging in the flower beds and planters to bury nuts and other salvaged treasures. At one point, sensing a shadow move across the pale sun, she looked up from her work. Hundreds of birds in tight formation were swinging over the rooftops, their wings beating rhythmically, heading south. When she looked down again, the squirrels had gone and the wind had dropped. In the sudden stillness, she could almost hear, far in the distance, the stealthy tread of winter. She put the garden tools away and went back inside, stamping the dirt from her feet. She flicked on all the kitchen lights.

The doorbell rang, making her jump. FedEx. She couldn't remember ordering anything and asked the delivery man to double-check the address. Yes, it was hers. She looked at the pick-up location. Cairo. Back in the kitchen, she ripped open the seal and pulled out a small bubble-wrapped package. Inside this was a pewter tin with the symbol of the sun god *Ra* on its lid. She flinched. She could guess what was inside. She looked for a letter or note. Nothing. She took the lid off the tin. The Eye of Horus stared back at her, black and white and lapis lazuli, the silver of the ring catching her own warped reflection in its bright shine. She sat down. Her body and mind no longer belonged to her and the free will she'd fought ten years to sustain was draining away. "There is no such thing as coincidence, Rachel," Karl always maintained. "There is always a plan, a grander scheme than you or I are capable of imagining."

In the cupboard in her study was an old shoe box with elastic bands, pencil sharpeners, rolls of tape and other things she rarely used. She put the pewter tin inside and shoved the box to the back of the shelf. For the rest of the evening, she paid bills, read, tried watching television. Nothing held her attention. In the end she took a hot bath and went to bed. She thought about tomorrow: lunch with Nigel and Philippe. Real life. It would do her good.

Chapter 17

On a Victorian rosewood table near the back of Nigel and Philippe's antiques store, stood an exquisite bronze lion of uncertain origin. Rachel ran her fingers over it, letting them linger in the folds. "Possibly British, 1900 —1910," said the little card propped beside it. For three thousand, five hundred dollars, someone could take it home and admire the proud tilt of the head as the lion leaned into a slight wind, clearly admiring his kingdom.

In Biggin & LeCler, *Antiques and Fine Art*, the frenzy of the day was coaxed into a lower gear. When the door closed, the hustle of Toronto's ritzy mid-town shopping district was silenced and only the assertive tick of the grandfather clock in the corner could be heard over the hushed voices of customers, or 'clients' as the boys called them. Every piece of furniture was polished to a fine glow, every ornament placed to best advantage and all were accompanied by descriptive tent cards, hand-written in italic script. "German mahogany gentleman's traveling case, 19th century.,"; "Tulipwood writing table from the end of the reign of Louis XV. Note the delicate *pied de biche* (hoof feet)."

Nigel and Philippe were happily consumed with their work, scouring the antique fairs and art auctions of Europe, exulting in the rare find, fussing endlessly about how things should be shipped, where they should be placed in the store. Rachel put her jacket on a commode cabinet, "Dutch, 1896," and lifted the lion to feel its full weight. It was about three inches off the table when she heard a familiar voice behind her.

"Now you have to take it home."

She stopped, bracing to steady the lion, and replaced it carefully. "Steven Farrow." She turned to face him. "I thought so."

He was leaning against the grandfather clock, its big white face crowning his own, his hands shoved deep into the pockets of a thick parka. "I knew you'd pick it up—despite all the 'please do not touch' signs."

"You're never tempted to touch?"

"I'm an artist. Looking is fine."

"Not too curious, then."

"Ambiguous and cowardly, I think you said."

She looked away. Six weeks after the review and he was obviously still rattled. "Sorry if you were offended. We see things differently."

"No. I see things that you don't."

She checked her watch. The boys should have been here by now.

He joined her at the Victorian table. "What d'you think of this lion? Want to buy him?"

"No way I could afford him. Anyway, he'd turn up that nose at my modest town house."

"You can't wheedle a special price?"

"They don't do that for anyone. They say they work too hard to find the stuff."

He turned up the collar of his jacket and thrust his hands back into the pockets, as though he were suddenly cold. "Since you're not buying, what brings you here today?"

"I'm having lunch with them."

He let out a long breath. "Oh shit."

At that moment Nigel bustled in, tossing out solicitous greetings to customers and waving his hands in the air. "Hello, you two." He kissed Rachel on both cheeks and grasped Steven's hand. "A lovely surprise, don't you think?"

As he guided them to the door, Rachel whispered "What the hell is this, Nigel?"

"It's called 'socializing' my dear. Perhaps you've heard other people talking about it. Come along. Philippe is already at Sorano's and we're late."

Rachel felt the miserable chill of the rainy day sink through her, turning her irritation into a thoroughly bad mood. Now she would have to make pleasant conversation with a man she had been trying to forget and who clearly disliked her. Inside Sorano's, she stamped her shoes dry and handed her jacket to a deferential *Maître D'* without acknowledging his courtesy.

Philippe approached with a flourish to escort them to their table. "Rachel, Steven, a lovely surprise, *non*?"

"You're pathetic, Philippe," Rachel muttered as she submitted to his hugs and kisses. She pulled out her chair, snatched the fluted napkin from the table and flicked it across her lap before the waiter could do it for her. She caught the boys exchanging "this could be harder than we thought" glances and noticed Steven shoot them an irritated look as he sat down.

"Clearly, we need wine," Nigel said. He signaled the waiter and held up a finger, more or less forbidding conversation until he had debated the merits of the pinot grigios and finally chosen. Then, with a grand gesture, he clasped his hands together and rested his elbows on the table. "Well. One hardly knows where to begin. For pity's sake, Rachel, put the menu down."

Philippe took it from her and placed it on the table next to them. "And please, enough with the sour faces. If we'd told you, neither of you would have come. The last we saw you, Rachel, you were charging out of George's gallery like the devil himself was behind you. Then you disappear for weeks."

"Surely my work didn't upset you that much," Steven said.

"I do have a few other things to think about."

He grimaced and she felt momentarily sorry, and then angry again, just wanting to be somewhere else, not having to deal with these erratic swings of emotion.

"Silly pair. We've brought you here to smooth over these misunderstandings, not make them worse," said Nigel.

Rachel felt the same heavy, claustrophobic squeeze she'd had in the gallery, the sense of being trapped in someone else's world. The restaurant was filling up, drafts of cold air gusting through as people hustled in from the sleeting rain and submitted to the clumsy disrobing of coats, scarves, gloves, umbrellas. The high-pitched chatter of the greeting of friends, the scraping of chairs, the melancholy tones of Andrea Boccelli in the background all clashed in her ears. These last few weeks she had struggled to regain some sense of control, to rationalize all her strange anxiety about this man and his paintings, and now here he was again, right back in her face.

The wine arrived and Nigel made a big show of swirling and sniffing. Eventually the glasses were filled and they clinked and sat back. Philippe pressed her hand under the table.

Okay, try and be reasonable, she told herself. She turned to Steven. "Do you paint more or less full time?"

"I do the odd commercial thing too. Pays the bills. Sometimes I hit long dry periods when I'm not happy with anything. Then I go play squash. Thrash it all out."

Rachel tried and failed to get a mental picture of him playing squash. It didn't fit. "Maybe all that thinking you do compromises your work," she said.

"What I'm hoping to get across ..." Steven paused, swirling the wine around in his glass, "is that everything should be questioned. There is always a darker side."

"Sounds like a grim place to paint."

"Painting is my sanctuary. It's what I run to."

"But all that cynicism will suffocate a real intensity, something very moving."

"You didn't see too much 'moving intensity' at the show," said Steven.

"I did see it, but not in the paintings." All three of them stared at her. She picked at the focaccia in the bread basket, crumbling it onto the tablecloth. "I can feel it. Somewhere between the artist and the work, like it's trapped in limbo."

"Rachel, that's creepy. What crazy thing are you saying?" Philippe removed her fingers from the basket, making tut-tutting noises as he scooped the crumbs off the table.

"It's as though there's another painting always trying to fight its way through." She thought about the unexpected familiarity of his work, the certain knowledge that she had once been part of some of those scenes. "They're kind of manipulative."

"Jesus. Must be nice to be able to dismiss months of work with a few choice words."

"It's only one perspective. You don't have to take it to heart."

"Just toss it lightly aside? No big deal?"

She dropped her voice. "Look, neither of us has to be here. I won't be offended if you tell me to F-off and then get up and leave." Nigel drew in his breath and closed his eyes. She braced for the sound of Steven's chair scraping backwards. In a split second, she saw him standing, placing his napkin on the table, wishing them in an acid voice a more pleasant afternoon. She saw him grab his coat and felt the gust of cold air as he walked through the door and disappeared from her sight.

And then she realized, with an unexpected flash of relief, that none of this happened. He was looking at her. He wasn't going to leave.

"Well, Ms. Covelli, I don't feel like leaving." He raised his eyebrows, braced with mock anxiety for another dismissal. "Because, despite your heavy-handed self-righteousness, you're making me think. And I'm kind of enjoying that."

"We'd better order," said Nigel. "I've been gulping so much pinot grigio, I'm practically levitating." He opened his menu.

Rachel reached for the olives in the centre of the table. "Sorry everyone. Order something for me, Philippe, would you?"

She watched Steven squinting at the menu's small type and finally pulling out his glasses. He kept dragging a hand through his hair. It was thick and brownish, with no discernable style, hanging unevenly around his eyes and ears. His face was pale and his body all sharp angles. He was wearing a sweat shirt with a Pearl Jam logo on it — quite different from the carefully constructed all-in-black persona at his exhibition. She guessed he was in his late thirties, although his eyes looked older. It must have been a deep pain that carved those ridges in his forehead. She felt a pinch of remorse. He looked up and gave her a lopsided smile that crept up the right side of his face before the left caught up. "Truce?" he seemed to say. She smiled back.

Ordering a meal with Nigel and Philippe was always an ordeal. They needed to know how everything was cooked, and whether this or that sauce was perhaps too heavy. And was the pesto home-made? At last it was done. Clearly anxious to steer the conversation to a lighter note, they held forth over the meal about their store, the Russian paintings they'd picked up for a bargain, the preposterous city by-laws holding up their expansion plans, and all the other day-to-day problems that beset the small business owner.

"Don't feel sorry for them, Steven," said Rachel, "they're making a small fortune."

"Not so," Nigel stuttered through a forkful of pasta. "People are haggling as though we're a common bazaar! The wealthier they are, the more they quibble. One has one's dignity."

"Are you going to the Latin Christmas Ball?" Philippe asked, refilling her wine glass. "So many super-duper artsy types." He licked his lips.

"Good reason not to go," said Rachel.

"Plus, you have nothing to wear," said Nigel. "You're the only woman I know for whom that claim is distressingly accurate. You must circulate more. Don't forget you met your latest squeeze at the Latin Ball. He lasted a whole year, I believe." He ducked as she swiped her napkin at his head. "Anyway, what's been consuming you all this time, if not designer shopping?"

"Nothing really. God, they always serve everything too hot here." She put her hand to her throat. "Pass me the water, please."

He filled her glass. "And 'nothing really' took six weeks?"

"I got back into that work I did in Egypt. Thought I'd write a bit more."

Nigel put down his fork "Not all that erudite ancient wisdom again? Honestly, one needs a painkiller for every paragraph."

"I'd like to have something new published, that's all. Anyway, it was you who got me the introduction."

"Condemned to live forever with the guilt of the *agent provocateur*. Steven," he dropped his voice to a heavily staged whisper. "We should tell you that in her dim and distant past, Rachel was a Sorcerer's Apprentice. I'm deadly serious. She dabbled in mythological cosmology or some such thing, way beyond my comprehension."

Rachel glared at him.

"You worked in Egypt?" Steven asked.

"Years ago. A writing project for the museum."

"And she met the Zeus of Zurich," Philippe giggled. "The Sinister Minister! Well, don't look so offended, *Cherie*. You spent all that time in his clutches, pondering the mysteries of the ancient world. He must have had some good lines. 'Come into zee kasbah unt I vill show you zee very meaning of life.'"

"Perhaps we're all a bit gullible in our twenties," Nigel said. "And Cairo ... dear God."

"Come on. You were there once too," said Rachel. "It's a wonderful city."

"Indeed. One couldn't get a cappuccino to save one's life."

"From what I understand, cappuccino wasn't what you were looking for."

"*Touché!* What a naughty girl you are."

"So, what's with the 'sinister minister?'" Steven looked at Philippe and back to her.

She stared at her plate, willing someone to change the subject.

"An Egyptologist?"

The innocence and persistence of Steven's questions alarmed her. She coughed as if she'd swallowed the wrong way, and drank some water.

"Isn't that the most exquisite risotto you've ever tasted, Steven?" Nigel asked.

Rachel silently blessed him for changing the subject.

"I'm not exactly a connoisseur. Food is fuel to me, I'm afraid."

"Food is fuel!" Nigel croaked, putting his hand to his throat. "What a painful concept. Good food is one of the best reasons to go on living."

"I hope you don't have bad feelings about our *petite charade*," said Philippe. "We were wishing the two of you could be good friends, *non*?"

"Maybe Rachel's got enough good friends."

"I'm surprised she has any at all." Nigel put an arm around her shoulders. "But we're terribly fond of her, despite her many weaknesses."

Steven leaned back, cradling the wine glass in both his hands, obviously amused by her discomfort. She fell to smoothing out the napkin on her lap, conscious of the expansion of the moment, its slow-motion fullness, aware of his eyes settling on her. She felt the trajectory of her life was changing and she was powerless to do anything about it. Looking up, she met his gaze and felt the tiny jolt of the course correction.

Chapter 18

After the lunch, Rachel knew Steven would call. She couldn't decide if she was looking forward to this or not. She thought he was charming and a little too sensitive, like many men in the arts world whom she had come to know, but also defensive, probably moody. In the end, it was curiosity that drove her interest, the need to get to the bottom of the anxiety she'd been feeling since they met. When he did call, the sound of his voice flustered her.

"Are you working?" he asked. "I wasn't sure if this would be a good—"

"It's fine. Just reading. I mean .... anyway... I was about to take a break."

And so on, like the stammer of a car engine when it won't engage. He said he was hoping they could go to dinner but the weather was lousy and it would be no fun going out. Maybe he could bring wine over to her place and they could order pizza? She couldn't remember how they decided on this, especially when she wasn't fond of pizza. It was as though she'd been selected to play a role in his life but there was no script to study and she had no idea how to act.

Now, nearly seven in the evening, she found herself pacing, waiting anxiously for his arrival. She went over to the bay window and peered outside. An icy December wind had picked up strength and was howling with renewed vigour, lifting the lids off garbage cans and sending them clattering down driveways, bending the trees into painful arcs and whipping the snow into peaks. In the light of the street lamp, she watched two black crows swing down to the top of the Colorado spruce on the other side of the road, their wings arched above them, their claws braced for landing. For a moment, they settled on the swaying branch and looked around, feathers rustling. Then, in unison, with a grand, downward sweep of their wings, they soared away again. Rachel watched them disappear into the darkness and wondered where they were headed, what they knew.

She looked around her living room and tried to see it from a new visitor's perspective. The overstuffed furniture that had been shipped across the Atlantic when her mother died, looked cramped and out of place. The 18th century walnut chest of drawers in the corner that Nigel had talked her into buying was surely ostentatious in her modest home? And there were still Ikea leftovers: a cheap side-table, a TV stand, a precarious bookshelf that Nigel threatened to put out to the curb one day. "How can you be so Italian with that mysterious aesthetic reverence and yet," he had spread his arms in disbelief "live like this? What a dreadful waste of genes."

Her eyes moved across her possessions, seeking something that telegraphed her personality, the texture of her days. The books, of course, almost all of them about art, art history, local artists, art criticism, but some on astronomy and Egyptology which she had brought up from the basement when she went through her old files. And the photograph album on the side table, cherished snapshots of her father, some of herself as a child stepping gingerly into the waves at Capo Vaticano, clutching at her older brother's hand as he squirmed away. Next to this was a decorative box containing postcards from her mother from the many places she had lived. Rachel remembered complaining once when she was teenager that they never stayed in one place long enough for her to make friends. Her mother had scoffed at this. "A popular person can make friends anywhere. Perhaps you should look for other reasons." Rachel had been on the point of throwing the postcards out but something—guilt, regret, a tenuous filial attachment—stopped her. Now that her mother was gone, she should consign them to the bottom drawer of the walnut chest with the tablecloths and fancy linen placemats she never used.

She loved only the paintings, one or two quite valuable now although these were not shown to advantage. She resolved to get Philippe in and give him free rein to move things around, suggest a few improvements. He had a softer touch than Nigel and would indulge her few whims.

Finally, Steven arrived. When she opened the door, the wind gusted in ahead of him, sending swirls of snow into the hall and blowing papers from the table by the stairs. They laughed in that new-relationship-embarrassed way while he stamped the snow from his shoes and grappled with his heavy coat, gloves and scarf. He gave her the wine he'd brought and she slipped off to the kitchen, grateful for the diversion of uncorking it, getting the appetizer tray she had assembled and dialing the pizza delivery because it would likely take a while to get here.

"Any preferences?" she called over her shoulder. "Mediterranean?"

"Whatever," he said.

When she came back, he was looking at three small landscape paintings on one of the living room walls.

"I see you like Jack Wilding." He moved closer to them. "Shit. These are the originals."

Obviously, he was wondering how she could afford them. She handed him a glass of wine. "They were gifts."

They clinked glasses and he took a sip, arching his eyebrows. "From him?"

"A while ago. We were friends, sort of."

"Guess he must have gotten a better review than I did."

They laughed and began to talk easily of other things—her work, his painting, the courses they found they had both taken, the people they knew. She watched him absent-mindedly spearing and dipping shrimp or taking handfuls of nuts and eating them without paying them any attention. He said he envied her Italian background because surely Italy with its deep colours and soft light would be the most perfect country for a painter to live. He had thought of moving there when his marriage broke up, he told her, but he couldn't speak the language and probably lacked the courage. Did she miss it, he asked? She was surprised at the feelings his question inspired. No one had asked her this before. She told him about her father and their home in Calabria, about her Uncle Vanni who lived there now and said the house would be hers one day. For the first time, she actually imagined herself living there, in her old age perhaps, and felt a sudden keen nostalgia for her homeland. She told him about her mother's affairs, her illness, their eventual estrangement, and the strange emptiness she felt when she died. He claimed that all families were dysfunctional and told her briefly about his divorce and futile attempts to nurture a civil relationship with his adolescent daughter. She enjoyed watching him as he talked, the light from the fire flickering across his face, his hands constantly pushing back his untidy hair.

"Did you always want to be an art critic?" he asked. "Like you always knew?" He slid back in the chair, almost horizontal, surveying all the art on her walls.

"Nigel bullied me. I was a mediocre painter but he said I had a good eye. Years ago, I dropped out of a course and—" Don't go there, she told herself. "Anyway, my heart wasn't in it. When I came home from Egypt, I did some freelance writing for the art gallery, promotional material mostly, so boring. Nigel and I met for our weekly coffee. I'll always remember. It was beginning to snow and the scene outside the window struck me like a painting by one of the impressionists, you know, blurred by the first flurries of the season, the colours running into each other. People were leaning forward, clutching their coats around them, fiddling with their umbrellas. They sort of melted into the scene with the snow. I tried to describe this to Nigel. When we left, he drove me home, came in the house and marched me to my computer. He made me sign up for a pretty serious art criticism course. Much more in depth than the one I dropped."

"Ah so it's all Nigel's fault then." Steven grinned.

"I'm sure there are many days he regrets it. 'My dear—'" she imitated Nigel's raised eyes, hand-to-the brow gesture. "'You now have a "reputation" but one is never sure how to interpret the word, how much one should apologize for you.'"

Eventually, the pizza delivery guy made it to the front door, clutching the heated pouch to his chest. Steven insisted on paying, then excused himself and went up to the bathroom.

"Whoa," she heard him say on his way back down. "Who's the photographer?" She knew he must be looking at the tall, black and white photograph of the city that hung on the wall over the stairs and could be seen only on the descent.

"Don Jaworksi." She paused, wondering again why she had kept the damn thing. "I don't think you'd know him."

"A professional?"

"Mostly freelance. News magazines."

"A friend?"

He might as well have said "another friend?" Jesus, how many more failed relationships was she going to have to admit to? Don Jaworski was a practical man and that had suited her at the time. After Cairo, she had longed for an ordered life, a sense of routine. But just a year into the relationship, she came home one day to find he'd moved out, leaving nothing but a cheque for his share of the balance of the lease on the apartment. Apparently there had been another woman almost from the beginning. "What?" Janet had yelled down the phone. "Aren't you just livid?" But it was Don who was angry. When they finally talked, he told her he had given up trying to break through the icy wall she'd built around herself. She would often look at couples on the subway, at restaurants, or simply walking down the street, and would marvel at how they were so natural, heads bent together over a newspaper or a menu, arms linked while window shopping. To her, these so-called normal relationships were such hard work. She couldn't admit to Janet that she felt a strange sense of relief.

"To be honest, I've got a bit of a problem with artistic photography," she said, handing Steven a wedge of the pizza. "All those supposedly great photographs make the subject, whether it's a person or a landscape or a building, look like it's been violated in some way. Painting is different." She stopped, unsure of this once very firm opinion.

Steven settled back into the wing chair by the fire. "How? Sounds like I might like this."

"Painting is a two-way thing. The painter explores and reveres the subject. And as he paints, he is offering part of his identity in return. In all great paintings you can feel the soul of the artist. The photographer beguiles or distracts his subject, waits for a certain light, a point of drama and then, snap, the photo is done. Not much empathy in that."

"Wow." He turned the word into two syllables. "I can think of a good number of photographers who would have you lynched. Did Mr. Jaworski know about these feelings?"

"We never saw anything the same way. He believed something was true or it wasn't. That was the drive behind his work, behind his life." She sipped her wine before continuing. "I guess his black-and-white personality was refreshing at that time. But ... old news. And we need more wine." She got up and cleared away the appetizer left-overs.

"This is good pizza, not too exotic," Steven said, when she came back. He took another slice. "Pizza reminds me of my brother, Colin. He used to make his own weird concoctions."

"Are you close?"

"He died years ago."

"I'm sorry."

"Yep. He was a great guy." He reached for his glass, drained it and poured himself another. "So, tell me a bit about the work you did in Egypt."

"A commission for the museum. They had this big show on ancient Egypt. I wrote the blurbs they put next to the exhibits, you know, the brochures, the narrative for the video, that kind of thing."

"You said at our lunch that you'd gotten back into it. Is there a new project?"

"A few articles I'd like to get published but it's just a hobby—the ancient rituals, the art, the astronomy."

"Astronomy or astrology?"

"At one time no one made that distinction."

Steven took a bite of pizza and chewed thoughtfully for a moment. "Weird stuff though. Do you think they were onto something we modern mortals don't get?"

She wiped her hands on the napkin and looked at him. She wasn't used to genuine curiosity. "Just because things aren't proven doesn't mean they aren't true." She took a deep breath. "I can show you some of the things I'm working on. I mean, if you're interested."

She opened the door to her study and let him walk ahead, then watched him pivot slowly on his heel, taking it all in: the table by the window covered with mathematical grids and charts, the map of the skies of the northern hemisphere lying to one side, big red marker lines across it, the giant globe reclining on its heavy wooden stand, and three of the four walls covered with Egyptian hieroglyphics and scraps of paper with notes, dates and symbols stuck on with masking tape. She saw a hint of wariness in his posture, like he was braced to run in the opposite direction if his deeper, doubting instincts proved true.

"Yikes," he said. "This looks like one of those rooms the police find when they've arrested the Unabomber or some serial axe-murderer."

"Guess that's why I don't talk about it."

From her desk, he picked up one of several prints of constellations. "Is this Leo?"

"Hey! I'm impressed."

"I only know because it's my sign. I know some of the stars." He pointed to one of them. "I think this one is Regulus, isn't it?"

He was holding the star map in one hand, the other idly spinning the globe. Rachel felt the same dizzy, trapped sensation she'd felt in the gallery as the realization of what he'd just said sank in. Leo. A fire sign. No matter how much she studied, no matter how hard she tried to embrace the ancient wisdom, some things were surely too fantastic to have any real credibility. Two voices competed in her head. One said drop it, right now, stop tempting fate, and the other: what the hell, fate is supposed to have its own agenda.

"Isn't it?" Steven asked again, still pointing to the star.

"Sorry. Yes. Regulus. A 1.36 magnitude, blue-white class B7 star. About 85 light years distant. The Arabs call it Qalb Al Asad —the heart of the lion."

"Holy Shit. Was that a button you pressed to get that information?"

She laughed. "The man I worked with was always reeling off the scientific data of the stars and all the mythology. Some of it stuck. Leo is one of the three fire constellations, as you may know. The ancient Egyptians connected it to the sun, and of course the sun-god Ra."

"So, what's your sign? Aren't I supposed to ask you that now?"

"No, you're not. Sorry, I get pissed off with all the crap out there." She ushered him out. "Come on, let's finish the pizza."

Downstairs, clearly light-headed from the wine, he sprawled out on his stomach on the floor and looked through one of the books he'd taken from her study. She knelt by the fire and began coaxing it back to life, prodding the embers with a poker.

"Planets dictating our destiny. You don't believe that, do you?" Steven asked.

The fire sprang up and spit out a shower of sparks on the rug and they batted at them with table napkins. Air and fire, Rachel thought. The wind is howling, the fire is spitting. The elements are angry. "I'm not sure what I believe any more. The planets are only one part of whatever the hell is going on out there. I'm more interested in the ancient Egyptian concept of fate. *Shai*, it's called," she said. "They believed that from the moment you are born you're surrounded by forces that affect your destiny in different ways and that your life could be lengthened or shortened depending on your good or bad deeds. And then there's what they call *Ma'at* which is basically karma. If you mess with the natural order of things, the rhythms of the universe, you'll create negative energy and upset destiny. And you'll pay for it."

"Negative energy." Steven rolled over and propped his head against the sofa. "Plenty of that around. It's a shitty world. I wouldn't want to be a kid today."

She remembered Nigel's comment "a daughter who won't talk to him."

"How old is your daughter?" she asked.

"Thirteen. We're not close. She doesn't like me."

Through the window came the whirring scream of a car's wheels spinning in the snow.

Steven got up, his wine glass wobbling in his hand, and walked to the window, pulling back the drapes to look outside. "Idiot," he said. "He'll never get the stupid car out that way." Rachel flinched when, turning around, he knocked into a table and sank clumsily onto the sofa, spilling wine on his sweater. "It started years ago. Things went wrong. You don't want to know." There was a challenge in his voice, an anxiety she would one day learn to recognize in an instant. "I don't buy into this whole karma thing. How come good people keep getting such bad luck?"

The clock struck the half hour and she felt as though the great cosmic machinery paused for a heartbeat, waiting for her response. "Some would argue everyone gets what they deserve—good or bad—in the end. It's just a question of time."

He scowled. "Like there's some kind of a grand scheme? I doubt it." His voice was thick with wine and melancholy. "I'm sorry. Something happened once ... someone ...." His words slurred together. "Shouldn't have drunk this much." He dipped a paper napkin in his glass of water and rubbed ineffectually at the wine he had spilled on his sweater. "I think I'm annoying you. You probably wish I'd go."

She felt he expected that people wouldn't like him and, when they didn't, got a glum satisfaction from being right. The wind fell silent for a moment, as though catching its breath. She fancied she could hear the snowflakes outside and wished they would never stop falling and the house would be cushioned in whiteness. No one would be able to get in. Through a narrow slit in the drapes, a yellow beam of headlights from a passing car swung through the room.

"You're not annoying me. Don't be silly. I'll go make some coffee."

When she came back, they talked of trivial things, a tacit agreement to avoid any more heavy stuff. He decided to take a cab home and come for his car the next day.

She took her time clearing things up. He had kissed her goodnight and there was a second or two when it could have gone either way. Both of them hesitated, their hands on each other's arms. If he had lingered on the kiss, would she have asked him to stay the night? Probably. There was something enigmatic about him. She put the glasses in the dishwasher, slammed its door and wondered why she was always drawn to difficult men.

Up in her room, she struggled with the casement window. A big wedge of snow fell as she pushed it open and a cloud of snow dust blew in, dampening her face and hair. There was no sound of traffic, only the tired moan of the wind, clawing through the branches and whistling under the eaves, as though looking for a place to sleep. Through a break in the clouds, she could just make out Hamal, the brightest star in Aries, on its final descent below the horizon.

She thought back to his comment when he was getting all negative. “Something happened once.” What happened? If she knew that, would it shed some light on all this anxiety she couldn’t shake? He had told her his birth date, August 12. It meant nothing to her. So why the hell was she so drawn to this man and yet, at the same time, left with such an uncomfortable feeling, almost dread?

With two hands, she took down a heavy, leather-bound book from one of the shelves. *The Concept of Ma’at, Explorations from the Egyptian Book of the Dead.* She opened it slowly, giving the sharp stab of prescience time to subside. She doubted she would sleep tonight.

Chapter 19

A few days later, Rachel got a call from Nigel. He told her Steven had received an invitation from a respected art dealer who was opening a new gallery in Vancouver. "Imagine my surprise and delight to learn that Steven was at your home the other night. How painfully sly you both are! Not a word to the dear friends who contrived to bring you together."

"Is he interested? In the exhibition I mean."

"Rachel, as you surely know, Penelope Pagonis has the credentials to make most artists grovel shamelessly. I told Steven his reputation could stand a little spit and polish. Don't you agree? Or did your cozy soirée banish all doubt? He needs some help to select the most appropriate work. No doubt he'll be calling. Ah, how the world turns."

Steven did call an hour later and suggested she come by for coffee.

The snow was thick on the ground as she drove through the tree-lined streets of the older neighbourhood where he rented a duplex apartment. She picked her way along the icy path to his door. He was immediately apologetic, explaining that clearing snow was supposed to be the landlord's job. This was the first place he'd found after his marriage break-up, he said. He intended to stay only until he decided where he wanted to live but, after six years, he still hadn't figured that out. It had a spare room for his daughter when she ever decided to visit, and the living room had great north-facing windows looking out to the trees ... although that heavy storm had damaged the old Manitoba maple. All this he spilled out as he took her coat and ushered her in.

She scanned the living room while he made coffee. An old leather couch, a sports bag with what looked like squash rackets sticking out, a paint-stained pine coffee table, a haphazard 'entertainment unit' sprouting a mess of cords and playing some obscure blues she couldn't identify. Otherwise, the whole room was given over to his painting. She counted four easels, one of them straddling a blanket box laden with tubes of paint and stacks of sketches. Everywhere, against the walls, leaning on the legs of the easels and the sides of chairs, were his paintings. She wondered if the women in his life felt diminished by this clearly possessive passion.

She noticed a series of four black and white inkings featuring a young woman, half clothed, sitting on the edge of a bed. With only a few deft strokes he had captured the subtle but arresting changes in her expression. Rachel stepped closer to read the titles: *Hopeful, Submissive, Humiliated, Cynical.* Where did all that scorn come from, she wondered.

She heard Steven in the kitchen rattling around in cupboards and called out, asking if he needed any help. "Nope," he called back. "Kitchen's a disaster. I'll be there in a minute."

As she looked at the paintings, she sensed that many started with hope and then the hope died, as if the feeling had surprised him and he'd ground it down with his heel before realizing what new dimensions it might yield. In some, the central figures appeared to be trapped beneath the paint, as though their lives had been arrested at that moment, their heartbeats stopped. Her eye was drawn to a familiar painting against the far wall: the naked, falling man that she'd seen at the gallery. It was partially concealed by others. She moved these aside. The man's mouth was twisted in anger.

Steven emerged from the kitchen, passed her a mug of coffee and stood beside her.

"What's going on with this guy?" she asked.

He hesitated. "I guess he doesn't want to die."

She stepped away, startled by the sudden chill in her stomach.

"Anyway, it didn't sell." He pulled the other paintings back in front of it.

She picked up an unfinished painting of a purple sky and rolling hills, stands of cypress trees. There was a faint outline of a man climbing a steep slope.

"That's what I feel Italy must be like. Am I right? I mean you see travel photos but they don't capture the soul of a country. I gave up. It wasn't feeling right." He moved over to a stack of unframed landscapes, almost ethereal in their treatment of colour and shape. "What do you think about these?"

"I like them. But," she lifted one of them onto an empty easel and stood back, "I don't love them. They're unresolved, as though you worked hard and then forgot why you started."

That's when he suggested dinner that night, saying he was afraid she had a lot more to say and believing he could handle it better over a bottle of wine.

***

Edouard's was a slightly dated French bistro near her home. It was built like a cellar, half underground, flanked with racks of red wine, its white stucco walls adorned with waxy candles wreathed in fake holly and mistletoe and, here and there, elaborately framed prints of Manet classics. The shallow windows under the ceiling gave straight onto the sidewalk. As Rachel waited for Steven, she watched people walking by: legs encased in high-heeled boots under long coats, treading warily through the snow, pants stuffed into snow boots striding with greater purpose. She felt disconnected from the urgent Christmas rush outside. A pair of running shoes skidded across and she knew this was Steven.

"So sorry," he said, squeezing into place at the corner table. "I know what you're thinking. These artist types. Always late."

"No worries. "I've ordered wine already. The Pinot Noir is good. Hope that's all right with you?"

Steven raised both hands. "I'll drink anything."

When the wine was poured, and they had ordered the meal, he talked about the weather and the traffic and the Christmas advertising he was getting so tired of and she knew he was stalling, unsure of how to bring up the only subject he cared about. "Never mind all that," she said eventually. "Tell me what you're working on right now."

She sat back and listened, watching the expression on his face change rapidly with his thoughts. He explained the hope and effort behind his art, the frustrations, the techniques he'd adopted and abandoned, and the brief, beautiful flashes of certainty.

He kept pausing to look at her, clearly waiting for some response. She began to explain where she thought his painting could go, how he must let his work take deeper breaths and longer strides and stretch and punch its way out of his heart and onto the canvas. "There's a filter between you and your audience," she told him. "Your doubt and distrust are too obvious."

He took a gulp of wine and set the glass down heavily. "Is it any good at all?"

She ignored the plea behind the question. "The brushwork gets cautious. You've got to trust what you feel, even if it's plain old happiness. Otherwise you'll never engage people."

He attacked the food on his plate, then stopped and poured himself some water. "You were more generous with the free-form style in your review."

"That's the more honest side of you. Anger, love, pain." He was still looking down at his plate but had stopped eating. She gave him a smile. "But I feel optimism too, a kind of brightness. You know it's there but for some reason you won't let it in."

He stirred the rice about on his plate and she concentrated on her own food. Finally, he put his fork down and leaned on the table, one hand to his head. She tried to gauge if he was being melodramatic but didn't wait to find out. "What's in the middle of all this, Steven? What's at the heart of you? That's what you should paint."

He made a sound, as though his words were stuck in his throat, and turned away, holding the napkin to his face. Alarmed, she reached over and tapped his arm. "My God. What's wrong?"

"Colin," he said. "Sorry." He coughed and turned away. "Can't get past it."

"Your brother?"

He looked down through several seconds of silence. "He was my half-brother. My Dad was married before." He cleared his throat. "Everybody liked Colin. He looked for the good in people. He spent his life counselling fifteen-year-old girls having babies or talking some desperate kid out of holding up a convenience store. You know, that kind of thing."

The candle on the table had burned low and he turned the base of it round and round, getting hot wax on his fingers. "He used to look at me and shake his head. 'Our Dad left my Mom to go and have you?' he'd say, then turn the hose on me or something. But, you know, he cared. He was really struck that I could draw and paint. He liked to show me off to his friends. 'Look at this cool shit my baby brother's done.' Stuff like that."

It was as though he were laying the memories on the table like old photographs from a shoe box, out of order, unconnected, each one surprising him or making him shudder.

"So, here's a guy who tried to do the right thing and it turned against him. He was eight years older than me. He liked to think he was showing me real life. 'Come on, buddy,' he'd say. 'Stop mooning around, help me do something useful.' I'd go with him to parts of the city I didn't even know about, dropping off clean syringes, watching him talk to the junkies, bring them food. Some guy he was trying to help might scream at him to fuck off, or we'd come back to the car and find a piece of it missing. He'd shrug it off."

The waiter hovered. Rachel gave him a slight shake of her head. He moved away.

Steven picked up the napkin ring from the table and began twisting it through his fingers. "When we both got married and my daughter came along, we didn't see each other so much. His wife's people had a little country house out near Lake Simcoe. Both families used to go up every year. So, we're all out there this one time and Colin gets a call. One of his probation cases hasn't checked in. He thinks he knows where the guy would be and decides to go look for him. He asked me to go along with him but I wasn't in the mood."

A little country house out near Lake Simcoe. Rachel swallowed and coughed. *It's nothing. Breathe.*

"I guess I was pissed because he and I were shooting the shit, drinking wine," Steven said. He dropped the napkin ring and it clattered to the floor but neither of them moved to pick it up. "Something we didn't get to do very often, you know, with work and all that. It was one of those great summer afternoons. Then it all changed.

Colin was the only person I could relax with. He never judged me. And now he was driving back to the city, and who knew how long he'd be. His wife was shaking her head at me, like, let him go, you won't stop him." Steven frowned and dragged his hands through his hair. "He was half way down the drive and I ran after him. We get into this fight on the side of the road. I felt bad and said I'd go with him but he said 'forget it, man.' He drove off—I couldn't stop him. All I could do was punch the side of the van in frustration."

The sounds of the restaurant had receded and Rachel felt untethered, weightless, far away. Her mouth was dry but she didn't trust herself to reach for the glass of water.

"I felt such a stupid ass. I start running along the side of the road, thinking he's going to stop. Some other guy comes along then and Colin pulls away. I watch the two cars climb the hill. And then, right on the bend of the road, I see this deer jump out. It's a stag. Huge. The antlers, everything. Enormous thing. They both swerved and disappeared round the bend. The deer ran off. So, I'm thinking okay, nobody hit him, everything's fine. I turned and went back."

Rachel's hands were trembling. She put them in her lap and clenched them together.

Steven looked away, fighting tears. "I'm still sitting in the damn chair in the garden an hour later when we get the call. Reading a book, drinking the wine we'd poured, hoping he'd come back that night, that he wouldn't be too long."

The News, his painting of the chairs she'd seen in the gallery swam into Rachel's mind. She remembered how she could smell the spilled wine, and how deeply sad she felt, staring at the empty chairs.

She needed to say something. Ask what happened. "So, then ...."

"He'd gone over the edge. Some farmer saw the flames. The van had caught fire." He looked up at the ceiling. "Colin was already dead. I hope the fall killed him. Not the fire."

"God, Steven. I'm so sorry," she heard herself say. *I'm so sorry I'm so sorry I'm so sorry.*

Steven was still looking up at the ceiling. "I always wondered about the other guy. I saw him swerve too. But he must have gone past Colin somehow, before Colin went over. I don't know. I can't work it out."

The other guy. "When did this happen?" But of course, she knew the answer.

"Ten years ago. August. A few days after my birthday. That's why we'd all gone to the country place. We'd taken some time off. To celebrate. How ironic."

Thursday, August 16th, 2001. She felt the floor had given way and she was free-falling. She held tightly to the sides of the table.

"The stag. The painting I saw at your show....?"

"Twentieth or thirtieth attempt. I remember him so clearly. He was a stunning creature. But my brother died because of him. I wanted to paint him away. Get him out of my head. I wanted him to be beautiful but terrible. The painting sold, thank God. I couldn't look at it again."

Rachel reached over. He took her hand and held it tightly.

"If only I'd gone with him that night. Or at least if we hadn't yelled at each other. Ten goddamn years I've been battling with this. I can't ever forgive myself. God, I'm sorry Rachel. Now I'm making you cry."

"And his wife? Your family? Did they—"

"Nothing was ever the same. His wife moved out east. They never had kids. She's remarried now. I was a basket case. Lillian—my wife—said I freaked her out. Took our daughter and left me. Guess you can't blame her."

***

Everything that happened after they left the restaurant and went back to her home would always remain detached in Rachel's mind. It was her but it was not her. She was numb, outside her body, outside the physical experience, hovering somewhere above herself, looking down and marveling that this person who was her could keep going, that this person could stand up, walk, link arms with Steven, squeeze his hand, make love with him.

He was so gentle, nervous, running his hands lightly over her body, kissing the nape of her neck, cradling her face, stroking her hair, taking his time. And then he clung to her, moving with a kind of anguish, as though he feared she might slip from his grasp. She gave herself up to him, taking pleasure from his pleasure, feeling a sweet flush of calm with his release. She dared not open her eyes. Surely her eyes would betray her. She lay cradled on his shoulder, scarcely moving, until she knew he was asleep.

Gently, she disengaged herself from him and went down to the kitchen to make tea. She moved mechanically, her whole body taut with anxiety and remorse.

So, this was it. This is what that sick feeling of dread was about. What on earth could have brought them together other than the cruelest twist of fate? For ten years, this man had been part of her life, unseen on the very edge it. Now he had come to the centre. She had blundered unwittingly into his world that night. And it was she, not that beautiful animal, who killed his brother.

She sat at the table, staring through the window into the darkness until the birds announced the coming of dawn and the first glimmer of light gave faint definition to the world outside.

Chapter 20

In the days that followed, she steeled herself to end the friendship. If she walked away, put it all to the back of her mind along with the macabre coincidence it represented, maybe things would go back to some semblance of normal. Why live with the constant fear of discovery, she reasoned, why endure the knots of guilt and remorse that kept her from sleep when nothing could change the past. She wondered if she wasn't cut out for a serious relationship anyway. Nothing had worked since she got back from Egypt.

Yet, for some reason she was drawn to Steven. She convinced herself it was because of their shared passion for art, the two different skills they represented. But of course, it was deeper than that. They had slipped into a gentle companionship, a quiet kind of love. He had moved to centre-stage and she had the strong feeling that, even if she tried to leave him, she could never really get away.

At Christmas, she visited her brother and his family in England. She enjoyed these visits despite the scrutiny she felt she was under and the fact that she and her brother had little in common. Robert never understood her love of art. To him, art was something you collected if you had "that sort of money." But she adored his three young children and made fun of his rather clumsy brotherly concern. Going away was a distraction from her constantly vacillating state of mind. If she was going to confess, she should have done so right away, when he told her, at the dinner. Every day of silence made things worse. She could never explain her silence or justify her cowardice. Even though she knew that confessing was the right thing to do, she convinced herself that it wouldn't make any difference and only cause more hurt and distress.

***

In the new year they began to lead separate but interwoven lives. When he was consumed with painting she didn't call or go to see him. He'd emerge from these stints as though from a trance, not realizing that four or five days had passed. When she had reviews and deadlines, she would retreat to her study and sometimes come out late in the afternoon to find he had let himself in and was lying on the sofa reading, or listening to music with earphones on. It was an unfamiliar harmony. She felt they both moved cautiously within it, knowing it was fragile.

He told her that he had tried many times to paint away his guilt and regret, trying to exorcise the scenes of his brother's accident. The stag was the most significant attempt, but there were many others: *The Abyss,* the surrealistic attempt to portray all the smashing of the trees and branches on the steep slope down, the strange patch of blue at the bottom being Colin's van; *Stranded,* himself on the side of the road staring ahead to the bend in the road where it all happened. *Suspense,* the painting of the naked falling man, an attempt to imagine Colin released into another life. But the fact that he was dead was always at the forefront of his mind and the painting itself became lifeless. He told her he'd gone to the scene of the accident when they got the call and had looked over the steep slope, wanting to follow his brother, throw himself into oblivion. Later, he went into a serious depression and was hospitalized for a while.

Rachel listened to this, barely taking a breath. She dared not meet his eyes. When he talked, it was as though he felt he deserved nothing but a life of remorse. He admitted that on many days it was hard to find joy in the things that used to bring pleasure—music, nature, even playing squash, which he did now only to thrash out the demons.

Alone one night, unable to concentrate on work, Rachel sat hunched in the armchair in her living room. She thought about Steven's paintings, the way he seemed so tentative with some of them, so unsure of his feelings, and how they clearly reflected the way he felt about his life. A new resolution began to take hold of her. If his life were going to evolve differently, he would have to paint differently. It was as though the hand of fate itself were holding the brush. Maybe this was the kind of thing that Karl was convinced would happen. That's why she was here, why fate had manipulated its way to bring them together. This would be her way to atone. She would help him to see beyond the edges of the canvas into a brighter world. She would help him paint that different world. But as soon as she felt the relief of this, she stopped herself.

She kept thinking back to Karl's conviction that she would somehow be punished for not doing the right thing. But, no. All that was his weird philosophy, his insistence on striving for the higher consciousness of an ancient wisdom. This had nothing to do with any of that. She had been involved in a tragic accident but it was history. In real life, there was such a thing as coincidence. Cruel, unbelievable, frightening, but still coincidence. And this was real life and this was today. She was an art critic. She was simply helping an artist she cared about.

She thought back to the FedEx package she received and the knot in her stomach when she recognized the handwriting on the label. Why had Karl sent her that ring? It was more than ten years since she had taken it off and left it on the copper table in his study. Was he calling for her in some way?

She was drifting off to sleep but her eyes flashed open at the memory of the energy and passion he could summon and what it had done to her. She couldn't believe how easily he kept sliding back into her mind.

***

A pale April sun flooded the front porch where Rachel and Steven were having coffee. The trees were beginning to bud and robins were darting around in the rhododendron bushes along the path, a sign that spring was here to stay, she hoped.

Steven was getting nervous about the Vancouver exhibition. "The two other artists in the show… that's bound to create some kind of comparison. I'm not sure which pieces to submit."

"Penelope will have the final say and she's got great instincts. Stop worrying. You can trust her judgement."

"I might pull out. I can tell she's fed up with me, like everyone else."

"Everyone else?" she repeated.

He tossed the newspaper aside. "My daughter called."

"So? That's good isn't it?"

"It never ends up that way. She doesn't like her step-father. She needs to buy this, that and the other. She really needs a new iPad, etc. etc. Her mother is saying she doesn't appreciate half of what she's got and won't give her more than her allowance. So, she's calling me. She's miserable and of course everything is still my fault. Which it is."

"Right. Absolutely everything is your fault. The problems in the Middle East, global warming, the stock market."

"Glad you think it's so funny."

"It's hilarious. And a really good reason to pull out of Penelope's show and ruin any chance of another one."

He drained the last of his coffee. "Maybe I don't feel right about the show anymore."

Rachel took the mug from his hands. "*Dio mio*. How about you go get us some lunch. There's nothing in the fridge and I'm hungry. You need something else to think about."

"Now you're getting fed up with me."

"Yes I am. *Va via*. Get lunch or go play squash. But go!"

She watched him leave. His shoulders were hunched, his head lowered. A neighbour walking her dog stopped him at the end of the driveway. She was a talker and Rachel could see Steven was anxious to get away. He leaned over to pet the dog, then looked at his watch, obviously making excuses to move along. Pale, scruffy and vulnerable, she thought. The sun went behind a cloud. She gathered the newspaper and coffee mugs and went into the house.

Upstairs in the study, she pulled out a large box stuffed with notes, old texts and charts. She sorted through until she found the slim manila folder she was seeking. With a tiny catch of breath, she registered Karl's writing on the first sheet, the clear script slanting forward with strong intent. She sat in her office chair and read:

For the ancient Egyptians, everything on earth and in the entire universe has a special order and harmony, imposed and sustained by the Goddess Ma'at. Each person has a destiny, a path to follow and each person will recognize the rightness of that path if they are attuned to the rhythms of the cosmos. But they will be tested and challenged on their journey by others, by circumstance, by many temptations. It is easy to stray from the path but they will be forgiven if they right the wrong. If they do not, they will always be vulnerable to the whims of fate. Some have called this 'karma' but to the ancient Egyptians, it was an all- encompassing way of life, a question of working with the forces of destiny, not against them.

From the back of the cupboard by her desk she retrieved the old shoe box and pulled out the small pewter tin with the sun god Ra engraved on it. She hesitated a moment before she pried off the lid. The all-seeing Eye of Horus ring stared back at her. "May I come to the Abyss as the Eye of Horus," she whispered, surprised to feel a sense of comfort from the ancient words.

She looked at the phone and checked her watch. It was 9.00 p.m. in Cairo.

***

Later that same evening after Steven had gone home, Rachel's doorbell rang and there was Nigel, one hand planted firmly on his hip.

"You'd better let me in. Philippe says he's been talking to Steven. I need to understood this hare-brained idea of yours."

"*Madonna,*" she muttered. "Why all the fuss?"

"I am making a fuss because, damn it all, this is worrying. Are you going to invite me in, or must I stand here on the doorstep and let the whole neighbourhood know our business?"

So, Steven had already talked to Philippe. She had told him her plans when he came back with the lunch and he didn't seem to be bothered. But perhaps he hadn't bought the casual act she'd tried to put on after all. She was not prepared for Nigel's inquisition.

He slid off his gloves, removed his coat and sank onto the sofa, motioning for her to sit down. "Please don't think of this as interference. That's insulting. We're your friends. Do your best to put our minds at rest."

"I just want to do some more writing and a bit of research."

"The Middle East is not exactly a relaxing place to get in touch with one's creative muse these days. The Arab Spring, Rachel! The Muslim Brotherhood. Civil unrest I believe they call it, if one can label the fire and brimstone one sees on the news as 'unrest.'"

"None of that affects me and what I want to do there. I'm not going to incite revolution, for God's sake."

"Can't you work with people in this country? Why does it involve going back to that Svengali character?"

"He's not a Svengali—"

"Yes, yes, whatever you say. Charming Swiss gentleman, then."

"I want to see him because of all that he knows and believes. That's one. And because he can help me. That's two."

"And three?"

"I won't do anything foolish."

"Tell me the details and I'll try to be satisfied."

Part of her wanted to blurt out the whole story, take the burden of guilt that hung around her neck and put it on the table between them for more objective and skeptical analysis. "It's something that happened ...look, it's complicated. I just want to revisit a couple of things."

"With the help of a few choice stimulants, I wonder?" He raised his finger and shook his head at her. "I was there before you, remember. Primarily for the sex, of course." He gave her an arch look. "At least we have that in common."

"I was on a commission, dammit. I worked very hard."

"I'm sure you did, darling. Earned every penny. But all that transcendental business, trips to the astral plane to 'get closer to the ancient wisdom,' 'know thyself.' Been there, done that. We all have to come home in the end."

"Why did you give me Karl's name if you don't approve of what he did?"

"Recreational drugs? A mere hobby I thought. Surely we've all grown up."

"I'm not going for the sex or the drugs, Nigel."

"Goodness. What else is there? How much did you tell Steven?"

She and Steven had been sitting at the kitchen table eating the ham and cheese baguettes and ready-made salads he'd bought. Affecting nonchalance, she said there was something she'd been meaning to tell him. He had paused, his fork half way to his mouth. "Shit. You're married and your husband's coming home tonight."

She was relieved by the easy opening. She told him she'd been going over the work on Ancient Egypt that she'd taken up again in order to write some new articles and that, for these to be any good, she'd need new research.

Steven raised his eyebrows. "What d'you have in mind?"

Through the window she could see that the last layers of snow were melting. A few hopeful perennials poked through. The world turning as it should. "The guy I worked with in Cairo, he got in touch a while ago. I just got round to following up. I thought I'd go over there again. Good way to kick-start some new ideas."

The radio began a high-speed advertising pitch. He frowned and leaned over to switch it off. Without the radio, the silence gave the whole thing unnecessary drama.

"You'll be back for Vancouver?"

"Of course." She leaned over to kiss him and got up to clear the table. An awkward silence fell as she rinsed the plates and stacked them in the dishwasher.

"Why did he get in touch?" Steven asked.

"Sorry?"

"The guy you worked with. Why did he contact you after all this time?"

"Some work he was doing made him think about the old project. He wanted to chat. He agreed to lend me a hand with the new research. That's all."

She shifted now under Nigel's gaze and felt sick with the lies she had told Steven.

"I don't think Steven's thrilled at the idea of your taking up with an old lover. Not to mention throwing yourself into trances in the middle of the desert. *Salvia divinorum*, I believe you told me." He enunciated the words with exaggeration. "Not exactly Club Soda. One can go to some very strange places."

"He doesn't know any of that."

"He's not naïve."

"We don't question each other that way. We don't have that kind of relationship."

"What kind of relationship do you have?"

"We're ... I don't know... quietly happy."

Nigel gasped, hand to his throat, with mock disbelief. "That we could all be so lucky. And yet you're prepared to risk this 'quiet happiness' by messing around with the past?"

"Look, we've both got our own lives. I don't have to account to him for every decision I make." She went over to sort through the stack of CDs on top of the cabinet and put on Sarah Brightman. Corny and comforting.

"Rachel, if you must fidget, at least make it productive. Get me a brandy. This conversation is giving me the heebie-jeebies."

She brought back two brandies, worried now about Nigel's concern.

Nigel went through the ritual of swirling and sniffing, then took a deep draught. "I suppose you know about Steven's little bout with anti-depressants? All to do with the brother's death, I heard. Bit of a mystery. Has he told you anything about that?"

With an abrupt stab of clarity, Rachel realized that Nigel must never know the details of Colin's death. He'd remember her accident, and would put two and two together. "It's a sensitive issue," she said, a little too quickly. "He doesn't want to talk about it." *Oh, what a tangled web.*

"Far be it from me. I'm not good at all those hand-wringing family dramas. Suicidal tendencies, I heard."

She felt a tight squeeze in her chest. Suicidal. He had told her he wanted to fling himself over the edge, follow his brother, but she had not taken this seriously.

"Steven's one of those dark, brooding types, that's all," Nigel went on. "So are you. The two of you should go to some Caribbean resort, where they make you dance the *Macarena.* Nice ring you're wearing by the way. Can we expect a Nefertiti costume soon?"

She wondered if Steven had noticed the ring.

Despite the lecturing, she was glad Nigel had come to see her.

He drained his glass and gave her a long stare. "Be careful over there."

"I'll only be gone a week, ten days maybe."

"Promise you'll be back for Vancouver?"

"I already bought a new dress at Holt's for the opening. Red, décolleté—rather daring."

"Goodness me. On sale, was it?"

She threw a candy at him from the bowl on the coffee table, relieved he had dropped the inquisition.

"I'm glad Penelope's featuring three artists," he said. "It works better for Steven. Puts him in a certain class." He eased himself out of the chair. "I must be on my way, my dear."

Rachel gave him a hug and showed him out.

Backing down the driveway, he called from the open window. "If you need anything, phone me. There are people over there who still owe me favours."

***

It had taken all the courage she could muster to make the call. She had stood by the window in her study so she could watch for Steven coming back with lunch. As she dialed, she had a strong conviction that Karl would be home but her throat tightened when she heard his voice. "It's Rachel," was all she managed.

A long pause. "So. The time has come."

His words reached through the years and sank deep into her, filling the old spaces she thought were sealed off long ago. Her hand trembled as she pulled out the chair. She sat down clumsily. "There's something I need to talk to you about."

Another pause.

"I haven't decided anything yet, Karl."

"You decided to call."

"It was you who got in touch. You sent the ring."

"That was November. A time for caution." She heard the shouts of young boys in the background, the rustle of papers being pushed aside. She imagined him sitting at his desk beside the open window.

"Caution?"

"A long time ago, we began a journey together. It was a powerful force that drove us. It cannot be stopped."

"But it did stop, Karl. I have a normal life here. I have a career, bought a house. Things that ordinary people do."

"Your normal life is a façade. You are not ordinary and you don't pretend well." She started to protest but he cut her off. "You thought you could choose a different path but it was merely a detour. You're feeling vulnerable now. I think that's why you are calling."

Goddamn it, she thought, the arrogance of the man, calling the last ten years of her life a fucking detour, telling her she was vulnerable. Her hand gripping the phone felt numb. She switched to the other ear. "Look, I'd like—"

"Rachel," *Ray-chelle*, just the way he always used to say it, the hard "ch," the "el" drawn out. "You are welcome here again. Surely you have always known this."

Was that true, she wondered—was that, in the end, what she had wanted to hear? "I'd like to come. Just a few days. To talk a few things over." She pulled the paperclips on her desk in and out of their magnetized container, fighting the hot flush that crept across her neck. "Karl ... why did you send the ring? What do you mean 'a time of caution'?" She closed her eyes.

"Have you lost all your interest in the stars, *mein Schatz*? It was very clear. Something from the past has come back. I am right, yes?"

Chapter 21

He was standing at the back of the pressing crowd at Cairo International airport, his thumbs hooked into his belt, his feet planted slightly apart. She noted the cream linen jacket over blue jeans, the pale blue shirt open at the neck, that unassuming elegance that European men pull off so well. He would be forty-four in November. His face, always deeply tanned, was thinner and there were a few fine grey streaks in his hair. It was dragged behind his ears and still hung well past his shoulders. She thought his eyes looked older, almost deeper, but he carried himself with the same easy grace, as though time itself flowed through him and never chose to linger.

He watched her coolly as she jostled through the crowd.

The confident greeting she'd rehearsed on the flight deserted her. He gave her the traditional two-cheek kiss, the merest brush of his cool lips, took her luggage, and guided her to the exit.

Everything passed in a blur as they emerged into the loud brightness of the outside world. He suggested they go to his home first. He had prepared a light meal, he said. The heat and clamour of the city pushed in through the open windows of his car as they made slow progress in the labyrinth of narrow roads she once knew so well and loved so much. A street urchin thrust a bunch of jasmine under her nose as they stopped at a light. She gave the boy the smallest bill she had. He scampered away, calling to his friends.

"Jasmine always reminds me of Cairo," she said, feeling the need to justify the purchase.

"You have an Egyptian soul."

She glanced at him but caught only a knowing smile.

Copernicus had died. She knew this as soon as she walked into the store, and wondered why it saddened her. She and the cat had not liked each other particularly, but he was so much a part of the memories that still haunted her. Hermes was there now, a tabby, bigger and slower to move. Hermes, the 'trickster,' invading our lives, helping us make connections, she thought. She tried to stroke him but he melted away.

Karl told her to wait upstairs. He would make tea and bring the food.

The stairs creaked a little louder, the leather chairs in the study were missing more studs. But much was the same as it had been all those years ago: books from floor to ceiling, the quiet whir of the ceiling fan, the wooden desk with the lilac lamp, the musty scent of cold incense. She quickly scanned the room for signs of a woman's presence but there was nothing to indicate this. She went to the open window and caught her breath, delighted to see Abdul's bakery still there, the broken window now repaired. She sniffed deeply and smelled warm cinnamon.

Several charts were lying on the copper table. One was a map of the movements of the planets from last summer, through the fall and up to this spring. There were many symbols and notations on it, all in Karl's fine sloping hand, all in English. With a start, she realized it was similar to one she'd been looking at back home.

She sat at the window and watched a small boy playing with a handful of stones in the narrow street below. When she turned, Hermes was on the desk staring at her. Karl appeared in the doorway, carrying a tray of jasmine tea. The familiar scent encircled her. This is a dream, she thought. If I speak to him, he won't hear. He motioned her over to her old chair.

She had not smoked for a long time but hesitated only a moment when he offered her a Turkish cigarette. She leaned forward to let him light it, alarmed that she could not summon even this small gesture of self-control. He poured the tea and handed her the cup with the same tender look he'd had when she was ill. She became aware of the music in the background. Rachmaninov. Of course. Had it been playing all the time? She had no memory of him putting it on. The wheels of time must have jammed, she thought, paralyzing her years ago in this very chair and now unlocking and crunching once more into motion. She drew her legs underneath her, trying to hold on to some sense of independence.

"It's good that you're here." He tilted his head back and blew a smoke ring in the air.

She tried to decipher the look on his face, the tone of his voice. Relief, pleasure, a quiet sense of triumph? She still couldn't read him.

"Ten years is a long time to pretend to be someone else," he said.

She bristled at the implication that she had wasted the last decade of her life and felt the need to tell him again that she had built a life in Canada, established a career, bought a house. But the words leaving her mouth sounded irrelevant, defensive. She stopped in confusion.

"You're tired from the flight," he said. "Everything can wait until tomorrow."

She wondered if he ever regretted the past, if he had ever missed her. He had always said so little about his own life. *What has he done all these years? Surely there's been other women?*

"Tell me a little about what you've been doing," she said.

He shrugged as though this was surely of no consequence. "I was in Turkey for a while. And Morocco. A few years ago, I was invited to lecture for a term at the Carnegie Science Institution in Washington. I still contribute to their program."

"You were in the US?" She fought the swell of humiliation. He had been so close and hadn't even called her. But he only nodded and she learned nothing more.

He was silent in the car as he drove her to the hotel. She felt compelled to ask what he was thinking about.

He widened his eyes. "The return of Jupiter. The planet of fortune and chance, over six thousand kilometres away. It's in the same place as when you first came." He pulled up outside the lobby and turned to face her. "The long years it took to come back seem only a moment now."

The return of Jupiter. For God's sake! He took her case and they made their way to the front desk. He stood back, half turning to go. Clearly, he had no intention of walking her to her room.

"I'll come for you tomorrow evening at seven," he said. "We'll go and have dinner."

"Not until then?" She winced, furious with herself for sounding needy.

"I'm busy tomorrow. And you should rest." He left. A slight raise of his hand in farewell.

She fumbled her way through the registration and followed the bellboy to her room, unsure how much tip to give him and resolving to at least go to a bank tomorrow. Dammit, I'm going to be busy tomorrow too, she thought.

Before going to bed she took a sleeping pill because she couldn't face another jet-lagged sleepless night and, the next morning, woke with new resolve. She reminded herself that it was intellectual curiosity that had driven her here. The whole concept of karma and destiny and *Ma'at*. She simply wanted to better understand the ancient Egyptian interpretation of these, look more dispassionately at her feelings of guilt and the desire to atone. The rest ... an old affair. Intense but over. Nevertheless, as the evening drew near, she found herself trying on different outfits in front of the slightly tarnished mirror which hung in an awkward place near the door of her room. Jeans and T-shirt for casual indifference? *Too scruffy*. Cream pants and a structured navy top? *Too uptight*. She hesitated, then shimmied into the red dress she'd bought for Steven's Vancouver opening and thrown in the case at the last minute, its tags still hanging at the neck. He did say dinner and it might be a dressy place. She looked critically in the mirror. Even with the jet lag and the dark shadows under her eyes, she didn't look too bad, she thought, holding her hair up and twisting to make sure the dress hung right. *Shit*. She slumped down on the bed. She thought back to Janet's incredulity when she told her. "Are you fucking crazy? Don't give me this new research bullshit. What is it about that guy? Ten years and you're still not over him." She tore off the dress and flung it aside. In the end she settled for well-tailored jeans with a loose white shirt that she ran the iron over. She left the top buttons undone. The lace of her new bra could be glimpsed if she leaned forward. She chose hooped silver earrings and a deep red lipstick. Let's see if he breaks a sweat, she thought, grabbing her purse and letting the door of her room slam behind her.

When he pulled up outside the hotel, she noted with some satisfaction that his eyes slid over her and she caught the glimpse of an appreciative smile. But he made no comment.

They sat outside at a restaurant farther south on the river, away from the lights of the city. Karl glanced at the menu and pushed it aside. He looked up at the sky. "Leo," he said. "Where the sun rose after creation, according to the ancient Egyptians, as you know. You can see Regulus and Denebola quite clearly. Look." He pointed. "Regulus, one of the four guardians of the heavens. And Denebola?"

"Bad news, loads of misery. And why not ask me about Algieba, Zosma, Ras Elased Australis, Adh—"

He gave her a wry smile. "Sorry. It's in my blood. Yours too, of course."

His accent had softened. It had lost some of its Germanic precision.

He chose the dishes of a *mezze* meal for them, claiming she needed to rediscover the great Egyptian food she had forsaken, When the waiter had opened the wine and left, he raised his glass and clinked it with hers. "So?"

And now, faced with that single loaded syllable, words almost failed her.

She told him about Steven's paintings in the gallery: the abyss, the two chairs with the spilled wine, the steep slope of broken trees. But particularly the stag—how terrifying and mesmerizing he was.

"I could think only about the accident. It was the same paralyzing effect. And I could even hear that fire engine in my head. I didn't know anything about this painter but when I met him, it was like I knew him."

He was watching her carefully. She sensed a glimmer of excitement in those cold eyes.

"And then... we got to know each other. We—" He shook his head slightly as though her attempts to describe her relationship with this man were of no interest. "I couldn't stop thinking about the accident, you know, the deer jumping out. I got these cold, clammy feelings. I thought I'd come to terms with it. I hadn't thought about it in years."

She stopped, needing some acknowledgement or encouragement from him. He merely gave her a questioning look.

"We had dinner. It all came out. Remember I said there was a guy on the road the night of the accident? He looked angry—he had punched the van? It was him. Steven." She put her hand to her throat. "It was Steven's brother in the van, Karl. They were arguing." Her voice gave way. "It was him I crashed into. I killed his brother." She put her head in her hands and began to sob. The sudden weight of the guilt sank through her and she realized that in all these years, she had never actually cried. Guilt, remorse, fear but never genuine sorrow.

Karl got to his feet and went to the edge of the restaurant patio which overhung a part of the river. He stood with his hands behind his back and raised his face to the stars. Rachel thought she could see his shoulders move, as though he were taking a deep breath. When he came back to the table, he leaned toward her. She could see the reflection of the candle in his eyes.

"Of course," he said. "Retribution. What a clever way for destiny to assert itself."

She was shocked by his tone, the admiration in his voice. "Well thanks a lot for all your understanding. It was a coincidence, Karl. A horrible twist of fate, maybe, but not orchestrated by a higher power. It was a nasty, unbelievable coincidence."

"Why are you here, Rachel?"

The question was like the slide of a knife under her ribs. The reasons she had given to Steven, Nigel, and Janet seemed insubstantial now.

Karl shook his head slowly. "Have you forgotten everything? You were once a fan of Jung. 'Synchronicity' he called it. Coincidence is mere chance. Synchronicity is evidence of something much more profound at work, something with meaning and purpose."

"So, this man coming into my life was all destined? He's here to punish me. Is that what you're saying?"

"We can never know the machinations of fate. Yes, possibly. You were involved in a serious accident and you failed in your duty as a citizen. You tried to run but fate caught up with you. Or perhaps it is deeper than that. Perhaps it was this man, his life force that influenced you to leave Egypt. It caused you to doubt the power and legitimacy of what you were learning here."

"Oh, come on! He and I knew nothing of each other. I went back to Canada to take that course, not to meet him. He's totally—"

"Innocent?" He smiled. "I doubt he feels that way. If he had gone with his brother, there would have been no delay at the side of the road. They would have been far ahead when the deer jumped out. So, it could be argued that it was all his fault and he is now using you, manipulating you to make you atone and to make himself feel better."

"Karl, that is such bullshit. He knows nothing of my involvement. He'd be devastated if he knew."

"He doesn't have to know. There are greater forces at work." He raised his hand to stem the protest she was about to deliver. "You will no doubt deny this like you are denying everything else you learned. But then I ask again —why are you here?" He raised both hands and gave that questioning look, the one that suggested so plainly that he already knew the answer. "You are here because you want to rationalize what happened, you want me to help you come to terms with your guilt."

He could read her so easily. Could he read her deeper motivation, she wondered?

"Well, it's not that easy, Rachel. Last November when I sent you the ring, I knew nothing of your meeting with this man. But I saw the signs in a reading of the stars. Have you read his charts, this painter?"

"Why would I do that? I got into all that stuff because of the project I was doing. I never fully accepted it."

"What did you learn about him?"

Ten years of so-called independence and here she was, still unable to hide anything. "Leo. Sagittarius rising."

Rachel watched for the self-congratulatory air but he remained impassive as though this knowledge was never in doubt. "And there is Leo watching over us now." He pointed once more to the constellation. "The ancient Egyptians likened the powers of Leo in anger to the wrath of Sekhmet," he said, eyebrows arched, clearly waiting to see if she remembered who Sekhmet was.

She took a deep swallow of her wine and speared an olive from one of the dishes. "The lion-headed solar goddess. Blistering the earth in her fury. Gee, I'll look forward to that."

"But it is the very wisdom behind that mythology that you want to reacquaint yourself with. You believe that if you learn more and try to embrace it, it may heal the guilt."

She put the table napkin to her eyes, heading off the threat of tears. "I can't bear to think I might have caused that man's death."

"What if you didn't? What if your friend was supposed to die instead? Even if you find a way to assuage your own guilt, what about his? You don't know what fate had in mind before you stumbled into his life." He twirled the wine glass in his hand. "But now we can only be concerned with you. You made a serious mistake and you want to atone. Isn't that right?"

He tilted his chair back against the wall. His left hand rested on the table inches from her own. In the past, he would have reached to clutch her wrist, wanting her to listen hard. She felt her fingers straying towards his, as though to a magnet, and snatched her hand away. He raised his eyes to the stars again. "Different dimensions of time, different spheres of lives collided. Cause and effect are rarely logical or predictable." He turned to her. "What are you hoping for?"

She watched the waiter seat another couple at a table across from them. They were in their fifties, she guessed, both attractive, holding hands. Tourists, probably. The man said something in a low voice and the woman laughed.

"Rachel?" Karl touched her arm. His hand stayed there and she could feel its warmth.

"I know we can't change the past."

"But the future is another story, you think. You want to help this man. Maybe you can make him famous. Then you will both feel better." He removed his hand, called the waiter and asked for two glasses of the hibiscus-flowered *karkade* tea, a specialty of the restaurant. He tapped his fingers on the table and said nothing more until it arrived.

He clinked the tea glass against hers. "*Prosit, mein Schatz. Auf die Zukunft.*" To the future, she echoed to herself, an anxious prayer.

The tea was hot and she felt a flush creep up her neck. She was aware of his eyes sliding over her, lingering at her neck, the deep opening of her blouse. Was he drawn back in time the same way she was, was he recalling the long nights of love and lust, the confusion of sunrise and sunset, rising in the dark to drink more wine, to smoke more hashish, falling back onto the bed, restless hands gripping and probing, always needing more?

"You're not thinking clearly," he said, reaching in his pocket for the slim case of pastel coloured Turkish cigarettes. "You believe this man is a victim and you want to help him, not only because you think that's the right thing to do..." He took a sip of tea, "...but because you've grown fond of him. You surely don't need my approval for that."

She noticed that he didn't use Steven's name. She searched his face for feelings she could understand: hurt, even jealousy. Nothing but that calm certainty.

"I guess I was so shocked by the coincidence —okay, the synchronicity. It made me think of all the work we did here, all the things you believe, the things you warned me about. It's so weird that I should be an art critic and he is a painter and maybe that is destiny at work. And if so, then it's maybe because I can help him. Through my work, through the skills I've honed all these years." She tried to make this sound like an academic pursuit. "I felt the need to open my mind to ... well, to that ancient wisdom. Maybe it would help me. Bring me some peace."

Was that right? Was she even telling the truth to herself? None of it rang true when she said it aloud.

He was nodding slowly, his eyes never leaving hers. She wondered, as she had so often, what was going on in that mind of his. "Anyway, why did you encourage me to come?"

He moved his hand a fraction closer to hers and she thought he took a deeper breath. She tried to keep her own breathing steady. But he didn't answer. He reached for his wallet, anchored some cash under his empty glass and motioned to her. "Come, it's getting late."

***

For the remaining days of her visit, she picked her way through the jumbled streets of her old neighbourhood to join Karl at his home. She remembered every twist and turn and realized how much she had missed it all, the sun-faded colours of the buildings, the glint of copper and brass in the early light, the smell of baking *aish baladi*.

Despite all the upheaval that the country had endured in her absence, she could still sense the old magic at work. No wonder Karl stayed. Some of the merchants she used to know stopped in disbelief when they saw her. They coaxed her in to greet others she had known and gave her the Turkish coffee she loved. She explained that she and Karl had remained friends and she was back in Egypt on business. They grinned, saying things in Arabic that she didn't understand.

One morning, when she arrived at the store, she heard voices in the kitchen. On the threshold, she stopped in surprise. Karl, Da'ud and Ahmed were standing by the counter. Da'ud hastened over and took her hand, exchanging the traditional Arab greeting.

"I heard you were doing some more research," he said. "Welcome, welcome."

But Ahmed stood open-mouthed, staring at Karl and Da'ud as though waiting for an explanation. When nothing was said, he seized his bag from the table and left abruptly.

"So, Ahmed came back?" Rachel said when Da'ud had gone too.

"He went to Morocco until all that business with Mustafa blew over."

"Well, he obviously still doesn't like me."

"He's just superstitious, same as always." Karl moved to the stairway. "Come, let's delve into some of the files I've pulled out."

They studied the old charts and astral mathematics, analyzing the cosmic choreography that had played out before she left Egypt, on the night of the accident itself and in the troubled months that followed. Karl made her read extensively from the Egyptian Book of the Dead and re-learn the philosophies and beliefs she had once studied with such passion. She had forgotten the gentle exactness of his manner, his obsessive neatness, the rhythm of his movements, the sometimes-hypnotic cadence of his voice. He was never in a hurry, never anxious. He blended seamlessly into his surroundings as though by camouflage and yet, at the same time, stood out in sharp contrast to the frantic world around him.

Once, looking through some of the charts on his desk, she came across a note he had written. *Fire: cause of death; rekindled candle—first ritual; Leo sun—day of accident; Leo/Sagittarius repetitive star patterns.* Was he actually linking all this together, she wondered, and still going right back to that damned candle which sparked to life again that first night they made love? She could not, would not, accept this. But she couldn't deny the twisted logic of the whole thing either.

He told her he would like to see his old mentor, Osman. Osman lived quite a distance away, near Aswan, so perhaps next time. He wanted Rachel to meet him. Osman would be interested to learn of the sequence of events that had brought her back. He may have guidance. Rachel had no idea how to react to this and wondered what was so compelling about her story that Karl would make that effort. Going to see Osman was surely a lot of trouble. But what startled her most was 'next time.' He simply made the assumption that she would be back.

Sometimes, they would finish each other's thoughts, just as they had long ago or she would glance in his direction after a short silence, to find him looking at her. Each evening when she was packing up to leave, or when they were paying the bill at a restaurant, she found her breath coming faster, causing her to swallow hard and fight the ache of anticipation in her stomach. Would he touch her hand, ask her to stay? And what then? Would she be strong enough to pull back?

Sleep was elusive. She woke at odd hours, doubting herself and all her decisions, realizing that Karl had caused these doubts. Her resolve to think objectively slid farther away with the taste of jasmine tea, the smell of the lemon aftershave that he still used, the closeness of him. He had loved her for what was at the very core of her being, not because he needed her, not because she could help him. How simple it would be to put herself once more in his hands. How hard to deny the ease and pleasure of that surrender. In the ten days they spent together, he never once touched her. But every moment in his company, she was alive to the union they once had and distressed to find it took so much effort to push it from her mind.

In her hotel room each night, she thought about Steven with a stab of guilt. She was doing all this for him because she cared about him, because she wanted to make up for what she'd done to his life. Because she loved him. This last thought always stopped her short. If she loved him, why did she find herself falling so easily under Karl's influence? Why did she feel so alive in his presence as he deftly wove his strange spell on her? She made herself remember how naturally she and Steven were drawn to each other, despite her early attempts to resist the relationship. Of course, Karl would say. Destiny finding its way, nothing more.

And still she wondered: was it too late to confess? Years had gone by. How could it help? Steven would never forgive her, never want to see her again. Word would get out. Her career could be over. She swallowed hard at this thought, acknowledging the cowardice it betrayed.

Chapter 22

Her townhouse looked cheerful, she thought, as the airport cab turned into the road. The tulips were in full bloom, some of the petals already fading and starting to falter and the fattening buds of the lilac looked promising. She smelled the fragrance of the new season in the air. Spring. She said the word out loud. It felt strange after the barrenness of Egypt.

She flicked through the mail that her neighbour had stacked neatly on the kitchen table, but nothing registered. Propped against the coffee pot was her booking confirmation for the flight to Vancouver. Steven and the boys were already there. She checked the date. Two days to clear her head.

She went from room to room lifting blinds and opening windows to let in the evening breeze, trying to reconcile the welcome familiarity of her home with the powerful sense of feeling out of place. In the living room, she stood for a few moments, then flopped onto the couch and began to open the mail that she still held in her hands: flyers, bills, charity requests, a personally written card from Penelope Pagonis, excited that she would be at the Vancouver show. The words went out of focus and she put her head back to rest. Images of Karl hung in the doorway of the quiet room. She buried her face in the cushion but he glided in and out of the gathering darkness. She could smell the jasmine of the tea and reached out for the cup he offered in her half dream.

The carriage clock on her mantlepiece struck nine. Waking with a start, disoriented in the darkened room, she rubbed her eyes and tried to collect her thoughts. She saw her suitcase, still at the foot of the stairs, the mail, fallen from her lap and lying on the rug, the big cream cushion on the couch smudged with her mascara. The edges of dream and reality blurred. Karl had never touched her, so why did she feel the press of his hands on her shoulders, the warmth of his breath on her face? Why was she fighting tears, yearning for that touch? She remembered the look in his eyes when she was sure he wanted her, perhaps still loved her, the rare tenderness fighting with the need to stay in control. He was in no hurry. Surely that wasn't love. Love was always in a hurry.

Dammit, she told herself, getting up abruptly from the sofa. You're more than ten years older, way past the time for silly infatuations.

***

In Vancouver, the sun and fine rain had made the shrubs burst with flower in all the gardens on the long road from the airport. Rachel leaned her head against the cab window as she watched the green, wet city slide by. A grey mist hovered half way up the mountains but the sun pushed through, making the roads gleam. It was late afternoon, the day before the exhibition. She checked into the hotel and found a note in the room. "I'm either in the bar or with a group of students. Can't wait to see you."

He wasn't in the bar, but there was Nigel, sipping a martini and leafing through a catalogue.

"Well, praise be," he said, getting to his feet with a big sigh. She submitted to his bear hug. "I see the Middle East has given you a becoming sunny glow." He looked her up and down. "I wonder what else it has given you."

"Give it a rest, Nigel. D'you know where Steven is?"

"Last I saw, he was down in the coffee shop surrounded by young art groupies hanging on his every word and making eyes at him over their Coca Colas. You might have arrived in the nick of time." He signaled the waiter over.

She settled onto the swivel chair. "Is he pleased with how Penelope has set things up? I'm afraid to go and look, I'm so nervous for him."

"It will be splendid. The paintings all look rather good together. This time, at least, he'll be spared one of your acid reviews." He ordered her a glass of wine from the waiter. "I've got some homework for you, by the way. That Belgian agent, Henri Lesard will be in Toronto soon. Here's the catalogue of the artists he represents." He pushed it over to her. "Steven's not on his 'maybe' list but I've been leaning on him. He owes me—had me track down a Japanese lacquered plate with dubious provenance. You must get Steven to select a few choice pieces for him to see. You know, play up the northern aesthetic." He swiveled on his bar stool and clinked glasses with her.

"Northern aesthetic. What's that?"

"I don't mean loons and lakes, all that tiresome stuff. Long cold winters bringing out one's sharper edges, that sort of thing. Lesard will get his jollies on that."

She made a face and stuffed the catalogue in her bag. "Anyway, how is he? You didn't answer my question."

Nigel took off his glasses and polished them with the cocktail napkin. "To be honest, he seems a tad vulnerable. It's as though he seeks company and then has no idea what to do with it." He lay his glasses down on the bar. "Rachel, delighted as I am to see you safe and sound, I have to say that Philippe and I are most upset with you. Why didn't you call or email?"

"*Per piacere*—I was only gone ten days. Steven knew I'd be back for this." She took a deep drink of her wine and wondered what cavalier advice her mother might give her now, whether she would understand the tugs she felt in two different directions. A telephone conversation she had overheard between her mother and one of her excitable theatre friends came to mind. "Cast a wider net, Hettie," her mother had said. "You'll never get everything you need in one package."

Nigel smoothed back his thinning grey hair. "Well, are you going to divulge anything, or must I pry and risk a hissy fit?"

She looked down, battling her indecision. "I got lots of material. It was worthwhile."

"Did you sleep with him?"

"Jesus, Nigel." She was embarrassed by the prickling flush that crept over her neck.

"The Grand Wizard must have been fairly brimming with enthusiasm over the return of one of his subjects."

"He doesn't brim with enthusiasm over anyone. I think you know that."

"Indeed. A study in Teutonic understatement as I recall. Well, I can see we're not in a communicative mood. You'd better go and look for Steven. Rescue him from those nubile seventeen-year-olds."

In the doorway of the coffee shop, Rachel stood for a moment to take in the scene. Steven had his back to her, talking to a group of earnest students as they looked through brochures of his work. An attractive woman, their teacher, she thought, with a mass of spiraling red hair and a gaunt face like a ballerina's, sat off to the side, nodding slightly as he spoke. One of the young girls looked up and caught Rachel's eye and they all, including Steven, swung round.

He grinned, the uneven smile she had grown to love. She had missed him. The realization hit her unexpectedly. They exchanged a quick kiss on the cheek and she was dimly aware of the introductions. There was a lot of chattering and fussing. Someone made space for her to sit down, someone else brought over another chair. She smiled and nodded at the praise of Steven's work, hardly listening. A few minutes later, the lovely red-head cast her eyes at them and made a clear move to go, urging her charges to drink up, thanking Steven profusely for his time. You are a beautiful woman, Rachel thought, silently thanking her for her intuition and shaking her hand goodbye.

She and Steven sat down again, the table between them strewn with empty glasses and half-eaten sandwiches.

"Here you are." He pushed the clutter aside and took her hands. "Tanned and healthy."

They looked at each other in silence. Curiosity, worry, relief, pleasure all slid behind his troubled eyes. She squeezed his fingers. "What? What are you thinking?"

"Just glad you're back."

The elevator to the room took forever. She leaned into him and held tightly to his arm. She wanted to close her eyes and never open them again.

At the opening cocktail reception the next evening, she stopped before Steven's painting of a man climbing a steep cliff, his body bent at the waist, his head tilted back, gazing up to where the ground flattened out. Beyond the edge of the cliff the landscape fell away, a wash of colour, swirling blues and greens. Barely visible beneath were faint shimmers of gold. She wanted to race up the hill and grasp this man's hand, make him run with her to the top. She thought back to the half-imagined, abandoned painting she had seen at Steven's home on her first visit there and realized with delight that he must have felt a stronger inspiration this time. She asked him about it later.

"You seemed to like the one I gave up on," he said. "So, I started again. Somehow I thought the view from the top should be a bit mysterious so this guy's not quite sure why he's struggling so hard to get there."

She saw the same struggle in Steven's eyes. Stop thinking about how hard everything is, she wanted to tell him, just keep moving.

***

The exhibition was well attended. She stayed in the background, leaving Steven to the clutches of his admirers. Penelope, the gallery owner, looking magnificent in a bright turquoise kaftan, a gold silk belt at her hips and earrings that hung almost to her shoulders, swung by with her practiced grace, accepting the compliments of the crowd. She waved across the room to Rachel and gave her a discreet thumbs up sign.

On the last day of the show, Rachel and Steven walked through Stanley Park which glimmered in the sun after another misty rain. The mountains were veiled in skeins of grey, the harbour sleepy. Resolute runners passed them, hoods up, heads down, their Nikes squelching on the rain-slicked path. Steven stopped to look north over Lion's Gate Bridge, and west to the wide sweep of the Pacific Ocean. The wind from the sea blew the hair back off his face, and Rachel was reminded of the bronze lion he had admired in Nigel and Philippe's store, taking in the scents of his kingdom.

"There's something deeply Canadian about this landscape, a kind of wild splendour," he said. "Like you're part of the land, but not hemmed in by it. Maybe it's the scale of everything—huge trees, big mountains, the ocean. You feel so alive. Don't you think?"

"Maybe you need a change of scene, something to inspire different moods in your work."

"I've been thinking about that." They continued walking. "Especially while you were away. Last winter was so long and I still feel listless. God forbid it starts to show in my work. I could use a shot of colour ... and warmth. I keep trying to paint that way but I can't quite feel it." He pulled her close.

A land of colours from the summers of her childhood took shape in her mind: gentle slopes of lavender and gold, curving around each other, trees shimmering with silver leaves, endless rows of vines heavy with grapes. The colours blended together and fell off the edges of the world. She imagined a house filled with light, high on a hill—somewhere in Italy, somewhere like Tuscany. Surely this was the land that Steven wanted so badly to paint?

She stopped in her tracks. "You should move to Tuscany," she told him.

Chapter 23

Both patrons and critics deemed the Vancouver show a success and demand for Steven's work began to increase, but he was unsettled in the weeks that followed. Rachel hoped his moods were nothing more than artistic temperament but couldn't help thinking that he enjoyed wallowing in self-doubt.

On learning that Nigel's Belgian art agent contact was not interested in any of the paintings he had shown him, Steven went into an even deeper funk. Rachel suggested they go to a local pub for dinner, hoping it might distract him. They sat at the bar, ate nachos and pretzels and half-watched a baseball game on one of the huge televisions. She made suggestions about the European representation he should be seeking, and offered to contact a few people on his behalf.

"For fuck's sake, Rachel, all artists are insecure. Let me suffer."

She looked for the self-deprecating smile she loved but his face was dark and sullen as he fished for the broken pretzels in the bottom of the dish. He signaled the bar-tender for the bill.

As they walked home in silence, Rachel felt the energy drain from her. She began to wonder whether she really could make him paint his way through this bout of depression, reach deeper and pull out the emotion she knew was wound up tight inside—and how much effort this would take. The summer was well under way and she hadn't once taken her bike out along the lake, something she used to do regularly, nor attended any of the Italian community events she used to enjoy. Janet accused her of becoming a recluse. When she wasn't with Steven, she was holed up in her study, immersed in Carl Jung or ancient Egyptian mythology, trying to embrace the philosophies that Karl lived by. In her quiet, candid moments, she questioned whether her real motivation to steep herself in that ancient world again was because it helped her come to terms with what she had done, or because it reconnected her to a life she had once found so enthralling.

She felt heavy with doubt and struggled to quieten the clamour of the persistent questions in her head.

On the warm evenings she would have liked to sit on the porch, drink a glass of wine and talk about art and life and the latest gossip. Instead she watched Steven pace, fighting his anxieties. There were many favourable critical reviews of his work but the more his reputation grew, the more he retreated inside himself. He stopped playing squash and rarely left the house. Before his recent acclaim, he said he had painted as a kind of repentance for all the things he had not done well. Failure was somehow fitting and reassuring. Now he was punished by success. Success was more malicious, he said. It was fleeting and phony. Either way, there was no joy. He drank as he told her all this, and she felt his greatest comfort came from the grim certainty that happiness was only ever temporary. All through this, she was thinking about another trip to Cairo but kept putting it off for fear of leaving him alone.

***

On a particularly hot, humid night, she drove to Steven's home, the car's air conditioning at full blast. She hadn't heard from him for a couple of days and her calls and texts had gone unanswered. She was worried.

When she turned her key in the lock and called out to him, he didn't answer. She stepped into the living room and stopped in disbelief. Empty easels were stacked against the wall, magazines littered the floor, and brushes, hardened with old paint, lay scattered everywhere. Steven was slouched in the armchair, nursing a scotch. He looked up but barely met her eyes. Something inside her snapped.

"Goddamn it, I was getting frantic about you." She gripped the back of a chair to stop her hands from trembling, not recognizing her own rising voice. "I thought you might be ill. Now I realize you like playing the martyr. That you're selfish and self-indulgent. I don't know what the hell you want from me." She couldn't believe what she had just said.

Slowly and deliberately, Steven swallowed the last mouthful of scotch. He placed the empty glass clumsily on the table beside him.

"Isn't this interesting?" he said. "I don't want anything from you. I never asked you to care." He enunciated each word. "You were the one with the high-minded ideas about relationships. But maybe you're hanging around so you can feel good about yourself. Maybe this relationship is all about you."

"You can't bear to be happy, can you?" she said, reeling from the accusation that it was she who was being selfish. "You've painted this great tormented picture of yourself. Undeserving brother, bad husband, rotten father, mediocre artist. Pick one." She knew she was trying to hurt him but she couldn't stop. "You use what you've been through like one big excuse. You're capable of so much but you prefer to stay in your own little melodrama of despair."

He got up, stumbled past her and opened the door. "So why bother with me? You can leave any time. I'm not stopping you."

She hesitated for just a moment, then left. The door slammed behind her and the resolute crunch of the lock stayed in her head as she walked back to her car. Maybe this was the excuse she'd been longing for. She couldn't help contrasting all Steven's anxiety with Karl's calmness of spirit. Yes, Karl was controlling, but it was always in such a reassuring way. When she'd gone back to Egypt, after ten years, he had shown no trace of bitterness, no moral indignation. Maybe this fight with Steven was also the working of fate; maybe it was trying to tell her it was too late to make up for the past and she should leave, right now.

She found herself getting tired easily yet she couldn't sleep. In her dreams she saw the stag. He was walking slowly along the edge of the road whereas she was running, out of breath, to get away from him. But no matter how fast she ran, every time she turned back, he had gained a little on her.

Over the next few days, she left a few voicemails for Steven. To make sure he was all right, she told herself. But he didn't return her calls. She tried to keep herself occupied with work, new initiatives and various household chores she'd been putting off. Nigel called to get the latest news and cheer her up but she got the impression he enjoyed the drama. "A lovers' tiff, my dear. And surely just the usual artist's angst. All of them close to slicing their ears off, if you ask me."

Janet insisted on taking her out. "You have appalling taste in men, Rache. They're all emotional cripples. The painter's too much hard work. A fucking cliché. Who has the time? Then look at your former live-in, Don. Full range of emotions from A to B. And don't get me started on Lawrence of Arabia. Geez, can't you find a stock broker with a Golden Retriever?"

Guess not, Rachel thought. She felt once again that the few people who knew her well believed she was a lost cause. "You're too secretive," Janet said as they parted. "Even with me. You don't share your emotions so you scare the decent men away."

She thought Janet might be right. This persistent belief that she was trapped, fulfilling an inescapable destiny, would not release its grip—so perhaps there *was* something wrong with her. And what did she see in Steven anyway, Janet had asked. She tried to explain that he was a quiet person, gentle, a great antidote to the anxiety she herself always seemed to be fighting under the surface. There was a lovely tenderness to him that made her relax and slow down. And she loved him. Didn't she? Yes, he was self-absorbed but all artists were like that. And she felt secure with him. "Quiet, gentle?" Janet had echoed. "So, what's with all the moody-needy-depressed shit?"

There was no simple answer to that.

Deep inside, she thought, Steven was a strong person with a yearning for expression. She had seen an optimism in his paintings at that first exhibition but it was buried in his recent work, waiting for air, for breath.

***

On a bright Saturday morning in late July she returned from a shopping trip to find a note pushed through her door. Steven's handwriting. All it said was: "Tell me about Tuscany."

He came over that evening. They talked through the night. They took long walks by the lake and into the ravines. They stopped at outdoor cafés and lingered over coffee. He tried to explain that he didn't understand himself when he was in these dark moods, that he let the old anxieties, the old guilt eat away inside him, undermining the resolve he knew was down there somewhere. But she cut him off and told him she only wanted to hear about the new ideas he had, the plans he was making for a whole new start. As he talked, she found herself clenching her crossed fingers, allowing herself to believe that her influence might be working. He could and would paint his way to a sense of freedom, a release from guilt. And then, just maybe, a release from hers.

On the long summer evenings, they sat outside until the sun went down, not needing any distraction or anyone else's company. They ate whatever they could find in the fridge, drank wine and let the dirty dishes pile up on the patio table. They stayed until the nights began to cool or the persistent mosquitos got the better of them. He began to paint again.

Three months later, he left Canada for Italy.

Chapter 24

Rachel had told him to find a place "filled with air and light," a high place, close to the sun. But as he drove through the scattered villages in these sunbaked Italian hills, Steven thought he'd never find such a place and doubted its existence at all except in her imagination.

Eventually, he stumbled on it by accident, though of course she said these things were never accidental. He was lost one day and, looking around to get his bearings, saw the house *"In vendetta"* high above him and walked up the steep, winding path, hoping to find someone who could help. The house was empty, yet full of warmth and welcome. He loved the dark wooden floors which complained beneath his step, the creamy stucco walls, the narrow stairs that plunged down to a musty cave-like wine cellar. Everything about it was heavy and solid and generous and he felt immediately at home. On the north side, he found a large room with a high, vaulted ceiling and windows on two sides. He threw open the shutters and the light poured through in giant shafts, flooding every corner. This was where he would paint.

***

At first, he felt like an intruder. His inability to speak more than a few words of Italian made everything complicated —from the relatively simple task of shopping for groceries, to the far more complex business of buying a car, and then the house itself. But word soon got around that a single man, an artist, had come to live in the neighbourhood, and the locals welcomed him. He would arrive home to find a loaf of bread, a small basket lined with leaves containing fresh plums or peaches, a bottle of San Gimignano's famous *Vernaccia* white wine on his doorstep and, once, a heavenly *schiacciata alla fiorentina* sponge cake in a box tied with a bow. There would be notes in broken English, a name, sometimes a telephone number. Gradually he got to know his generous neighbours and visited their homes or joined them for coffee at the café in the village.

In the twelve months Steven had been here, he had grown to love the early morning. He would wake, always at the same moment, when the colours of the day were still charcoal and soft grey and the chilled air quickened his senses. He would dress hurriedly and make coffee, warming his hands on the mug, while his two dogs grunted awake and nosed around him, their paws making little slapping sounds on the cold tiles of the kitchen floor.

Today, he slid back the iron bolt of the heavy wooden door and stepped outside with a sharp sense of anticipation, his feet crunching on the gravel, his breath a fine vapour before him. The dogs loped ahead, knowing the path to the ridge, knowing where an unsuspecting small, brown rabbit might still be half-asleep in the scrub grass. On the horizon, a thin amber glow began to burn through the grey. The first glint of light caught the tips of the vines below and the medieval spires of San Gimignano nudged through the mist on the far hills. Steven walked to the end of the path where the ground sheered away and the terraced vineyards, studded with groves of cypress trees, began their steep march down. Standing on the very edge, he breathed deeply, arched his back and stretched, lifting his arms way up towards the sky. He waited, not for the sun to rise, but for the Earth to spin him through space to meet it.

A faint breeze ruffled his hair and he stretched higher. It was going to be an excellent day, he thought. He dropped his arms and smiled at the pleasure this little ritual gave him, knowing he must cut a foolish figure to the two dogs who always stopped their scrimmaging around to look at him, heads cocked to one side. He walked back to the house with a light spirit, made a big breakfast and ate ravenously. Today, he would paint and might forget to eat again.

***

He never noticed the hour, only the changing of the light so, when the long-fingered shadows curled around the French doors of his studio, he stopped and looked about as if waking from a dream. The sky was mauve, the cicadas had begun their nightly drone and, in the near distance, the dogs were barking. He widened his eyes and smiled, cleaned up quickly and walked through the house to the garden.

She was waiting at the far corner of the terrace that swung out over the hill, near a crumbling stone fountain. It was her favourite place. The whole countryside was spread out at her feet in shades of purple, sage and gold. The silver-backed leaves of the olive trees flickered in the breeze, and the water at the base of the fountain sparkled so brightly he had to shield his eyes. On the table beside her was a basket of fruit, a bottle of wine and two glasses.

He hurried down the stone steps. "Rachel! Why didn't you tell me you were here?"

"I knew these two would find me." She petted the two dogs who were leaping around and licking her face. "I heard music and guessed you'd be painting so I snuck into the house for the glasses. I thought I'd sit here for a bit, watch the sunset."

She stood and raised her arms to gather him in. It was over four months since her last visit. He buried his face in her hair and wondered how she could always sense his moods, how she always knew when to come.

***

They talked until the deep hush of early evening fell over the valley and the tiny lights of distant farmhouses began to shine through the gathering dusk. He told her of the gossip in the village, his feeble attempts to improve his Italian, the amateur art classes he'd been pressured into giving in the local church basement for several ex-pats who had bought properties nearby.

"How's the new painting?" she asked.

"Guido wants it for the Rome show. You can see it in the morning." He leaned back, his hands clasped behind his head, and thought how wonderful it was to have her attention again. He hoped she'd stay a while this time, do some writing.

"I'm still working on that damn book," she said, guessing his thoughts. "There's a limit to how much art appreciation people want. Nigel and Philippe are trying to help. I met up with them in Rome. They're always looking for some a new antique store or some undiscovered 'to-die-for' restaurant. They're appalled that I was born in this country and can't tell them these things. They ran me off my feet and made me drink too much."

"Will they ever come and see me, d'you think?"

"They've never forgiven you for leaving. They claim you're eccentric. Nigel said he'd be terrified to open your fridge. Philippe claims Italy's wasted on you because you don't appreciate good wine. But they pump me for every little anecdote. I bet they exaggerate it all shamelessly back home."

"Back home." He turned the words over in his mouth. They felt like two stones, cold and hard. "They've got a nerve, claiming I'm eccentric. The two of them are crazy as loons."

"One day you'll see them staggering up the drive, loaded down with Gucci and Versace bags."

"I'll go hide in my cellar."

He still struggled with people, savouring every moment of his freedom yet suffering from small, unexpected bouts of loneliness. He watched as she absently plucked at the few grapes left in the basket. She had a deep tan and her dark hair looked lighter —probably from too much sun. She looked tired. He leaned back and scanned the night sky.

"And where else have you been?" He tried to make the enquiry sound casual.

"How do you know I've been anywhere else? I could have been holed up in my study writing your biography." She took another sip of wine and gave him a coy look over the rim of the glass, but he wasn't going to play along. "I did go there again for a while," she said, finally. "He rarely leaves Egypt and I needed to talk to him. There's a lot I still want to work on."

He got up and walked over to the parapet to gaze at the hillside below. The lights of San Gimignano, *'delle Belle Torri,'* glowed faintly in the distance. The moon had climbed higher and he could still make out the contours of the valley. He had studied this landscape at every hour in every season and could almost feel it breathe. A chill had cut into the night air and the fall winds would soon sharpen the colours in the tapestry below.

"And what great wisdom did he dispense this time?"

"He's not a witch-doctor."

"Really? I thought he was all-seeing and all-knowing." This was dangerous old ground, but he couldn't let it go. Three times she had been back over there, spending longer on each visit. "Why is it so necessary to be there? Can't you phone or email?"

"There's so much material there. Some things can't be done from a distance."

He winced, not wanting to imagine what they might be. "I don't like having to worry."

"I'll always find my way here as long as you care to see me. You know that."

"And I'll always care to see you. You know that."

Most of the time, he stifled his concern. He knew they could both pull the loose fabric of their relationship tighter, trapping the other in a cocoon of intimacy. But it would never hold. The strange burden of dependency would burst it apart. And that was why, though he struggled with the weight of the unanswered questions, he didn't ask her more about her trip. And probably, he thought, why she didn't offer any more, though he was sure she longed to tell him. He pulled her to her feet and kissed her with the longing he fought so hard to keep in check.

***

Early in the morning, while she was still asleep, he crept downstairs and made coffee, the old dog Monty by his side. He didn't go to the ridge; he was too anxious to finish the painting.

His studio was his kingdom. It had a palpable energy, the fusion of hundreds of colours, textures, memories, moods. He would place his easel with its back to the door so he could walk around it, then turn quickly to get a fresh perspective on his work from the day before. Sometimes a weakness would register and he would stand and wrestle with this while drinking his first coffee of the morning.

Gradually he had gained confidence. He painted rhythmically, the picture building beneath his hands like a symphony under a skilled conductor. For such a long while he'd been heavy with guilt over his brother and his obvious failure as a husband and father. He was sick with the sour taste of the promises he couldn't keep. Then he had met Rachel. Slowly and cautiously, he began to drop the defenses and dip into the goodness of life with a more open mind. With her patient encouragement, an old, forgotten optimism had begun to surface, a capacity for joy.

He adjusted the easel to capture the best light from the windows and picked up the charcoal sketch he had made of the scene on the terrace when it first inspired him. In his mind's eye, he saw the movement of the breeze that night, the blend of shape and colour, the strange light that made him catch his breath. He wanted to inspire that same catch of breath on the canvas before him.

After a couple of hours, he stood back for a critical look, not quite willing to call it complete. But he was keen to show it to Rachel. He looked at his watch. Ten o'clock and still no sound from above. Goddamn it, he thought, this latest stint in Egypt has really tired her out.

"Come here, Monty," he called to the dog curled up on a nearby chair. Monty barked and clambered down. Steven guided him to the stairs. "Go and wake Rachel up. There's a good boy. Tell her all decent people should be out of bed by now."

Chapter 25

It took Rachel a moment to remember where she was. She lay still, wanting to prolong the pleasure of a lazy morning. The sun squeezed through the half open shutters and she surrendered to its warmth.

A scratching sound on the landing diverted her thoughts and she opened her eyes, squinting against the light. The heavy bedroom door creaked open and Monty padded in, placed his huge paws on the bedspread and stared at her in what looked like admonition.

"Monty." She reached over to stroke his head. "I know. Daytime."

She got up and stumbled over her suitcase, lying open but not unpacked, along with yesterday's clothes, abandoned on the floor. She rummaged through the case for her robe, pushed the shutters back fully and leaned out over the terrace. The air tasted like fine champagne. She could pick out the scents of the valley: lavender, mint, wild thyme, and the pungent smell of the dark peat that fed the vineyards. Memories of another view from another window flickered through her mind: hot sun, dark doorways, the lingering smell of hashish, the haunting wail of the muezzin across the rooftops, calling the faithful to prayer. She rubbed her eyes and straightened up. Far below she could hear several cars gearing down to tackle the sharp curve of the hill into the village. It must be market day, she thought.

Down in the kitchen, she coaxed the old espresso machine back to life and took a coffee with her to the studio. On the threshold, she stopped and fought back her usual flutter of nerves about what she'd see, how confident Steven was, what new expressions he might be exploring.

He looked around his easel. "Finally. *Signora* has risen." He took her hand to lead her into the room. "Come on. I need you to be a critic again." He kissed the top of her head and nudged her forward to face the large painting on the easel.

It was a woman asleep on the terrace in the late evening. She was lying on her side on a slatted wooden lounge chair, her hair covering her face, limbs almost lifeless, as though she had fallen there. Rachel's eye was drawn to a fold of the white gauze dress which caught the moonlight and seemed to be floating, as though lifted by a breeze. She scanned the backdrop of the hard stone surfaces of the terrace but they were painted with less definition and defied close scrutiny. Her gaze returned to the white on white of the fabric of the dress and the strange quality of light on the body of the woman.

"You've done it," she said. "That's it. Exactly."

He let out a long, exaggerated exhale. "Honest? And it's you —you feel that?"

"It was so humid that night. Everything still, surreal. It doesn't matter that it's me. It could be a dream you had. It's wonderful."

"I'm not happy with this bit in the corner where the moonlight hits the flagstones. It's not ...will you get over here and look closer. It's not quite there."

"Leave it." Rachel took the brush from his hand. She could tell he was delighted and trying not to show it. "Every painting should have a slight flaw. It shows the vulnerable part of the artist. A testament to his humanity." She pulled him away from the easel and out to the back patio. "Just look, it's a glorious morning."

Behind the studio, the hill rose steeply and the old house clawed into the earth as though it were afraid of falling away. This was the neglected north side, lacking the grandeur of the terrace and its view. Caper flowers grew tenaciously in the cracks of the yellowing stone and the creeping vines were taking over. The low stone wall that edged the patio had started to crumble, reclaimed by the same ground from which it came.

They walked a little way up the hill until they could look down over the terracotta roof of the house, past the clusters of chestnut and pine trees, over to the valley beyond.

"This is one of those 'master of the universe' views," Steven said, staring straight ahead. "I feel I could jump off and actually fly. Scary."

Her heart skipped one tiny beat and she pulled at his shirt to get him away from edge. "Let's go. I need to get showered and dressed. Will you paint some more today?"

He made a sweeping gesture to the landscape. "We should go for a drive. What the hell —maybe we could rustle up a picnic."

Back in the house, Rachel contemplated the contents of the fridge and settled on cream cheese, a few apples, a tomato, some celery hearts. Among the many jars of pasta sauce in the pantry, she found a bag of walnuts and a few biscotti that did not look too old. They could pick up a focaccia loaf in the village.

She began to wash and trim the celery. The cupboard door beneath her kept swinging open and banging her leg. She slammed it shut but it popped open again. Steven was not exactly a handyman. She pulled out a few drawers, looking for the only sharp knife, and eventually found it in the dishwasher that had clearly not been run for a while. She wondered what on earth he ate when she wasn't here. He had dinner out occasionally, he said, usually at Vittorio's, a nearby trattoria that attracted the ex-pat crowd, but she bet he lived on spaghetti bolognese.

From her quick glance around his studio earlier, she thought his recent work was good, revealing a deeper, more passionate intent that she was happy to see after the fits and starts of her previous visit. On some days, she had had to beg him to go walking in the hills and he'd stride ahead of her, hands shoved deep in his pockets, barely noticing the splendour around him or acknowledging the polite, guarded greetings of his neighbours. She feared he was giving in to the old anxieties, second-guessing himself again.

But last night, he told her the urge to paint came in waves that made his blood tingle. He had made numerous sketches and taken lots of notes, excited by new colours and textures that were more vivid now, more alive and he could hardly wait to commit them to canvas. Maybe, she thought, the old guilt was finally wearing itself out.

She made herself another espresso and sat at the wooden table. It was littered with art magazines and English language newspapers, long out of date. She thought about the articles she had to write, deadlines approaching, and the book she was struggling to bring into shape. And she thought about her last trip to Egypt. These trips clearly bothered Steven and he was obviously suspicious about her motivation. And now she had so much more to hide. Maybe she wasn't doing a very good job of it.

She wondered for the thousandth time if she should risk everything and come clean.

Chapter 26

They drove into the hills and stopped in a clearing to eat their picnic, to drink a little wine, to read and doze in the sun. Steven walked down the slope of the hill to where the ground dropped away. He picked a stem from the mounds of lavender flowing over the rocks at his side, crushed the tiny flowers and brought his fingers to his nose to savour the sharp, sweet smell. The grape vines below sagged with the weight of their fruit, some of the leaves already turning the red of autumn. Soon, the valley would bustle with the cheerful commotion of the late harvest. A few days ago, shopping in the village for the fruit that was so abundant now, he paused to look at a pyramid of yellow plums caught in a shaft of light. He admired the soft curves, the pools of dappled gold. Behind the stand was a young woman with gaunt, Slavic features. She plucked a fat plum from the top of the pile. Looking directly at him, she sank her teeth into it, her eyes laughing in unmistakable sexual invitation. He thought about this now and wondered if he could paint it from memory. Maybe tomorrow he'd sketch it out and see.

Rachel was propped against a scraggy fig tree, trying to write. He watched as she pushed away her notes in frustration. He resolved to make her put her work aside for a while.

"Paolo will want us to help with the olive harvest," he said, walking back up.

"Great. Up at dawn, swiping the foliage with sticks under a lashing rain." She rose to her feet, clipping her hair at the back of her neck and brushing the dust off her clothes. "No point coming back at this time of the year unless you're prepared to be a real *contadina*."

"Let's go look for blackberries. It'll get us in that harvesting mood." He grabbed the hamper with one hand and pulled her up the hill with the other.

Rafiki, the German Shepherd, came bounding out of the undergrowth, aware that they were on the move again, but old Monty, asleep under an oleander bush, had to be jostled awake. They half-pushed, half-lifted him into the back of the car which sizzled with the heat. The little Fiat laboured up the winding hills and they drove for a while in silence, tired from the wine and the sun. The road curved through a tiny hamlet with warm coloured houses hugging the edges, paint peeling in gentle curls from their sides, shutters closed to the afternoon heat.

Steven reached back to pull the hamper away from Monty's inquisitive nose. "I'll have to build some kind of compartment for these animals," he said, looking in the rear-view mirror. "God knows where Rafiki has been. Somewhere disgusting, by the smell of him. He was supposed to be a guard dog. I was really duped there." He geared down to handle a sharp turn in the road. "We must go and see Rico soon. He's always asking about you. He can barely see now, but the more his eyesight weakens, the better his stories."

Rico was one of Steven's first acquaintances, showing up one day on the doorstep, unannounced. A sharp rapping had interrupted his painting. He thought it was probably another tradesman looking for work and wondered why they were all so keen when, once engaged, they were suddenly busy elsewhere. Irritated, he swung open the big kitchen door. My God, he thought, it's Rumpelstiltskin. Before him stood a short, spry old man with a walnut face and wispy grey hair, his walking stick raised to strike again. A wolf-like dog sat at his feet.

"You are painter, they say, *signor*," said Rumpelstiltskin in a lyrical Tuscan accent. "I am an artist, too. Well, one time I was. Now I cannot see well enough to work. You will need a dog. Every painter must have a dog. Here he is. He will guard you well."

When Steven objected, the little grey man said "*Posso?*" and walked right past him into the kitchen. "He is Germany-shepherd. Very intelligent. I show you, signor." He issued a number of commands which, as far as Steven could make out, meant variously "sit, lie down, bark, bark louder," and "walk back and forth on two legs."

"Does he understand English?"

"You will teach. He is young dog. He learn fast. Very smart."

Rico was a wood-carver and sometime carpenter and had spent some of his younger years in Africa, whittling his way, quite literally, through the continent, enchanted with the strange shapes of that vast land, its older, faded colours, its beautiful soft woods that yielded like butter to the knife. But eventually the need to "make a proper living" forced him home. Steven learned that "Rafiki" was Swahili for "friend," a hopeful sign, he thought.

"I can care for this dog no more. He is a good guard dog. I leave small bag of food outside but he eat most everything. Need too much exercise for blind old man." He patted the dog and, from the depths of his worn jacket, produced a fine, embossed card printed in Italian and English. *Enrico Pariselli, Master Carpenter, Decorative Wood Carving*. "You will visit me. I'm not far from here. Come soon."

The next morning, Steven was woken very early by scratching and whimpering sounds followed by a sudden chorus of joyful barks. He fought to disentangle himself from the woolly skeins of sleep and slowly remembered that he had a dog now and that this dog was barking enough for two. He cursed his way downstairs in the dark to the kitchen where Rafiki was leaping repeatedly at the door. "Down, boy," Steven tried, before remembering the dog's limited linguistic abilities. He threw back the latch and swung the door open to let Rafiki out. Instead, a large, scruffy mutt catapulted into the kitchen and ran round and round in tight circles while Rafiki pranced about, barking non-stop. Steven sank into the kitchen chair and swore profusely.

This was Monty, Rico explained when Steven tracked him down to a small house on the other side of the hill. Monty was Rafiki's friend. This is good. Every painter must have two dogs. Yes, yes, all is well. *Alle bene.*

Steven could not be angry. Despite his reservations, he had become fond of his two new friends. And he had made an important discovery the day that Monty arrived. Sunrise. On that morning, as he moved to close the kitchen door, he saw the first glimmers of light way beyond the cypress groves, and stood transfixed. Always a late riser, he rarely saw the sun's first light. Inexplicably, he felt the tilt of the earth, as though the sun were pulling him like a magnet towards the warmth.

He walked to where the path forked, one part descending steeply to the road below, the other trailing off through the trees to the ridge. The two dogs stopped their barking and howling, and sat a few feet behind him, watching with interest. As he stood at the fork in the path, he resolved to adjust the mechanism of his daily life. He would rise with the sun. He would live longer days.

"I'd love to see Rico again," Rachel said. "Let's call him and fix a date. We can take him some blackberries."

The day was winding down and the sun's rays hit the windshield at an angle, causing them both to squint. God, I love this country, Steven thought, wishing he could stretch and fatten each moment. He glanced at Rachel and wondered how long she'd stay this time. At least a couple of months, he hoped. He needed her company, her encouragement, her belief in him.

To their left, the hill climbed steeply. To their right it tumbled over into the green and gold valley. Steven pulled into a small clearing. "I spy blackberries."

The little tableau was back-lit by the dying sun. Steven watched as Rachel, silhouetted against it, reached deep into the thorny undergrowth (where the best ones always were, she said), the dogs getting under her feet. All four of them cast long shadows that bent up sharply behind them to take the shape of the hill. *'The Blackberry Pickers,'* he thought. Should he try to paint this, too? No, some things were meant only to be memories. He would pull it into his mind again on a colder, lonelier day.

***

As he walked back from the ridge the next morning, Steven felt a change in the weather and began to think about the things that needed to be done before it turned cold. Most important was to order another pile of logs which Paolo, the local *tuttofare* man, would hopefully deliver. He poured himself a coffee and went to check out the big stone fireplace in the living room. It needed cleaning and the chimney should be swept. His eye was drawn to the books and papers that Rachel had set out on the long trestle table under the huge tapestry on the far wall, a passable replica from the *Lady and Unicorn* which had come with the house. A magazine was open to a review she had written. He read a few lines.

Few can match the passionate flights of fancy Olivia McCall has delivered so imaginatively with her stunning impasto technique. Under such a vigorous brush....

He picked up a few of the nearby books. *The Egyptian Moral Code, The Sacred Tradition in Ancient Egypt, Night Skies of the Northern Hemisphere.* She'd tried to teach him about the stars, a passion she had inherited from her father, and showed him what to look for at different times of the year. But he could never retain it. Anchored under a mug of pens and pencils, he saw a To Do list: Food!!, Tea, Philippe re. collector, Robert—not Christmas, K—fix date.

Robert, her brother. She usually spent Christmas with his family in England. Looks like she didn't intend to this year. Then where was she planning to be? *K—fix date.* He felt a nasty churn of the stomach. Mr. Egyptology, he assumed. And what sort of date would that be, he wondered—a writing deadline? The date she'd be going there yet again? His good mood from the walk turned sour. He leafed through more papers: sky charts with hieroglyphics and photocopies of what looked like pages from a book of Egyptian art. What the hell am I looking for, he thought, feeling embarrassed with himself and shoving them back roughly. He found a relatively recent copy of *The Florentine*, and settled down with it to finish his coffee.

He was still reading when she came down. She sat on the arm of his chair and leaned on his shoulder. "Why didn't you wake me? Have you had breakfast?"

"What does 'K fix date' mean?"

He felt childish afterwards. She had laughed at him. She said she knew lots of people whose names began with K and began to reel them off: Kelly, Kyle, Katrina. Even though he could hear the petulance in his voice, he goaded himself into the old argument. He said he knew it must be Karl and why was it important to be there? What did this guy have that she couldn't find on Google? She'd told him this so many times but he wanted to hear it again, feel the reassurance in her voice. Surely, he wasn't jealous, she said. She told him about some gorgeous painter the boys had introduced her to in Rome, a real Italian stud by the sound of it, who'd taken her to dinner one night. Now there was a guy he could be jealous of. She kissed him, promised to conjure up breakfast with the remaining food and said they really must do some shopping today.

But she never admitted which Kit was or what the date was about.

Chapter 27

Steven had asked no more questions about "K" but Rachel could tell he was brooding. She had always believed their relationship was free from possessiveness. When he bought the house, they decided she'd come to Italy as often as possible and they rarely questioned each other about their time apart. Once, she answered the phone and a woman, an American, she thought, asked who she was. When she said her name, the woman hung up. She never raised this with Steven. Somehow it didn't matter. For her part, the odd casual date she had back home was scarcely worth inquiry. But of course, she thought, things had changed now.

That night, sleep eluded her. She tried again and again to shut down the guilt, to convince herself that she was doing the right thing. Steven was painting so beautifully and she felt he was on the brink of something new and exciting. So why, she asked herself, did she keep on going back to Cairo. "What part of your past is really troubling you, Rachel?" Karl would say. Of course, he knew the answer.

At three in the morning, she tiptoed downstairs to the kitchen to make chamomile tea.

Several art magazines, well-thumbed, lay on the table, along with tattered copies of *The Florentine* and a paperback crime thriller. Reading and walking the dogs, that's mostly all Steven did with his 'down' time, he said. She noticed a pamphlet advertising his painting classes in the local village church. He obviously enjoyed doing this and, a bonus, he'd met a wealthy guy with a villa and a tennis court. Not as satisfying as squash, he claimed, but at least he had a chance to work off those melancholy moods that snuck up on him. She poured her tea and stared at the stars through the small kitchen window, trying to make out the constellations. Pegasus, perhaps, over toward the east. But light clouds were scudding across the sky, confusing the patterns.

Still not sleepy, she took a flashlight from one of the kitchen drawers and, feeling like a burglar, walked along the hall to the studio.

She hesitated in the doorway. He was always encouraging her to come in, to sit with him a while when he was painting. The reluctance was all her own. Despite the comfort of her hard-won credentials and the knowledge that she had guided him to new expression and considerable success, she could never shake the feeling that she was an intruder in his art, his life.

In the beam of the flashlight, she saw he had removed the painting of her on the terrace. The easel stood empty, giving off a sense of hunger. She told him once it was bad luck to leave easels like that, insisting he put a new stretched canvas on the stand as an inspiration to start a new painting. But he rolled his eyes and said he didn't realize easels had feelings. She could not see any blank canvases and fretted for a few moments about his motivation. Several large paintings were stacked against a wall and she separated them, shining the light on each. Maybe he'd picked these out for the Rome show. Most were landscapes but others focused in exquisite detail on a defining characteristic of the local countryside, the sway of a tall cedar in the evening wind, an unexpected burst of orange poppies growing defiantly at the side of a gravel road, an elderly man pushing a wooden cart of shiny green apples. In the blueish beam of the flashlight, they had a strange serenity, so different from the anger and cynicism of his earlier work.

Later in the morning, when she finally rose after a fitful sleep, she left Steven painting and walked to the village to get groceries. Their neighbour, Paolo, waylaid her in one of the stores, excited to see her, she guessed, because he welcomed as much help as possible for the olive harvest, but also because "*il signor,* so lonely." His poor English and her rusty Italian made conversation difficult. He clutched both hands to his heart, saying she and signor must both be crazy with "too many go and come back." He stroked her cheek with the back of his hand. "*Signora* is tired."

The shopping took longer than she expected and she was glad to see the terracotta roof of the house through the trees up ahead. She wound her way up the steep road, stopping to take in the views of the valley between the stands of cypress and hawthorn trees. The groceries were heavy. On the stone bench at the curve of the driveway, she sat down to catch her breath. A bee buzzed in and out of the cyclamen and dahlias around her but otherwise it was deeply quiet. Summoning a little more energy for the driveway's last steep curve, she thought about what she had to do: phone a few friends, write to Nigel, get going on the most critical of her articles. She entered the house with new resolve, warding off the dogs who hurtled towards her, sniffing with interest at the grocery bags.

Steven was cleaning up. The smell of turpentine was strong and the chaos of the studio was now in a clumsy kind of order. He was wiping a fist full of brushes.

"So, what did you think?" he asked, pointing to some paintings against the wall.

"I couldn't sleep. Do you mind?"

"Only that you didn't tell me. And that you can't sleep."

"I just need a few days to unwind." She turned to go. "I'm going to put the groceries away and then write to the boys."

"But what did you think?"

"Wonderful," she called from the hallway. "That's all you're getting for now."

Steven called back. "There's a package for you, by the way. Kitchen table."

She hesitated. "I'm not expecting anything. Where from?"

"Gee, let me think. Somewhere in the Middle East, I believe."

Was he teasing her or was he still pissed off, she wondered? She wasn't going to trouble herself to find out. In the kitchen, she opened the large brown envelope from Karl. In it was a series of night-sky charts for various dates over the next few months. A simple handwritten note was included:

Rachel, you must study these. Look at the patterns, look at the beautiful cosmic choreography that is playing out now. It is time to accept the future rather than continually trying to manipulate it.

She turned it over. That was all. No reference to what had happened on her most recent visit. A tiny shiver went down her spine as she thought about this.

She took the charts with her to the wooden lounge chair by the broken fountain. Why would he ask her to study them, she wondered? He must know by now that she would never come to the same conclusions as him. He could see patterns and meanings and portents and warnings, he would invoke the wisdom of the ages, wisdom she had still barely tapped into. Even now, after all that had happened, she could never fully buy into what Karl believed.

From where she sat, she could see the whole valley and smell the tenacious thyme and cat-mint that grew along the edge of the wall. In the terraced fields below, she watched one of the neighbours, Alfredo, on his tractor and wondered why he was zig-zagging so erratically. Then she heard a high-pitched shriek of laughter and realized his grand-daughter Anna was at his side. The little girl was grabbing the wheel, making it twist and turn about. What a wonderful place to grow up in, she thought, remembering her own childhood in Calabria, the long warm nights on the terrace, sitting with her father while he pointed out the stars: *orione, del toro, dei gemilli.* Uncle Vanni lived in the house now. He was keeping it for her, hoping she'd come back one day.

Her eyes drifted over the wall to the distant hills now surrendering to the shadows of the late sun. She always found it so hard to do any serious work here. Nigel was always pushing her to be more aggressive in her career. Over the years, he kept encouraging her to get to know "people who count," professing despair at her reluctance to grasp the importance of this. With his help, she made brave forays into journalism and eventually developed a good reputation in the erratic world of art criticism. She loved her work but the unpredictable income made her very grateful for the money she had inherited from her mother. It was not a lot but it allowed her to hold on to the independence she had once forsaken so willingly.

She opened her laptop and typed quickly to Nigel and Philippe, anxious to get her mind off Karl. The boys would be thrilled to know that Steven had signed the deal with Guido and Annette, the art agents in Rome, that the show had finally been booked for May and that he was clearly dedicated to its success. She filled them in on the local news: the 'foodie' events of the harvest, the village fairs, the upcoming wine festivals. She imagined Nigel re-reading the email alone, lighting a thin cigar and shaking his head, staring through the huge windows of their sky-high condominium, over the tops of the office buildings, out to the lake beyond. She knew he worried about her state of mind. He didn't know the whole story, only that she wasn't telling it.

Chapter 28

Steven leaned back in the wicker chair on Rico's porch, nursing his espresso, and watched Rico guide Rachel through his generous herb garden. He was pointing out his horticultural achievements with his whittled cane and with obvious pride, bending down to smell the herbs and verify their identity when his rheumy eyes failed him. The sounds of their voices, one lilting and frail, the other deeper and tender, floated up in fragments on the light breeze. He reached down to pet old Monty who lay at his side. The dog rolled over with his paws in the air and rubbed his face on the leg of the chair.

Another perfect Tuscan morning—almost paradise, he thought. He stretched his legs, letting the sun pour onto his upturned face. Almost. The word snagged in his head. A smooth, deceitful word, starting with such plump promise and ending in a spiteful hiss. His thoughts were diverted now, trying to sort out the splinter of discontent in the otherwise flawless day.

"Not wholly original." That's it. That's what she'd said. The swift kick of the words in his stomach took his breath away a second time. He opened his eyes and squinted at Rachel. She had walked farther down the sloping garden and was deftly removing some plants with a crooked little trowel. Rico, sitting on a wooden bench, held a shallow box ready to receive these unearthed specimens, no doubt destined to supplement Steven's own neglected garden. Perhaps sensing his eyes upon her, Rachel looked up and waved, but he closed them quickly, preferring to wallow in his renewed sulk.

Over breakfast that morning, he told her he was going to experiment more with landscape colour, relying only on the memory of the scene captured in his mind's eye. She was pleased, telling him the paintings should reveal his feelings about the landscape rather than its true texture. She went on about the lights of darkness, the deception of color intensity and so on. Then she blurted out "Would you consider impasto for these?"

He took a deep breath. "We've had this discussion before. It's not exactly original."

"But what you're doing isn't wholly original either."

"I've enjoyed a little success despite your critical insight," he managed. He wondered how often she had to steel herself to make a comment. Lately, one painting had followed another with only a few days of scary uncertainty in between. Was he becoming predictable? Is that what she meant? Was he too comfortable now that he had a reputation? He spent the next hour brooding in his studio and trying to tidy up.

As he had stacked sketchpads and put paint tubes in order, an old idea wrestled its way to the front of his mind. He had thought about it many times but never felt he was up to it. From his wallet, he took out a photograph, well-thumbed, worn at the edges, and taped it to the top of his easel. He propped up a portrait canvas, then took a few paces back, imagining the way he would like to paint it. He didn't want the photographic intensity, he wanted the spirit, the vitality, the essence of the person. Could he really do it, he wondered. He took a decisive step forward and sketched it out in broad strokes. Beneath his hands, the face began to come to life, the hair a little wild, the eyes curious, laughing, the chin tilted, perhaps in disbelief or surprise or ready to tease. He could already feel the intensity coming through.

He shifted position in his wicker chair and Monty opened one eye as though to check on him. Rachel could always sense his doubts, smell them out. What she was saying, of course, was that the old anxiety still inhibited his work. Being "wholly original" meant working with real freedom, no imaginary censors. Ah, but in the end, freedom was the most frightening thing of all.

Perhaps, he thought now, the critic in her is disappointed each time she returns. He shivered involuntarily. He would tell her about the portrait, see what she made of that. He leaned back defiantly in the comfort of the sun and watched a plane far above him, trailing a white plume across the sky.

Rico and Rachel were walking back up the path, chiding him for his slothfulness.

"We're going to make lunch," Rachel said, putting the box of herbs in a shady corner.

"Want any help?"

"You just stay right there and concentrate on breathing." She squeezed his shoulder as she passed behind him. "I'll bring you a glass of wine."

He would always think of that light squeeze of his shoulder as the end of the goodness of the day. After that, the seed of worry about her dug deeper into his stomach and began to sprout its thin, sinuous roots. He remembered everything so clearly: the clattering of plates and cutlery through the kitchen window, the smell of the crusty bread, the sharp taste of sun-dried tomatoes, the creak of the faded patio umbrella as it swung about in the sudden gusts of wind. So why hadn't he felt a finger on his spine, a sudden sweat ... something, anything, to alert him to the cold work of fate on such a beautiful day.

"There is our lazy boy." Rico waved his cane at Steven, as he made his way to the table on the little patio. "Maybe he dream of new painting and we should not disturb."

"Just closing my eyes and counting my blessings." He sprang up to take the tray from Rachel and help Rico into his chair.

"Many blessings for all of us. I don't see so good but God give me other things. Maria-Theresa coming always to help me, good neighbours, plenty sunshine, many birds singing."

"Well, your eyesight sure hasn't affected your cooking."

"*Grazie, grazie*. Another blessing. When autumn is come, I feel like animal. Make a lotta food, stay inside and sleep."

As they ate and chatted, Steven surveyed the scene with painters' eyes. He squinted, a habit he had formed to diffuse sharp edges and determine the governing colours. Rachel and Rico became two figures arrested on his imaginary canvas: a woman pouring the amber harvest wine, her sun-glasses propped on her hair, their frames catching the glint of the sun; a mellow old man, his body stooping forward; the tiny garden of falling, golden leaves.

"Can you believe, it Rico?" he said. "All my life I've dreamed of living in Italy, painting in Italy, and then along comes this sort of Italian woman here." He leaned over and kissed Rachel's shoulder. "And somehow, here I am. What a beautiful coincidence."

"There's no such thing as coincidence," Rachel said.

"What? Okay then, fate, karma. Whatever, whatever."

"You shouldn't joke about fate," she said. "You give it the energy to turn against you."

"Whoa, don't go all weird on me. I'm just teasing." He noticed that Rachel wasn't smiling. He wondered if she'd had too much wine or if the sun was getting to her. He busied himself passing the food, filling the glasses. "This is good wine, Rico." He held his glass up to the light.

"Florus, I think. Maybe you read label for me."

"*Castello Banfi Florus Moscadello di Montalcino*," Steven read with what he hoped was passable Italian flourish. He took another sip and sat back. "So, I started a new, 'wholly original' painting this morning. It's a portrait. So far I've only sketched it out."

Rachel turned to him. Good, he thought, she's smiling.

"A portrait? Anyone in particular?"

He pulled out his wallet and showed her the photograph. "This guy."

"Who is it?"

"It's my brother Colin."

The photograph fell from her hand to the table. She stared at it, saying nothing, her face frozen.

As though in slow motion, Steven watched the wine glass she was gripping so tightly break into pieces. He looked at the pool of liquid on the tablecloth and all he could think, absurdly, was that they'd been drinking white wine and the liquid was red. There was no sound coming from anywhere. His own voice was stuck half way down his throat.

After what seemed like a long time, Rachel spoke calmly. "Look what I've done."

"Jesus." He stood up. "You've really cut yourself. Quick—" he gave her his napkin, "put pressure on it."

Rico was trembling, confused. "Something break."

"A glass. It's all right. Have you got any bandages?"

"In the bathroom maybe. Maria-Theresa buy many things I don't know."

Steven hurried Rachel inside, made her sit on the edge of the bath and held her hand in the sink under the cold running water. "Shit, it's bad. Does it hurt?" He rifled in the cupboard for gauze and bandages and pressed down on the cuts to try to stop the bleeding.

"Go back to Rico. I can manage."

"You can't, damn it. Take off this ring. There may be glass underneath." He started to pull at the Egyptian ring she wore, but she snatched her hand away.

"It's too tight, leave it."

He looked at her a moment, trying to weigh the mix of panic and defiance that skittered across her face. "It's got to come off, Rachel. What's the big deal?"

"No big deal. Stop fussing."

He fought back the desire to wrench the stupid ring off and toss it down the toilet. In silence, he fixed the bandage over a gauze pad, weaving it in and out of her fingers. She stood and leaned her head against his shoulder. He hugged her. She seemed remote, fragile.

He cleared up the broken glass on the table and retrieved the photograph. There was a spot of blood on it that sent a chill up his spine. He wiped this off quickly with a napkin and, for the rest of the lunch, kept the conversation light, trying to reassure Rico that all was well.

When it was time to leave, Rachel went ahead to put the box of herbs in the car and get the dogs settled. Rico walked unsteadily down the driveway, clutching Steven's arm.

"Steven, *amico mio*." He stopped and held him back. "Something wrong."

"What? Aren't you feeling well?"

"Rachel. She has trouble. I feel it. Very strong." He reached for a handkerchief in his pocket and Steven saw that his hand was shaking.

"She hasn't been herself lately, Rico. Probably just the pressure of work. Those cuts on her hand will smart a bit, but she'll be fine."

He watched her trying to cajole Monty into the back of the car.

Rico reached up to touch Steven's face. "God be with you both." He gave a faltering wave in Rachel's direction and turned back towards the house, leaning on his cane.

Steven stood in the middle of the driveway, watching him go. He struggled to hold on to the time they had just spent together but it seemed to have happened long ago. He walked towards the car as though in a trance and felt the colours drain from the day.

Chapter 29

He finished the painting of Colin quickly. It was as if, after years of being held back, it wanted to spill out of him all at once. As the face of his brother smiled back at him, Steven knew that he would never sell this, never show it, not even to Rachel. It couldn't be shared. If Rachel asked, he'd say he had put it aside for a while. But she never did.

They had resolved to go to Siena on a day when the weather was fine. He was keen to climb the *Mangia*, the bell tower of the Palazzo Pubblico and take in the view from the top. Rachel had perked up over the last week. She was focussing on her work, pecking away at her laptop with her bandaged hand. He thought a change of scene would do her good.

But now, as she followed him resolutely up the four hundred stone steps, stopping several times to catch her breath, he wondered if this was a mistake. They leaned against the parapet and gazed over the honeycomb of terracotta roofs, the newer ones gold and bronze in the afternoon light, the oldest faded to a warm tawny brown. Here and there were the crooked spires of churches with their heavy bells poised to swing and, in the distance, the dark green patches of cypress groves. Below lay the famous fan-shaped square, edged with ornate palaces and busy cafés, waiters like tiny stick figures scurrying about. Steven pulled out his camera to take a few shots and raised his hand to shield the sun.

"You okay?" he asked Rachel over his shoulder. "It's not like you to get winded climbing stairs." He put his arm around her. "Rico's still worried about you."

She frowned. "That's because I broke that glass. He probably thinks I'm—" she put her finger to her temple, "*strano*."

"Worse. He thinks you're under an evil influence." He felt her shoulder tense.

He had spoken to Rico a few days after the lunch and the old man was strangely insistent, claiming there was something troubling Rachel, something that was working through her. He said she might be *"posseduto."* Steven tried to laugh it off. Rachel was not feeling well, he told the old man, but she was certainly not "possessed." He put this notion of Rico's down to his traditional Catholic sensibilities but, in the pit of his stomach, was a persistent gnawing concern.

But what the hell was bothering her, he wondered. It had to be something about these stupid trips to Egypt. Each time she came back she seemed weaker. She used to be energetic and now here she was getting out of breath all the time. Was she into drugs, the way Nigel once confessed he'd been? If so, he'd seen no evidence of it since her arrival. Once, when she'd gone shopping, he went through her things in the bathroom and the bedside cabinet, vacillating between shame and justified concern. He found nothing out of the ordinary. He looked through her work again but understood so little. One text had some notes underneath it in her hand-writing. He read a few lines.

Destiny vs. free will. If a person does wrong, he has upset the four elements of nature, the fine balance of the universe and his own place within this, his own destiny. The ancient Egyptian concept of Ma'at would suggest he must right this wrong to restore the balance. But are we only destined to do right? If every single thing is predestined, then doing wrong is also predestined, part of the grand and mysterious scheme of things.

The words had left him with a queasy feeling.

The *Mangia* bells began to toll, catching them by surprise.

"Rico's melodramatic," Rachel said, when the bells went quiet. "Like most Italians, you would say. A few more weeks in this part of the world and I'll be fine."

***

When the colder weather began to set in, they dressed warmly and walked in the hills, not wanting to miss the waning glory of the late fall. The dogs loped about, sniffing and digging into every bush. From the high path that ran upwards behind the house, the valley looked tired, its colours muted and fading at the edges. The last leaves of the chestnut trees clung on stubbornly, then gave up and broke loose, pirouetting through the air to the thickening carpet below. Today, the regular 'thwack' of an axe echoed from the far hill and they could just make out the farmer working through his pile of logs, his two young boys helping to stack them by the barn.

Steven stood with his hands on his hips, surveying the landscape he loved so much. "I think winter has won the battle. It's turning round and round on the land the way dogs do before they snuggle down into their baskets."

A fine rain started and the clouds thickened. They put up the hoods of their jackets and linked arms. The rain gathered strength and slicked through the olive groves, making a pitter-patter on the canopy of leaves, darkening the surface of the narrow road that wound through the hills beneath them and silencing the few birds who were out for their last meal. The axe fell silent. Father and sons retreated to the house.

"I've been thinking," Steven, said as they quickened their pace toward home. "You should stay longer. You need time to get over all the drinking and late nights with the boys in Rome. And that visit with your Egyptology friend. Last night you were talking in your sleep again. You kept saying 'Ozman' or something. Who is that?"

"What?" She looked the other way. "No idea. I get weird dreams."

"Well, I'm taking a stand. Forget about leaving before Christmas. See out the winter. Another three months or so. It'll do you good."

"But you're painting so beautifully. I worry about crowding you. You need space now."

He tightened his grip on her arm. "Then give me space. But don't leave. I don't need to be alone twenty-four hours a day. It's a big house. Meant for more than one person."

Over the hill he could see the roof tiles of his home and he thought how the house was at its coziest now, the warmth of summer still trapped inside. They hurried on in silence and he worried that she was working up another excuse to leave. He stopped and turned her shoulders to make her look at him. "If you're thinking of going back to Egypt again any time soon, put it out of your head. It can wait."

She looked at him for several seconds, biting her lip. "Maybe I can re-arrange a few things. I guess I can help you get ready for Rome."

"Rome. Jesus. I still can't believe my luck, landing that show. Guido's almost too enthusiastic. He's making me nervous. Shit we're getting drenched."

They sprinted up the final slope to the back door of the house.

"You've landed the show because you're good," Rachel said, leaning with both arms against the door to catch her breath. "Nothing to do with luck."

Steven lit a fire and they curled up on the couch, the two dogs at their feet, watching the flashes of lightening at the window. Rachel put her head on his shoulder. "You're very quiet. What's going on in that head?" she asked him.

"A painting that came to me this morning. It will be a big challenge."

The painting had taken shape in his mind as he stood on the ridge, waiting for the sun to rise. He would try to capture the feeling he always had when he raised his arms to the sky: the sense of being both grounded and suspended, whirling through space yet anchored firmly by gravity.

As he described it, she became immediately excited. She pulled away from his shoulder and faced him. "Yes, yes! You need a huge canvas. It's got to be large, generous, uplifting. It's got be free-form, soaring—"

"I know, I know. It has to be the work of the brave Mr. Farrow, the one who's not 'scared by the strength of his feelings.'"

"What?"

"She doesn't even remember! That nasty review you wrote." He affected a supercilious tone. "'When Mr. Farrow ceases to be afraid of artistic freedom, he may be a great artist.' Well, watch out. Steven Farrow, *grande artista*, is on his way."

Chapter 30

If she had known how her most recent trip to Egypt would end, would she still have gone? Rachel would ask herself this many times in the weeks to come, wrestling with the undeniable truth of her feelings.

They had flown to see Osman, Karl's old teacher and mentor whose unexpected phone call Rachel had been surprised by all those years ago in Cairo. A driver took them through the lushness of the town of Aswan, south along the river swarming with *feluccas*, past Elephantine Island and into the hard, barren hills beyond.

Rachel watched the land roll by. To the right, the ancient river pushed north, carrying its secrets to Alexandria. Near one of the narrow canals, a farmer tended his crop of beans while the boy at his side picked off the cutworms with his bare hands. All the goodness of the land must be wrested from it, inch by inch, she thought, and yet surely the elements plied their magic more sweetly here than anywhere else on earth. On the road ahead a young girl walked behind a line of donkeys laden with bales of straw. She flicked a skimpy cane to urge them along.

They moved away from the river and climbed towards a small, yellowing village that clung to the side of the hill, the buildings leaning against each other, sheets and towels drying on ropes strung from door to door. The rough road ended in a square with mud-brick houses clustered around it.

A man emerged from the shadows. He hurried to the car and held the door open for them. "Osman is very tired. He is waiting for you," he said.

Rachel pulled her scarf over her head.

The room was dark and cool after the burning heat outside. Thin woven rugs hung at the open windows and others lay on the floor, barely covering the hard sand. Karl spoke softly in Arabic to several men standing by a cot against the far wall. They came to his side with words of welcome, clasping his shoulders and gripping his hands. Osman lay still, his body thin and wasted. A blue vein at his neck pulsed weakly, as though his very blood were tired. Karl sat on the edge of the cot and the old man's watery eyes fluttered over to focus on him.

They spoke quietly in Arabic for a while until Karl took Rachel's hand and pulled her into Osman's line of vision. "She is here. This is Rachel," he said in English. One of the men brought a raffia stool so she could sit beside the bed.

Osman clutched at Rachel's sleeve and she leaned closer to catch his rasping, broken voice. "Destiny may be diverted but never cheated. Remember this. There is no immunity." The buried guilt rose up like bile from her stomach to her throat.

A woman brought candles and a tray of food to the bedside. Rachel scooped a little hummus with flatbread to be polite but did not register the taste in her mouth.

In obvious pain, Osman gestured to Karl to give him the star charts that were lying at the foot of the bed. He leafed through them for a while, his hands trembling.

"Your soul was guided by the influence of the gods," he said to Rachel. "But you left the path that was chosen for you. Great sadness came and much regret. Ten years you have craved forgiveness and a way of atonement has been granted. But the stars are angry. A final step must still be taken. You must find the courage. Until then, the fire will use up all the air within you."

His voice was failing. Rachel leaned even closer. "The two of you are two rivers destined to flow together as one now, inseparable. But destiny works in mysterious ways."

He and Karl talked on in Arabic, the sound and cadence of their voices like a strange lullaby. Rachel watched, marvelling at Karl's fluency in this beautiful, rough, expressive language.

Osman dropped back to the pillows and lay still for a while. "Go with the river," he said, switching back to English. "Khnum controls the waters of the Nile. He will watch you. Satis and Anukis will watch you. And always beware the fire. Water is your element, my good friend. It will take you home."

They sat with him until he fell asleep.

Outside, the world had fallen into darkness. Karl went to speak with their driver who was waiting on the other side of the little square.

"We're taking a boat to Cairo," Karl said, walking back to Rachel. "We'll leave later tonight."

"What? It'll take days."

"A few days only. This is Osman's advice: go with the river. The driver knows a boat we can take. He'll cancel the flight and hotel and fix everything. He'll be back in an hour or so."

The sense of unreality enveloped her again and she felt the need to pinch her skin to make sure she was here. "What was Osman trying to tell me?"

"Osman is a seer, a diviner. He told you something I feared years ago would always haunt you."

"The step still to be taken." She felt that familiar pitch of her stomach, like the one from the sudden downward lurch of roller coaster. "Confession." She took a few steps away. "Still? Now? Is that what you think too?"

He said nothing for several seconds. "I fear it may be too late. For all we hope for."

"What do you mean? What did he tell you? You spoke together for a long time."

He took her hand. "Come, let's walk a little way and look at the stars,"

There was no moon and, after the dim lights of the tiny village, the darkness surged around them like water. As their eyes adjusted, Karl guided her to a stony ridge on the slope of the hill, lit a cigarette and stretched out full length on his back, staring at the star-laden sky. She sat nearby and followed his gaze. There was the centaur Sagittarius in the centre of the Milky Way, his arrow trained on Antares, the heart of Scorpio, as he chased him over the horizon.

She looked at Karl, his hands clasped behind his head. His shirt had come loose at the waist as he stretched out. She imagined moving over to him and easing it out further. She imagined the feel of his leather belt in her hands as she slipped it from the keeper and peeled it back to release the buckle. She could feel the hardness of him as she slid the zipper down. If she leaned over him, her own shirt falling away at the neck, her breath coming quickly, would he draw her close and pull her to him or would he push her gently away? On the two previous occasions she had come back to Egypt, she had to fight this intense and overpowering need to make love with him.

"Rachel."

She opened her eyes and realized she had drifted off and was lying awkwardly at the edge of the rock. She sat up and rotated her left shoulder which had gone stiff.

Karl stood and helped her to her feet. He kept hold of both her hands. "I was dreaming," he said. She could smell the lemon aftershave and the jasmine smokiness of his breath. "I dreamt you came to me." His voice was a whisper she could hardly hear. "I think you know this dream."

She took a step back. "I don't know what I'm doing, Karl. I think I should go home."

With one quick movement, he clasped his arms around her back. He kissed her lips, her eyes, her throat, his hands moving under her blouse, squeezing her breasts. She held on to him, her arms fastened around his neck as though clinging to a life-raft.

She tried to stop, pushing herself away. "Karl. Please."

He gathered her towards him again, more gently. "Rachel, Rachel. Why don't you admit that the life you lead away from here will never be enough for you? Don't hide behind your old guilt, your old decisions. You came back, didn't you? And you keep coming back. Because of this." He swept his hand across the desert, the big bowl of the night sky. "Stop fighting with yourself. This is who you are. This is where you are meant to be. Here. With me. Together." He tightened his grip around her waist and buried his face in her hair. "And I cannot wait," he said, his voice breaking. "Not any longer."

Chapter 31

Rachel sat on the terrace clutching a large coffee, groggy with the after-effects of the sleeping pill. Last night she dreamed about the boat on the Nile, the long journey with Karl back to Cairo, the fear and the sheer joy of their surrender to each other, the long hours of love and lust, the peace and stillness of her heart, feelings she had pushed away and thought forever buried. In her dream the journey took weeks and they were lost. She could see the shore in the distance but, as they tried to draw closer, the shore drifted farther away. She felt the boat rocking and woke, dizzy and nauseated, to find herself clutching the side of the bed.

Now, she heard Steven and his neighbour Paolo coming round the side of the house and remembered Paolo had promised to deliver a load of firewood for the coming winter. They must have been stacking it at the back.

"*Signora!*" Paolo bounded over. "*La raccolta delle olive. Sabato! Tutto è pronto.*"

Oh God, the olive harvest. Saturday. "For sure, Paolo." He gave her a big hug, lifting her right out of her chair. "*Si. Si.* We'll be there. Right, Steven?"

"Wouldn't miss it," Steven said, with an exaggerated wince behind Paolo's back.

Harvesting olives would mean a long day of hard work. Paolo was a purist. No mechanization on his farm. Everything was done the old-fashioned way or, as Paolo said "*a mano con telo.*" The workers picked by hand, dropping the olives gently onto ground nets. But it was all worth it, she had to admit. At one o'clock everyone would take a break and gather around groaning tables of Tuscan food and wine. Paolo was generous with the lovely golden olive oil. Sure enough, when she walked back with him to his truck to see him off, he proudly produced two bottles of that very oil—a clever incentive to get them to show up.

Later that morning it began to rain and she was glad of the excuse to stay inside and rest. She was feeling increasingly tired and out of breath. Without telling Steven, she had visited the local doctor. He suspected asthma and gave her a puffer but it didn't make any difference. Could it possibly be true, she wondered, that the air she had was being "used up" just as Karl, and now Osman, had predicted. She shook her head at this crazy, but nonetheless disturbing, thought.

When Steven went to the village on an errand that afternoon, she called Janet in Canada. She had promised to do this as soon as she got to Tuscany but had been putting it off because she knew she'd get a lecture about the Egypt trips. She tried to adopt a normal tone, as though just catching up on news, but Janet cut right in. "How long were you there this time? Shit, Rache. All this star-gazing la-la land. Enough already." She burst into a dramatic rendition of the song from the musical *Hair*: "When the moooooon is in the seventh house and Joooopiter aligns with Mars. You've still got the hots for Lawrence of Arabia, I can tell. And he's bad news. He's messing with your head again. Why don't you live full time with the painter for God's sake? He may be hard work but at least he's harmless."

What would Janet say if she knew what had happened on this last trip? How to explain the thrill, the intoxicating power of that love without sounding crazy and out of control? Even liberal-minded Janet with her predisposition for recreational sex would shake her head in sad reproach.

***

The olive harvest went off successfully, the rain holding back until the end. She enjoyed the day and loved the chance to feel Italian again. But the exertion tired her and she found herself frequently feeling weak and having to sit down. The neighbours fussed around, offering her food and drink, encouraging her to live here full time because surely everyone in North America was too stressed, in too much of a hurry.

She watched Steven and Paolo working at the olive trees, laughing and teasing each other. Could this be home again, she wondered. But even as she smiled at this contemplation, she felt her inward gaze being pulled like a magnet across the Mediterranean and south along the Nile. Yesterday, when she was sure Steven was absorbed in his painting, she called Karl and told him she needed to stay a little longer. Steven's show in Rome would be a major breakthrough for him, one that she felt he could not have done without her constant encouragement. She had to make sure he completed everything, that he didn't second guess himself and back out.

"And after this, you will be ready?" Karl had asked. "For all you must do?"

Yes, she told him, though she still wasn't sure.

"Then come when it's right."

As the winter settled in, she tackled the few remaining projects she had committed to, finishing each with a sense of finality. In the early evenings, Steven would light the fire, draw the long velvet drapes at the French doors that gave on to the terrace and lie on the couch to read, the two dogs asleep at his side. She would sit at the trestle table underneath the old tapestry, her work spread along its full length. Hours passed in silence but a sudden movement would alert her and she'd look up to see Steven grab the sketch pad that was always at his side, discard his book and start drawing, his hand moving quickly, his face frowning with concentration. She struggled between the longing to help and the strange feeling that she must not get too close. She could guide and encourage him but she must never encroach as she had done once before, unwittingly driving a painful wedge into his life.

This conviction made her superstitious. She would not go in to his studio alone. Once, she did this without thinking, looking for something she had mislaid. The sun was streaming in, catching the floating dust in slanted shafts of light. Against the wall was a painting of a tree he had finished some time ago. She could feel its strength and vigour as it pushed up through the soil. But as she looked, she sensed a change, first in the painting and then in the whole room. The leaves of the tree began to fade and droop. Outside, the sun slid behind a cloud and the shafts of light vanished, making her suddenly cold. She fled the room, gulped a shot of whiskey and sat at the kitchen table until she felt calm. Don't be so goddamn stupid, she told herself. *Your imagination is off the charts. You'll be seeing ghosts next.*

***

A few mornings later, she woke to the faint sound of barking. It was still dark and Steven was not there. He must have gone to the ridge, somehow knowing that today the sun would rise in all its glory, no clouds or mist in its way.

She pushed back the shutters. There was a layer of frost on the ground and a sharp chill to the air outside. She pulled her robe tight around her shoulders. When the sun was higher, it would light up the bend in the driveway where the path to the ridge started. From the wicker chair by the window, she waited to see Steven walking back. As the shapes outside grew clearer, she felt a sharp pinch of worry. She shifted in the chair. Get a grip, she told herself—he's not going to jump.

Rafiki burst from the undergrowth, barking madly. *Where is Steven?* She saw the bushes move and he came into view. He was carrying Monty. She rushed downstairs.

"Get some water," Steven said as she flung open the kitchen door. He put the dog down gently and stroked him. Monty lay still, his breath coming in scratchy gulps.

"God, what happened?" Rachel nudged the dog's nose with the bowl.

"He was sniffing over the edge and he freaked and lost his footing. He slid down and landed on that ledge that juts out to the right, thank God."

"Poor thing. He hasn't broken anything, has he?" Rachel stroked his head, trying to still the pounding of her heart.

"Don't think so. He scrambled back but then he flopped down and wouldn't get up. Rafiki kept pawing him and prancing about."

"Come on, Monty." Rachel scratched behind his ears but the dog shrank from her touch.

"Let him be." Steven took her hand. "Maybe he'll wake up his old self."

They put some food and his favourite chewing things close by and went in frequently to check on him. He breathed quietly but he didn't move.

That night they went to bed early but Rachel couldn't sleep. A crackling fire sparked at the edges of her dreams and spat out glowing embers around the bed. Sometimes they caught, making little holes in the sheets that flared bright at the edges. She thrashed and jerked away from them under the covers.

Monty died that night. In the morning, they found him stretched out by the fireplace. Rafiki lay nearby, his face sunk deep into his front paws, staring at his old friend. Rachel sobbed until she was short of breath. The dog was old, Steven said, he'd had a great life. His heart must have given out. Rachel wondered if the poor dog had felt the same shiver of panic she had felt herself as she sat waiting at the window that morning.

They buried him off the pathway to the ridge later that day, both of them weeping and trying to smile through their tears. Rafiki stood forlorn, his tail between his legs.

Steven retreated to the studio to paint.

Rachel sat in the living room, unable to focus on anything. Her mind drifted back again to her last trip to Egypt.

Every night after she and Karl returned from Aswan, they went to the desert to gaze at the stars and marvel at the mystical splendour of the night sky. The ten years she had spent away from him felt like a strange dream of someone else's life. He would hold her steady as they drank from the liquid in the silver flask. He had lost none of his intensity and gave himself up completely to the energy they created together. The images of him in this state spun through her head: the light of the stars in his eyes, his long hair swinging, his shirt hanging loose, his black pants rolled above his ankles, his bare feet moving lightly on the sand. This was the real soul of the man, the mystic, the adept. The other man, the one who so patiently taught her the old texts, the plotting of the heavens, the interpretations of the hieroglyphics, who so carefully crushed the powders and mixed the tonics to help them feel closer to that ancient world, who read the books and tested her memory, willing her to believe ... he was just the vehicle for this finer being. And when he drew her close and they tumbled together on the blanket in the sand, there was nothing and no one in the world she wanted more.

She had felt his presence strongly when Monty died, reminding her she was an unwitting channel for negative energy. What force of energy had driven her back across the Atlantic all those years ago and then punished her for obeying it? What was it that had taken her from the path she once chose, from the man who had been her lover, mentor, friend, soul-mate? She lay back in the chair and drifted into sleep. Wasn't he just calling her home?

***

At the doorway of Steven's studio, she cleared her throat to draw his attention. He peered round the edge of his painting, brush arrested in his raised hand. The sun made the yellow paint on the tip of the bristles glisten like a drop of gold. Two easels were placed side by side to accommodate the large canvas.

He put the paintbrush in a jar. "This painting's because of you. Come and look."

The winter sun slid from behind the wisps of cloud and shone brightly through the French doors, lighting up the painting. Rachel immediately felt the sensation of leaving her body, floating into the air and watching the man in the picture from high up. The man stood at the edge of a cliff. He was leaning forward, his back arched, his arms raised to the sky, as a diver might before springing off. Far, far below was the valley, sketched roughly and washed with pale green. But what caused her catch of breath was the way the man was rooted to the very edge of the ridge, his feet planted into the earth. Even if he leaned farther, the gravity from the core of the planet would hold him like a magnet. He would never fall. He was spinning with the earth, through space and time, braced to greet the dawn. She dragged her eyes away from him, across the valley to the far hills. There, the sun was coming into view and into being. She could feel this sun pushing through the wash on the canvas, willing itself to life. The scene was ethereal, yet she could see it clearly from this lofty height where she soared among the clouds with the man's spirit.

She imagined how Steven would finish the painting, how the silvery leaves of the olive trees would shimmer, how the shadows, purple and grey, would slide into the valley. He had sketched in the cypress trees as they marched down the hill, and the narrow, winding road below. But she could tell these would only be a blur, a suggestion. He would not let the eye stray too far from the joy of the precipice.

She finally spoke. "It will be magnificent. It's you, your spirit."

"But?"

"Don't stop and think. Let the painting work through you. It will be unbelievable."

"Thank you, my love. If only you could do a legitimate review for my Rome exhibit. Too bad everyone knows we're sleeping together."

"Guido will want this as the anchor. I know it. What will you call it?"

"Something that captures the idea of freedom without the fear that comes with it. You know, being grounded, yet reaching far out for something."

"*Aphelion*."

"Which means?"

"When the earth goes round the sun, it's not in a perfect circle. It's an ellipse. So, there's a point when the earth is closest to the sun and one when it's farthest away. When it's farthest away, that's called *aphelion*. You could say that's as far as we can go without spinning out of orbit. The sun's gravity will hold us but, well, we're way out there."

"*Aphelion*? Perfect." He kissed the top of her head.

She watched him hustle about, whistling as he began to clean up. He must finish the painting with the same sense of possibility that started it. He must paint the precipice and the valley below without looking down, without fear. In the end, helping him to finish this would be the most important thing she could do for him. And for herself too.

***

That evening, Steven went to the village to give his weekly art lesson. Engrossed in her books, a banging outside disturbed Rachel. She opened the outer kitchen door and noticed some logs had fallen from the wood pile and rolled across the driveway. A *cinghiale,* no doubt, the wild boar that were such a nuisance. It was a clear night and her eye was drawn to Capella, the Goat Star, almost directly overhead in the Auriga constellation. She thought how, in the Arab world, many believed this star to be the grand director of the celestial game, the master choreographer. Ah, Capella, this is your doing, she thought—you're calling me out tonight. She went back in, threw on her coat and foraged around in the kitchen drawer for a flashlight. Unable to find one, she took a candle and matches.

It had rained all day, a fine misty rain that lay in puddles across the driveway and among the trees. The crescent moon glinted from every pool. She walked along the path that led to the ridge aware of the fluttering above her and the scurrying of tiny feet in the undergrowth. She sat on a fallen tree at the edge and looked for a while at the darkened valley, then took the candle from her pocket, dug it firmly into the earth in front of her and lit it. The moon kept disappearing behind the scudding clouds but she felt it was alert, keeping an eye on her.

She thought about Steven in the village church below. She thought about Nigel. When she told him her plans, would he listen, would he help her? She prayed he would understand. She stood and faced south-east towards the far desert where it had all begun. She looked at Capella. "I'm ready," she said and blew gently on the flame. The flame had burned low. It wavered for a second and briefly scorched her finger before giving itself up to the darkness and leaving a thin wisp of smoke to drift away with the breeze.

She would leave on March 21st, the vernal equinox. She would go to straight to Cairo and then for a couple of weeks to Canada. Steven was ready for his exhibition in Rome and she would promise to meet him there. *Aphelion* was almost done. He had made the valley come alive. His valley, his bid for happiness, all the golds and greens and lavenders blending together in a landscape of dreams.

***

On the night before she left, as Steven slept, she tiptoed down to his study, breaking her rule that she would never enter when he wasn't there. This time was different, she reasoned. She switched on the light and let her eyes roam around the room, taking in the intense, rich colours, the bold strokes, the layers of texture, the deep expression, the passion that had once been so bruised and stifled. All the emotions the paintings evoked coursed through her and she sealed them in, a reservoir of comfort she could dip into.

There was a lot of luggage. The little taxi that was to drive her to the train station groaned under the weight and the driver grumbled, waving his arms about. She stood with Rafiki, watching Steven as he tried to help. A breeze swept through the herb garden, bringing the scent of the early mint and chives. Rafiki whined, pushing his face against her legs.

A last hug, the goodbye words: "...see you in Rome, be careful, be safe, look after yourself, give my love to..., don't forget this, that..." the slamming of the taxi door, the tires spinning on the gravel, the wave through the window, looking back as the taxi dipped down the driveway, seeing Steven bend to grab Rafiki by the collar to stop him running after it.

Her body was tense and still so the tears flowed freely and in silence.

Chapter 32

Twilight lingered on the upstairs terrace of the gallery in Rome that was hosting Steven's exhibition. It had been hot all day. As the big sun slid finally behind the rooftops, the large terracotta flowerpots that stood along the railing turned to a burnished gold. Steven rested his hand on one of them and found it still warm to the touch. He broke off a leafy tendril of ivy and twisted it through his fingers, his eyes scanning the tourists in the winding streets below. He had intended to do so much that day —the Borghese, the Piazza Navona, maybe find a shady restaurant patio there for lunch. But he couldn't shake his bad mood. He took another generous sip of his whisky and soda.

Guido's wife Annette came out to join him. "Taking a break? Good for you. Guido is beside himself. All the praise for our gallery! He's thrilled we found you. What a pity Rachel's not here."

He looked away.

"Our friend Giuseppe bought *Treescape*. Did you know? It will look wonderful in his home. He needs your advice on where to hang it."

Steven struggled to be attentive as she chattered on, spilling her drink with each enthusiastic gesture of her hands.

"*Dio mio.*" She stopped in mid-sentence. "I almost forgot. There's a man inside who wants to see you. I promised to track you down."

"Patron? Dealer?"

She shrugged. "He was in the west annex with the landscapes. Long hair. Blond."

As Steven approached the annex, he could see the man she had described through the archway. He stopped. He knew who this must be. The visitor stood alone, thumbs hooked into his belt, his head tilted back to gaze at the major painting on the wall before him: *Aphelion.*

"Inevitable we should meet," the man said, over his shoulder. He turned to face Steven. "I'm Karl Gustav."

The curious, unexpected formality of this man, the slight bow as they shook hands, the almost imperceptible straightening of the shoulders unsettled Steven. He withdrew his hand and waited. His heart pressed against his rib-cage.

Karl gestured with his thumb to the painting. "This is good. I notice it's already sold."

"Thank you," Steven cleared his throat to cover his mounting anxiety. *Why is the son-of-a-bitch here? To collect her things because she doesn't have the nerve to come herself?*

"I believe this painting was a turning point, a different motivation breaking through."

"Let's cut the crap. I don't think you've come because of my work. Rachel knows you're here?" Steven could barely get this out. "Right?"

A slight softening of those stiff shoulders. "She might guess."

"Guess? She was with you."

"For a while."

The blood rushed to Steven's head and one sensation after another chased through his body. Relief. A huge, wonderful wash of relief that, after all, Rachel wasn't with Karl. But then, right behind the relief, flooding into every pore, the anxiety. Where was she? Something God-awful must have happened. "She left Tuscany a while ago," he said. "She was going to see you, I thought. And at some point, go back to Canada."

"She spent a month with me in Cairo."

Steven's gut turned over again. Here he was. The flesh and blood Herr Gustav. Undeniable, infuriatingly arrogant. "Then what?" he asked, though he hated needing answers from this man.

"Why do you expect me to know this?" Karl widened his eyes. He was framed by the painting behind him, blocking all it stood for, becoming its central figure. "Rachel is free to come and go as she pleases."

"Why the hell are you here then?"

The sly smile vanished and Karl leaned closer. "Perhaps I came to see you."

Fuck you, Steven thought, but bit his lip.

Two gallery visitors entered the room at this point and stood to admire the large painting, speaking to each other rapidly in a language Steven did not recognize. After a few moments, clearly picking up the tension, they exchanged a meaningful glance and left quickly.

Karl went over to one of the narrow windows that overlooked a pathway to a little square. Steven took in his sharp profile, his expensive watch, his finely-shaped hands now leaning on the window-sill. Lightning-fast scenes from a jealous imagination flickered through his head. Against his will, he followed him to the window.

"I came," Karl said, "because I wanted to see who had claimed all Rachel's attention, all her concern these last few years, whose life she'd had the misfortune to stumble into."

Steven felt he'd been punched in the gut. For a moment he couldn't summon the breath to respond.

"And yes, you are right," Karl went on. "Because I thought she might be here."

"Well, she's not." Steven fought to stay focused. "She must still be in Canada. Something must have happened. She would have been in touch. She wouldn't have missed this show."

Karl shook his head. "There are forces in motion that are stronger than all of us." He picked up the leather satchel he had brought and began to move towards the door. "Now I know Rachel's not here, I have no reason to stay any longer."

For many days, Steven went over and over the next scenes in his mind, trying to play them out differently. He cast himself in a more decisive, more physical role, grabbing Karl's throat, causing him to stagger and lose his maddening composure, throwing him out of the gallery. Or perhaps he would get Guido to call the police, claiming a visitor was acting suspiciously. He would try to dwell on these more satisfying alternatives but the pictures faded and he couldn't hold them fast.

Instead, the crushing humiliation of the real scenes persisted. It all started in the back office of the gallery. He had begged Karl to stay, to wait while he phoned some people, to help him figure out where Rachel might be. Karl leaned against the wall as though he were here on a casual visit, while Steven made the calls, aware that he was sounding desperate. He watched Karl saunter into one of the adjoining rooms to look at the paintings: Rachel asleep on the terrace, the young Slavic girl eating a golden plum, the *Woman in White* pouring wine for a frail old man in his Tuscan garden. Karl stood for a brief moment before each of them. Surely the paintings shrank back to the wall, sensing the indifferent eye of this stranger.

She spent a month with me in Cairo. The phone in Steven's hand was wet with the sweat of his clenched fist. Finally, he put it down, unable to reach anyone, not even Nigel and Philippe who must know of her whereabouts, and causing only consternation for her brother Robert in England.

"Do you know why Rachel is such a big part of your life?" Karl said, coming back into the office. "Has she told you anything about the past?"

"What? What do you mean? We met at my show in Toronto. I'm sure you know that. Not that's it's any of your goddamn business."

Karl shook his head, a look of thinly disguised pity in those hard eyes. "The fact is, long before she met you, you were already involved in her life."

"Involved in her life? Before we met? Oh God, don't give me some Egyptology mumbo jumbo like she knew me in a past life. Like we're both ancient spirits or some crap like that."

Karl sat down in the swivel chair on the other side of the desk. "Do you have any idea what Rachel has been studying in Cairo?"

There was an unquestionable challenge in the question. Steven felt the need to answer. "Some business about the stars. The way the ancient Egyptians interpreted them." He realized, too late, how uninterested this made him sound.

Karl was silent for a moment. He made a steeple of his hands, his elbows resting on the arms of the chair. "Not exactly. Rachel has been studying two interlinking concepts. They are known as *Ma'at* and *Shai*. You would explain this today as karma and how it is tied up with the whole idea of fate."

Steven got a brief flashback to the first time he had been in her study at her home in Toronto, all the maps of the sky, the prints of hieroglyphics pinned to the wall, the volumes of Egyptian books lying open, post-it notes all over them.

"You have played a role," Karl continued, "unknowingly of course, in a detour of the course of fate that now concerns us all."

Steven leaned forward across the desk. "Come on. What do you take me for?"

A burst of laughter from one of the exhibition rooms made Steven jump. It sounded harsh, inappropriate.

"It was your paintings that Rachel recognized first," Karl continued. "She'd seen some of those images before, had actually been part of some of the scenes. Later, when she learned more about you, she made the connection. She blames herself for your brother's death."

Steven felt like someone had plunged him in ice cold water. "What the fuck are you talking about?" he said, enunciating each word slowly. "What the hell do you think you know about my brother?" He half rose, his anger and confusion finally getting the better of him. "You're both into drugs. You've been messing with her head, making her believe all this psychedelic shit."

"Psychedelic shit," Karl said. "If that were true, it could be laughed off as an indulgence of youth. When you hear the whole story, maybe you will understand. It is no laughing matter."

"You're damned right, it's no laughing matter," he said. "Who knows what the hell has happened to her?"

Karl raised both hands in the air, like an exasperated teacher with a slow student. "You stopped me from leaving because you wanted to know the truth. I have started to tell you but you're not even trying to understand. You're dismissing it because you don't like what you hear. Rachel returned to Egypt because she had met you. She wanted me to help her come to terms with something that happened years ago, to try to make things right." He pointed his long finger at Steven. "And she did this for you. For your sake."

Steven's head reeled with the insanity of it all. "Rachel never met my brother. She has nothing to do with his death. I want her to explain all this. I don't trust you."

"That's up to her." Karl said. "But it may be too late. She will pay a high price for trying to help you. And probably, because I've been involved, so will I." He stared out of the office window for a moment, shaking his head. "She was very weak when she left. I feared she might come here and not want to tell me. I'm glad she didn't. She needs to take care. I doubt you'll see her again."

"What? And you will?"

Karl gave an almost imperceptible shrug. He slid his satchel onto his shoulder and looked directly at Steven "Now I know what a tragic waste Rachel's effort has been." He headed for the door.

Steven grabbed his arm. "Don't think you can just fucking walk out."

Karl wrenched his arm away and kept moving.

"Where is she?" Steven yelled, following him out of the gallery's main entrance, pushing past the people on the front steps. "You must have some idea!"

It had grown dark outside. He was vaguely aware of the tourists milling around the little street. On the edge of his vision people were posing for photographs, drinking, laughing, but he couldn't hear them, only a mad roaring noise in his ears. Karl was way ahead of him.

"Stop, goddamn it, I'm talking to you." He heard his shrill voice as he raced to close the distance between them. "Where do you think she is?" His words came out in ragged gasps. "If anything has happened ... your fault."

Karl stopped when he reached the square but did not turn round.

"If you cared about her at all," Steven said, stopping a few paces behind him, "you'd help me find her." He paused, breathing deeply. "Please."

Karl seemed to twist in slow motion, his long hair fanning in a wide arc across his face. "You are a fool," he said. "You're absorbed in your art because you can't cope with the rest of your narrow world. Why are you so concerned about Rachel? Do you believe she loves you? If she does, it is love born from a misguided sense of duty. Do you claim to love her?" He shook his head. "No. You used her. You're a selfish man. She made your life more bearable. She saved you from yourself. Well, now she's all used up." He began to walk away, then stopped and turned back. "Don't talk to me about caring, Mr. Farrow. You're not qualified."

Steven stood paralyzed. When the scene came back into focus, Karl was gone. The square was dark and empty; the waiter at the little café was slowly stacking the chairs.

Chapter 33

Rachel tried to focus. A nurse was replenishing the saline drip and had placed a thermometer under her tongue. A man in a white coat and a stethoscope was at the foot of her bed looking at a clipboard. He came and stood beside her. His expression was kind but stern.

"Miss Covelli. You have pulmonary fibrosis and possibly some kind of bronchial infection —we are waiting for the test results. And you are pregnant. Did you know this?"

Rachel nodded. She had known from the very night it happened.

"It would have been helpful if we had known this too. You need medical attention not just for yourself but for the health of the baby."

"Doctor, if I may—," someone said. Rachel turned sharply to the other side. It was Nigel in the armchair by the window. "Rachel was hardly able to discuss any of this. She was unconscious when we brought her in."

Hadn't she just said goodbye to Nigel? Philippe had come too. And Janet. The nurse had shooed them all out, saying she wasn't up to that many visitors. Wasn't that today? They had brought flowers and chocolates but the thought of chocolates made her want to retch. She checked that she could still reach the crescent-shaped plastic bowl on one of the chairs. She was so tired. She longed for sleep.

Nigel was saying something. "I know it's hard, Rachel. Terrible news. But we must talk."

No, no. He'd got it all wrong. She wanted the child. What did he mean?

He was talking to the doctor now, over by the door. "A state of shock," she thought she heard the doctor say. Nigel was shaking his head slowly.

The tears were coming back. She would not let them out. None of this was real. If she turned her face to the wall and closed her eyes tightly, it would all go away.

When did she talk to Karl? It must have been days ago, a week maybe. None of the days or nights made any sense any more. She opened her eyes to ask Nigel the time but the room was dark and she was alone. She remembered asking a nurse to find her phone for her, the nurse shaking her head as though a phone call was the last thing anybody ought to be thinking about. But she had been desperate to reach Karl. He didn't know she was ill. "Thank God you're being looked after," he told her when she finally got through to Cairo. "You have done enough. A new life is coming. You must take good care of yourself, Rachel." *Ray-chelle.* When he didn't hear from her, he was sure she'd gone to Rome. She couldn't bear to think that he had been there, that he and Steven had met.

He told her one of Steven's paintings had stayed in his mind: a small oil of a woman standing on a beach, her hand raised to shield her eyes from the sun. The water lapped around her feet and her bare heels were sinking into the sand. She was painted with little definition, fading into the scene. "It was you. You looked so tired. The energy was draining from you. He actually painted you fading away!" It made him angry, he said.

It was quiet now except for the sound of her own raspy breathing. She strained her ears and could just make out the whispering of two nurses in the corridor. An old woman in the room next door cried out for something. A trolley wheeled by.

How ill was she really, she wondered? She had caught only a few phrases from the doctors: "can be managed..." "unfortunately progressed..." "with good care ..." "closely monitored..." No one ever finished a sentence.

***

When she and Karl were together this last time, the vast, empty desert was their second home, just as it always had been. They stumbled through the heavy drifts of sand. They spread out the blanket and watched the sun go down, feeling the sting of the light breeze that skidded over the dunes. For a while, they could see the pyramids on the horizon but as the darkness fell, there was nothing but the two of them and the soaring constellations of the night sky. On the first night, the moon was new, a thin sliver. It looked fragile, barely visible behind the scudding wispy clouds. But each night, as it waxed heavier and brighter, Rachel felt the symbiotic swelling of her own body. She gazed at the stars and knew for certain that this time–*please God*–, this time the child would live. Once, she looked in the bag for the silver flask, wanting to feel the punch of that liquid, the rush that would flood her veins. But it wasn't there. "No more," Karl whispered. He knew.

He gathered her to him and she clung tightly to him as they made love. They would fall into a deep sleep and wake with the chill of the desert night and make love again, wanting the darkness to last forever. He would light the hash pipe and lie on his back, his head on her lap. The fragrance of the hashish was carried by the breeze and mingled with the scents of their bodies. She stroked his hair.

"What are you thinking?" she asked him once.

It was a long while before he answered. "The way things fall. What life gives you, and what it takes away."

She leaned down and kissed his forehead. This strange love was all she had now, and all that mattered.

***

"Time to take your blood pressure, Rachel." The nurse was cranking up the head of the bed. "Here's a fresh gown. You need to get ready for your breathing test." She tut-tutted at the untouched breakfast on the tray. "We're not going to get well on a hunger strike, now are we?"

Rachel fought through the soothing memories in her head and struggled to open her eyes. She squinted with the sudden brightness of the room: the white sheets, the white wall, the white uniform of the nurse, the clean, pale blue gown on her lap.

She let out a strangled sob. The truth hit her like a punch to the stomach, knocking the breath right out of her. The tears she had stifled with disbelief came unchecked now. She couldn't see. She groped at the sheets to wipe them away. She took big gulps of air. She tore at the blood pressure sleeve. She wrenched her arm free from the nurse who was trying to calm her. "Leave me alone," she tried to yell through the coughing and the tightness in her throat. Another nurse came running in. Measured voices: "Relax, you will be fine, everything will be all right." She curled into a tight ball, her hands over her ears, and stayed that way until they left.

Nothing would ever, ever be all right again.

Karl was dead.

***

"Rachel, it's me." *Nigel.* The face of her dear friend hovered over her. "Come on, let's get you sitting up here." He helped her lean forward and plumped up the pillow behind her. "I've brought you a coffee. Real coffee, not the dreadful stuff they give you in the visitors' room."

Between laboured breaths, she took a few sips and clutched the paper mug, taking comfort from its warmth.

"Don't rush or you'll start coughing." Nigel squeezed her arm. "Can you bear to talk about it now?"

The brutal details crowded into her head again. It happened only yesterday. Or maybe the day before. A fire at the store. Broad daylight. Karl was in the study. No chance. Massive blaze. Da'ud had called Nigel. Suspicious, the police said. They wanted to ask her some questions. Nigel told him to put them off. Not until she was better.

"They've arrested someone, Rachel. I have his name here." He took a piece of paper from his jacket pocket. "Ahmed Gamel. Do you know him?"

"*Ahmed?* What? I—. God, Nigel. No. No way." She coughed and the coffee spilled on the bedcovers. Nigel quickly took it from her. "Jesus, this can't be true. Surely not. Ahmed was a colleague. He used to work with Karl at the university. He was the one who would get us the salv—"

"The drugs. Yes, I know. That all came out I'm afraid. But the police are saying that he is, shall we say, mentally challenged. He was talking a lot of gibberish. This is where it gets tricky. I've heard all this from Da'ud who's been talking to some chap called Fadoul. I think you know him. Owns a café. Apparently, there was a bit of trouble with Ahmed in the past." Nigel hesitated. "He doesn't like you. Do you know why?"

Rachel fell back on the pillow and stared at the ceiling. "He used to think I had 'negative energy.' But that was years ago. He and Karl, sometimes they'd argue. But surely to God ... I don't care how crazy he is, he's not going to set a fire on purpose to get rid of Karl." She grabbed some tissues from the box at her side. The tears were taking over again. Her voice broke. "Why? It doesn't make any sense."

"Listen to me, Rachel. You've got to try to hold it together. I know there's a lot to deal with. But you see, Ahmed believed Karl went to Rome to bring you back. He didn't know you were here. He said you'd been gone ten years and then you start showing up again and now it looked like you were coming back for good. Things would start to go wrong again, he said, or some such nonsense. That's what Da'ud told me. And he's getting it all from Fadoul so who knows what the motivation really was." He shook his head. "Anyway, apparently by his own admission, Ahmed thought Karl had gone out that day and that you were there alone. It was *you* he wanted to kill."

***

Every day, Rachel yearned for the night, for the oblivion of the dark. That was when the noises stopped, the beeping of monitors, the moaning and the shouts of other patients, the busy-talk of nurses and doctors and orderlies, the endless squeak of those hospital shoes along the corridors. She was aware only of the low hum of the heart rate monitor she was hooked up to. And sometimes, if she concentrated really hard, she swore she could hear the tiny heartbeat of her child.

Karl had told her Steven was dismissive, accusatory and cared only about his own life. She had slid beneath the thin blanket on the hospital bed and held the phone closely to her ear, taking such comfort from his voice. It didn't matter what he was saying. All those years ago, she had felt so connected to the strange world around her, the world within her. She was happy. She loved and was loved. She mattered. Why did it all go so dreadfully wrong? She had tried hard to atone. But she must have been found wanting, for here she was, the weight on her shoulders so much heavier now. Crippling, unbearable.

***

Janet came by every day. She brushed Rachel's hair and helped her get washed and walked with her up and down the ward, rolling the IV unit beside them, insisting that she must get up and get her muscles working, and stop all that "croaking and vomiting like something out of *The Exorcist.*" Rachel found herself looking forward to her friend's visits. Sometimes she managed to smile through the tears.

A nurse bustled in with the spirometer and set it up at the side of the bed. "Up we come," she said, peeling back the covers. "You know what to do."

The deep breaths and the fast, deliberate exhales into the machine made Rachel weak, and she was glad to lie down again. She was dizzy and closed her eyes.

When she woke, Nigel was sitting in the chair beside her, reading.

"I've brought you some croissants and strawberries and a little camembert. And don't give me that look. You're too pale and too thin."

"Nigel, we have to talk."

"First, I have to talk and you have to listen. You are a little better. It's time to get serious. You must call Steven. He went through hell in Rome, as you know. You disappear into the desert for weeks on end and then show up at our front door. All we could get out of your frantic blathering was that you were ill, you were pregnant and under no circumstances were we to call Steven. Do you remember that? Probably not, since you collapsed in a heap before uttering another word. Out for the count for several days."

"Has he tried—" She coughed and then breathed in hard "to reach you?"

"Of course! He thinks we're travelling. His voice mails are getting increasingly angry and desperate. We daren't answer the phone. You can't treat your friends like this, Rachel."

Rachel maneuvered herself upright and reached for the plate and napkin he offered. If she turned her head, she could see the bright sky, the tops of tall buildings through the half open window. The spire of a TV aerial glinted in the sun. The hum of the traffic on the busy street below drifted up, punctuated by a squeal of brakes, an impatient blast of a car's horn. Normal life, just beyond her reach.

"Nigel." She turned back and held his worried gaze. "There's something else I need to tell you."

Chapter 34

Steven sold more than he expected at the Rome show but couldn't bring himself to care. All the praise from the buyers, the gallery's patrons, from Guido and Annette, sounded hollow. Several paintings had gone anonymously through dealers, including *Aphelion*. Probably better that way, knowing the work was truly valued somewhere, but not knowing where.

As he drove north on the long stretch of the A1, he went over and over the things Karl had told him, trying to contain his contempt. All that bullshit about his brother. What the fuck was that about? And what had made the son-of-a-bitch get on a plane and come to Rome? The only possible explanation was that he was seriously worried about Rachel. "Don't talk to me about caring, Mr. Farrow. You're not qualified." The knife twisted once again in his gut.

"Fuck you!" He blasted his horn at a Porsche that cut in front of him. The driver gave him the finger through his sun-roof.

Where the hell was Rachel? His calls to Nigel and Philippe had been in vain. Nothing but voicemail. The manager at their store said he didn't know when they'd be back.

The drive was slow and tedious. When he finally made it home, he stumbled upstairs, threw his clothes to the floor and collapsed into bed, dreading a long and restless night.

He was woken early the next morning by the sound of a dog barking. Paolo who had looked after Rafiki in his absence, was bringing him back. Through the bedroom window, Steven shouted his sleepy thanks and half-heartedly offered coffee, but Paolo was on his way to the market and Steven was grateful he couldn't stop. He got dressed, surrendering to the day and the full weight of his anxiety.

A movement in the corner of the kitchen caught his eye. Rafiki had slunk down into his basket and was looking up with mournful eyes, unused to any display of temper. Poor dog —not much of a homecoming. "Come on then, boy." He grabbed the leash. "The rest of the goddamn world can go to hell for an hour or so."

He took the dog off into the hills but, walking back, resolved to give Rachel's home number one more try. He'd wait until the evening – about noon her time. Maybe she'd had to leave suddenly and might be back now. Maybe there'd been some kind of emergency.

At five o'clock, unable to concentrate on anything, he picked up his phone and hit Rachel's number. For a few seconds he indulged in the beautiful belief that he had made a mistake. He looked at the digits on the call display. He knew them by heart. He swallowed hard and tried again.

I'm sorry, the number you have dialed is not in service. This is a recording. I'm sorry, the number you have dialed is not in service. This—

All the sounds and colours around him fused into whiteness and silence.

The sun was hot and bright when he woke the next morning and it was a few seconds before the full shock seized him again. He buried his face in the pillow, craving oblivion. He thought about Rachel's friend Janet, then realized he didn't even know her last name, much less her number. He was tempted to get a flight to Canada but thought if Rachel wasn't there, what a stupid waste of time that would be.

He walked in the hills, Rafiki at his side, or sat for hours on the terrace letting the sun burn his face, taking no comfort from it. The summer was advancing quickly, the colours brightening, bursting out of the valley. He slept fitfully and late. He didn't go to the ridge. He didn't paint.

A few days later, out on the terrace with a late morning coffee, he saw the mail van labouring up the driveway. His whole body shifted into a lower gear. He turned away from the van, scanned the valley, took in the house, the steps, the broken fountain, the flowers tumbling down the slope. He tried to reassure himself that everything was real, everything was fine. The mailman walked towards him, his hand in the air, clutching an envelope.

His fingers were clumsy as he tried to open it. In the end, he ripped it apart. A small purple drawstring pouch fell onto the table. He stared at this, his heart contracting, then pulled out the letter.

Steven ...

I have been ill and I have been a coward. Nothing I say will excuse my silence. I ask only that you read this and try to understand. What I have to tell you will be hard to accept and I know you may never forgive me.

When I worked in Egypt, I came back to Canada to take a course at Devlin's Point. It was August 2001. I was there when Colin died, Steven. I was in the car behind him. When the stag leapt out from the trees, we both went into a spin. My car clipped the back of Colin's van. I've replayed the scene in my head so many times and I still don't know if I caused him to go over the edge, if it was my fault that he died.

But nothing excuses the next part. I didn't report it.

The letter was shaking in his hand. The words were blurred. He wedged it under his mug so it wouldn't blow away. He reached for the coffee pot. But his hands felt weak and he didn't think he could lift it. He sat still for a few minutes, holding the arms of the chair. The letter rambled on more...reasons, mistakes made, excuses for the trips to Cairo. He skimmed ahead to the parts that made sense...

...I do believe it was fate that brought you and I together. You an artist, I a critic. I could never undo the past but perhaps I could influence the future. That would be my atonement. I wanted to help you with your own sense of guilt, to bring some joy to your life, and I hoped to do this through the medium of your work.

But I have learned that the Goddess Ma'at is not easily satisfied and there is a high price to pay for cowardice. Karl is dead, Steven, and I am pregnant with his child. He died in a fire at his home in Cairo. This, I believe, is my ultimate punishment. From now on, I must follow a different path. My child will be my only concern and I will not see you again.

I have talked to a lawyer here in Toronto. Tomorrow, I am going with her and with Nigel to the police. It is simply the right thing to do, albeit far, far too late.

We were so good together, Steven. But it couldn't last. It was a transition, a few beautiful years of some mysterious cosmic choreography. All the darkness and uncertainty are behind you. You are free and you are ready to move on. Because I know this, I'm happy and at peace.

All I can ask is that one day you might forgive me. And then forget me.

Con tanto amore, sempre. Rachel

Steven picked up the purple pouch that had fallen out of the envelope. Inside was the Eye of Horus ring. He slipped it into his pocket.

He walked to the end of the terrace and leaned over the wall. The day was bright and still. High in the sky above him, two larks circled each other. Very faintly, he heard one of their calls. He tried to imagine himself from their point of view, a small figure, inconsequential, carving out one single life here on the hillside. The tears smarting at the edge of his eyes would make not a jot of difference to the world.

That afternoon and for many more days, he painted in a fury. The colours flowed from deep inside, and the heaving sadness, the blunt rage, the sudden, unexpected surges of happiness, all of them rushed to the surface and spilled out of him.

***

A month passed. He walked into his studio one day and looked at all the work he'd done. Two young men, brothers, were in every painting. They were flying, spiraling around each other, dancing in every landscape, laughing in every colour. Their feet never touched the ground. They were held in exquisite limbo by a lighter gravity.

Early the next morning, he walked towards the ridge, Rafiki loping ahead. He stopped to gaze at the muted colours of the land, taking deep breaths, inhaling the lemon balm, the lavender, the moist tang of the earth that played on the wind. At the end of the path, he waited.

First, a wedge of gold pushed at the horizon, then a glow of pink, sparkling at the edges. The darkness on the top of the hills began to slide down, leaving a deep lush green in its wake.

He moved to the edge, his hands loose at his sides. The valley froze, the birds stalled in mid-flight. There was no noise of chugging cars on the winding road below, no barking of dogs on the distant farm. The olive grove ceased shimmering. The cypress trees stood tall and still, as though holding their breath.

He raised his arms, threw back his head and cried out with tears of pain and joy, his feet gripped by the earth, his body light and strong, ready to greet the morning sun. And it seemed to him the wind picked up again, the trees let out their breath, the valley sighed with relief and the world began once more to turn.

Rachel was right. It was a beautiful transition. It was time to go home.

EPILOGUE

At the top of the dune, Rachel stopped, out of breath. The little boy pulled his hand away from hers and sank down. She thought he might cry again but he was quiet, even when the wind rose and small gusts of sand spun up and stung his arms and face. The sun had long gone and the thin slice of moon gave little light. The darkness wrapped itself around them.

She sat beside the boy and pointed to the southern sky. "There's Sagittarius," she said. "Do you see him? He's crossing the meridian now, half way along his night-time journey."

From her pocket, she took a candle and a lighter, wedged the candle into the sand and lit it. They sat for a while, cradled against each other, watching the tiny flame. She took off her backpack and pulled out a wooden box. On each of its four sides was a hieroglyphic, inlaid in pewter.

"Fire," said the boy, pointing to one of these.

She nodded and turned each side to face him.

"Earth. Air. Water," he said. He looked proud to know this.

She kissed the top of his head. "It's time." She undid the clasps and set the lid aside. "Are you ready?"

The boy stood and took the box in both hands. He walked a few steps to the edge of the dune, his bare feet sinking into the sand. He steadied himself, twisted back and, still gripping the box, swung it forward. The ashes fanned out in a wide arc and hovered, weightless.

Out of the great valleys of sand came the desert wind, stronger now. It circled and lifted the ashes. Higher and higher they floated, spiralling upwards into the darkness, on their way home to the stars.

"Goodbye," the boy whispered.

Rachel came to his side and touched his shoulder.

He moved away. "I know what to do." He took a bottle of water from his pack, poured a few drops over the candle flame and pinched the wick hard.

Rachel watched him, her whole body overflowing with love and grief. Her son was crying again now. He began to run down the dune, stumbling in the soft sand.

-End-

ACKNOWLEDGEMENTS

While writing this novel, I was encouraged, supported and prevented from ripping my hair out by so many.

My thanks go to my stalwart writing comrades Ariane Blackman, Arif Anwar, Hilary Trapp, José Sigouin, Justine Mazin, Michelle Alfano, Michelle Boone, and Tina Tzatzanis – whose patience, kind praise and merciless criticism kept me inspired and motivated; to Canadian author Dennis Bock whose insight and craftsmanship steered me through the challenges; to my great friends Gary Hesketh and Louise Doucet who suffered through early drafts and whose enthusiasm was unflagging; to Shane Joseph, my editor and publisher who saw the potential of the story right from the beginning, and whose critical eye helped me to bring new dimension and impetus to it; and, most importantly, to my husband Jürgen, the love of my life, who has always been my anchor and my strength.

Liz Torlée

2020

AUTHOR BIO

Liz Torlée lived and worked in England and Germany before emigrating to Canada. Her fascination with the idea of fate and what is known as "coincidence" fuelled the ideas in this, her debut novel, ***The Way Things Fall,*** and her extensive travel in the Middle East and Italy inspired many of the scenes. She lives with her husband in Toronto.

CPSIA information can be obtained
at www.ICGtesting.com
Printed in the USA
BVHW030035260822
645556BV00007B/103

9 781927 882559